DATE DUE FEB - 6 1992

		MAR	9 1992
AUG 1 0 1991			
SEP - 5 1991		MAR 1 5 1993	
SEP 1 9 1991			
OCT 1 6 1991			
MAR 1 5 1993			

ROD   Roderus, Frank
         Mustang war

Mustang War

Also by Frank Roderus

J. A. Whitford & the Great California Gold Hunt
Billy Ray's Forty Days
Charlie and the Sir
Billy Ray & the Good News
Stillwater Smith
Finding Nevada
Reaching Colorado
Leaving Kansas
The Ordeal of Hogue Bynell
Cowboy
Old Kyle's Boy
Jason Evers: His Own Story
Sheepherding Man
Hell Creek Cabin
Easy Money
The Keystone Kid
The 33 Brand
Journey to Utah

Mustang War

FRANK RODERUS

A DOUBLE D WESTERN

DOUBLEDAY

New York London Toronto Sydney Auckland

063047

For Stephen and Michelle

A DOUBLE D WESTERN
PUBLISHED BY DOUBLEDAY
a division of Bantam Doubleday Dell Publishing Group, Inc.
666 Fifth Avenue, New York, New York 10103

DOUBLE D WESTERN, DOUBLEDAY,
and the portrayal of the letters DD
are trademarks of Doubleday, a division of
Bantam Doubleday Dell Publishing Group, Inc.

Library of Congress Cataloging-in-Publication Data

Roderus, Frank.
Mustang War/Frank Roderus.—1st ed.
    p.   cm.—(A Double D western)
I. Title.
PS3568.O346M87   1991
813'.51—dc20   90-22871
CIP

ISBN 0-385-41845-0
Copyright © 1991 by Frank Roderus
All Rights Reserved
Printed in the United States of America
July 1991
First Edition

10 9 8 7 6 5 4 3 2 1

ONE

HE WAS HALF AFRAID yet completely enthralled. It was so lovely here. And so tense.

There were more than a dozen people huddled in the small boat but the only sound was that of the gentle slaps and creakings as the squat and ugly little craft rode the slow swells.

So lovely, and yet . . . Oliver cleared his throat, acutely conscious of how loud it seemed, and surreptitiously snugged the straps of his life jacket. The cork-filled jacket stank of diesel fuel and sunbaked canvas and it probably was making his new shirt filthy.

The winter sun laid a shimmering path of pink and red and purest gold across the gently rolling water. The range of color streaming down from the distant sun was amazing. It caught on the water surfaces and reflected time and time again from the wisps of cloud that floated out to sea. It was getting late. Soon they would have to crank the engine and start back, he was sure.

Oliver peered off in the direction of the sun, his mind's eye following the bright sun-path to Tahiti, to Pago Pago, to Borneo and Sumatra and ancient Cathay. He smiled. Follow the Yellow Brick Road. Baum must have been beside a body of water when he thought of Dorothy making her way to Oz.

Because he was staring away down the Yellow Brick Road, Oliver was the first one in the boat to see the steamy, misty eruption that announced the arrival of the leading member of the pod they'd been told to expect. And then beyond it more plumes of spray leaping up from the placid, gold-tinged surface as the other whales came nearer.

Oliver's hand squeezed involuntarily on JoLynn's, and he heard her gasp as she too saw.

"Ballena," the dour pilot said, pointing. There was a collective yelp of pleasure from the other occupants of the boat, and the craft tilted alarmingly, gunwale deep, as everyone tried to shift closer to the approaching whales. The pilot said something—Oliver had no Spanish and this man apparently no English—then abandoned verbal communication and began gently tugging and coaxing at shirtsleeves to try to herd his charges back onto their seats.

Oliver felt his pulse and breathing quicken, felt JoLynn wriggle and squirm with excitement against his hip. The whales were close enough now that he could begin to see their slick gray backs breasting the surface, still too far, though, to gain any impression of size. The occupants of the boat, oddly, were silent.

To north and south alike there was the sound of engines firing as the pilots of other watch craft moved to intercept the course of the pod. Whale watching here had become quickly popular and commercial. There were seven small craft on the bay this afternoon that Oliver could see and probably more beyond the horizon.

The pilot of a big Avon inflatable brought his people in between Oliver's boat and the approaching pod. The discourtesy brought a rumble of protest from Oliver's boatmates and an unapologetic grin from the Mexican who was guiding the Avon.

A whale—a blue? a gray? Oliver had no idea what the difference between them might be—surfaced within a dozen feet of the Avon, and a woman's voice squealed. The people in Oliver's boat craned their necks for a closer look, and the craft lurched and rolled with an alarming lack of stability. Oliver grabbed for the solid gunwale and clung to it. He was glad JoLynn hadn't wanted to come out in an inflatable. The body of the whale was submerged and only a portion of its back showed. Even so, the impression of hidden mass was immense. Bigger than a breadbox. Bigger than a Volkswagen bus. Closer to a Greyhound. Oliver had been told that, of course. But he hadn't *appreciated* the fact until now. He began to grin and came halfway to his feet in an effort to see better. He felt a tug on the tail of his life jacket and reluctantly settled back onto the hard, oil-smeared Fiberglas seat. It was no longer at all distressing to think that one casual, unconcerned nudge by a massive fluke could upend the Avon or any other puny, man-made boat. Worries like that were secondary to the pleasure of seeing these marvelous creatures up close in their natural state. JoLynn whispered something, but he didn't register the words.

Everyone in the boat was staring over toward the Avon, willing to forget for the moment that the Avon was poaching on "their" whale. The huge cetacean took in a breath—they were close enough that Oliver could actually see the thick, meaty plug of flesh rise to close off the blowhole before it submerged—and sank out of view, leaving the ocean surface smooth and glassy and blank where it had just been. Oliver groaned his disappointment right along with everyone else.

He turned, grinning, to say something to JoLynn, and his eyes went wide.

A second whale, a smaller one, was lying at the surface beside her. Not two feet away from her. Only a thin sheet of Fiberglas and a few gallons of salt water separated her from the whale's body. The animal's head was toward the bow of the boat. Its body extended into the depths of the water for an unimaginable distance. Not five feet from where Oliver sat, the blowhole puckered, a monstrous belly button of rubbery flesh, and frothed. The whale exhaled, spouting warm spray at least a dozen feet into the air. Droplets of it rained down onto the occupants of the boat, and there was a smell of the whale's breath in the air. Not fishy really. Salty. Humid. Alive. It was a distillation. All the sea's primal appeal concentrated and encapsulated within the living body of this one immense mammal. The whale was all the reality and majesty of the sea made flesh. He shivered and felt a sense of awe at the beauty of the thing.

"Oliver!" JoLynn whispered.

People all along that side of the boat were leaning out now. Touching the whale. Petting it. The whale seemed, if anything, to welcome the human contact.

JoLynn reached out, leaned, extended her hand to the creature. She touched it. Stroked it. Fondled the mottled skin. "It's wonderful, Oliver. Here."

He found himself on his knees between the seats, his pant legs wet from the cold salt water that had collected on the deck and his belly pressing hard against the unyielding gunwale. He shifted a bit to take the pressure on the front of his cork vest instead and leaned out again.

He felt a surge of excitement as his groping fingers found the whale's side.

The great beast's skin felt cool to his touch. Not at all slimy or unpleasant. It was rather like stroking a wet football on a chilly autumn day. He hadn't really known what to expect. Whatever he'd expected or thought he should expect, this was better. This was . . . contact. From one species to another. Without greed or violence or dishonesty. One human mammal wishing love and well-being to one whale mammal. Oliver felt something—tears? possibly; intense gut level emotion, certainly—well up inside him and bring moisture to his eyes and a clenching lump into his throat.

Then the whale sucked in a breath—he could hear the fluttering, bubbling intake of air—and sank. Simply dropped away beneath the water and out of reach, its great form becoming indistinct within moments and then disappearing completely into the green belly of the sea.

Oliver knelt on the hard flooring of the excursion boat, his hand trailing in the cool waters of the Pacific, and stared into the water long after the whale was out of view. His and JoLynn's whale was gone now, but its memory would be with him forever. He turned to JoLynn, who was still sitting above him, and wrapped his arms around her waist and pressed his face against her chest. She was feeling the wondrous sense of connection, he could tell, and he wanted to hold on to the joy of it with her for as long as possible. He felt her stroke the back of his head, her hand still cold and wet from where she'd stroked the great whale, and he did not mind the salty water that dripped onto the back of his neck. This was another form of connection, a sharing, and it was good. He felt JoLynn's heart beating strong and steady against his cheek, and that too was good. He sighed and felt his love for her fill him almost to overflowing. His lips moved and he murmured a message meant not for her ears but sent straight into her heart.

"What, Oliver?"

He shook his head. "Nothing." He looked up at her and smiled. Then winked. "Secret stuff." She made a face at him and laughed.

Oliver pulled away from her and resumed his place on the boat seat. The others who crowded the small boat were already intent on looking at a whale calf—the baby was the size of a station wagon—that was hiding near the surface between their boat and the Avon. Oliver squeezed JoLynn's hand, and they resumed the pleasure of the whale watching as the pod assembled around the growing flotilla of tourist boats. No matter what else happened now, though, the whole trip was already worthwhile and then some.

OLIVER WOKE EARLY. A thin and watery predawn light filtered in past the bent, zigzag slats of the venetian blinds in the room. He had no idea what time it was but really didn't much care.

Dawn rising was not his habit, or hadn't been until this trip. He'd begun waking so early here simply because the motel mattress was lumpy and musty smelling and he didn't sleep well on it. Now he was discovering that he liked being awake an hour or more ahead of JoLynn. He enjoyed the silence. And the fact that he could sit quietly and look at her while she slept.

First things first, though. Moving as stealthily as a cat burglar, he slid his skinny, knobby legs out from under the sheet and inched sideways to the edge of the bed. A bedspring squealed softly in protest, and Oliver smiled. At first they'd found the howlings of the bedsprings distressing. But the things were so raucously loud in their advertisement of any and all activity that the noise became more funny than embarrassing. More endearing than aggravating. He paused for a moment at the lip of the sagging mattress to find the gritty floor with his left foot and slowly, cautiously transferred his weight off the bed. JoLynn's hand, held atop the pillow beside her ear, clenched and twitched a little but she didn't wake; the rhythm of her breathing did not alter. Oliver smiled again and stood fully upright.

He padded barefoot and naked into the tiny cubicle of a bathroom and quickly attended to his immediate needs. He put the lid down over the bowl but didn't pull the chain—he hadn't known anyone still used plumbing like that—to flush the john yet because it was even louder than the bedsprings and was sure to wake JoLynn.

Yawning and stretching, his tendons creaking and joints popping, he turned and looked into the bathroom mirror while he fingered the stubble that had begun to accumulate and to annoy him beneath his lower lip. The hints of daylight reaching in through the translucent window glass weren't enough to shave by. Not that Oliver did much in the way of shaving in any event. His cheeks and chin were covered with a dark, soft mat of red-brown fur. But he liked to shave his neck now and then and absolutely required a close trim beneath the nose and lip. Except for that, however, his morning sink-and-mirror routine was a matter of complete simplicity. Brush the teeth, brush the hair, brush the face, and all was done. That too could wait a bit, though.

There wasn't any other reason he might want to stare into a mirror either. Oliver found his own features to be ordinary and uninteresting. Narcissism was not among his faults.

Oliver Bendix was . . . average. In his own opinion, average shading to something less than. Average height at five ten but under average in weight. Dark brown hair. Perfectly ordinary brown eyes, although JoLynn swore she could see flecks and highlights of gold in them. Average features. Average American teeth, which was to say white and nearly perfect but hardly remarkable. Average nose. Average ears. Hairline receding in a perfectly average manner, even if at thirty-two Oliver was the only one who seemed to be noticing that quite yet. Average intelligence, Oliver told himself as he looked into a dim, streaked mirror in the rundown Mexican motel room. That, however, was a bit of a lie. Oliver did not really believe that himself, though he told himself that he did. If conceit is a fault, then modesty must therefore be a virtue. Oliver actively wanted to be able to think of himself as a virtuous person. And therefore he felt obligated to think of himself as no brighter than the average bear. He yawned again and went back out into the bedroom.

JoLynn was still sleeping. Oliver sank onto the grimy upholstery of the lone easy chair in the room and smiled as he looked at her. God, she was gorgeous.

She lay facing away from him. That didn't matter. She was gorgeous from any angle.

Her black hair, so long and lovely, spread over the pillow and sheets like a swatch of shimmering silk. She let it fall loose and full and free only at night, so that Oliver was the only other person who ever got to see her like this. During the day she wore her hair pulled back into a single severe braid that hung nearly to her waist even when shortened by the braiding. Brushing JoLynn's hair at night was one of Oliver's great pleasures. The nightly activity had become a ritualized part of their relationship. Braiding it again in the morning, however, was JoLynn's task alone. Oliver never could bring himself to draw the braids tight enough to suit her, although he used to try. She liked the sides drawn back so sharply that the corners of her eyes pulled and wrinkled. Oliver simply could not make himself tug and pull hard enough to satisfy her.

Now, loose while she slept, her hair continued to hold the crimps and wavelets imposed by the long habit of the braiding. Soft waves on a midnight sea. Oliver smiled, thinking both of JoLynn now and of the whale yesterday. Marvelous, both of them.

God, she was gorgeous, he thought, not for the first time and certainly not for the last.

Funny how it had taken him so long to see her real beauty, though. He hadn't been able to see it when they first met. All that had come later. Now he found it quite incredible that he had ever been able to miss seeing it. Now he could see nothing but beauty when he looked at her.

Beauty, not prettiness. And there is such a difference, Oliver knew. Pretty is a quality many women have, but it lies on the surface and can be lost to time or misfortune. Beauty is something that lies within and glows through to the surface. Beauty is a quality of the spirit, not the body, and it need not be diminished by aging or injury or any other external influence. What JoLynn Weaver had was beauty in the truest sense. A very great beauty, in Oliver's smug opinion.

As for the other, well, she was almost pretty as well. Her "day face" was as severe as her hairstyle but certainly not unattractive.

JoLynn was as tall as Oliver and even leaner. Two years older. Dark complected. He teased her sometimes about having AmerIndian blood hidden somewhere in her family past, although in truth there was none known. Her ancestry was a mixture of Mediterranean and Middle European, much like his own except perhaps with a little less English and a touch more Italian.

JoLynn's hair was as black as a raven's wing and her eyes a strikingly pale blue-gray. Her lips were thin and firm in appearance. But marvelously soft to kiss. Her nose was thin and her cheekbones high. Her figure was boyish, a great disappointment to her although a delight to him. She looked anorexic but wasn't. She could, and frequently did, continue to eat with gusto when Oliver was stuffed and groaning.

She presented to the rest of the world the physical appearance of a spinster librarian. Prim, plain, reserved to the point of seeming chilly. Oliver knew better. Her reserve was shyness hidden behind a mask of stone. But that particular stone could melt and, when molten, could sear and inflame.

Thinking about her, thinking about that, Oliver felt affection turn to desire. The seat of the emotions he was experiencing toward her left his chest and flowed south.

He glanced toward the window. The light outside was stronger now but still far from being the full, harsh glare of the southern winter sun.

There was plenty of time. The day's boats would not leave for hours yet.

He stood and went to the bed, lifted the sheet and crawled in on JoLynn's side, wedging himself tight against her back and having to be careful so that he didn't slide off the edge of the slightly too small mattress.

"Fibber," he accused gently. "You aren't asleep. I can feel that you aren't."

"Well, you certainly aren't either." There was no hint of sleep-huskiness in her voice, and he wondered just how long she'd been awake, if she'd known he was there looking at her and admiring her. She chuckled and pressed herself back against him, spooning herself tight to his body and wiggling her hips suggestively.

She was smiling when she turned into his embrace, and he found that JoLynn was quite as awake and ready as he was.

•   •   •   •   •

OLIVER WAITED until JoLynn was out of the way, then reached into the back of the Subaru to rearrange the bags and bundles packed there. The roads down here in the Baja weren't exactly freeway quality, and he didn't want any of their souvenirs broken.

Or, for that matter, wouldn't want anything on the Subaru to break either. He would have to do all the driving, at least until they reached the border. JoLynn was notorious for her disregard of road hazards. The battered little mustard-colored station wagon was tough but not totally indestructible, as JoLynn seemed to think. Her theory seemed to be that if a vehicle had four-wheel drive, it could handle anything.

"Is that everything?" he asked.

"Everything except that silly hat."

He grinned. "Hoping I'd leave it behind?"

Her answer was a smile and a shrug. Then she laughed. She might not fully approve of the touristy thing, he knew, but she didn't begrudge him having it. Just, perhaps, so he didn't wear it when she was present.

"I'll take a last look around, then we can go." He pulled the cargo hatch down and pressed rather than slammed it closed.

He turned toward the motel room that had been theirs for the past week, and JoLynn stopped him with a touch on the elbow. The look she gave him was serious, searching.

"You aren't sorry, are you, Oliver?"

It took him a moment to realize what she meant. Then he shook his head and reassured her with a light kiss. "No. I'm not sorry. It was everything you said and a hundred times more. Just that, that one moment"— he didn't have to specify which one moment, they both understood the special quality of being able to actually touch a free and living whale— "that made it perfect."

She looked pleased, and no wonder. They never actually fought about anything, but they had come close to it over this whale-watching trip to Baja. Oliver had agreed to come only because of JoLynn's passionate insistence.

Not that he had anything against saving the whales. Far from it. In fact, he had been the one accusing her of not truly caring about them. Oliver had wanted to donate the money to Save the Whales; JoLynn had wanted the relatively selfish pleasure of seeing the winter migration for herself.

They'd ended up in a compromise. They took the cheapest possible package excursion south and donated the rest of their vacation money to Save the Whales.

Now Oliver was glad he'd come.

He smiled and kissed her again.

"You better quit that or we won't get as far as the border tonight," she warned.

"Promise?"

"Go get your hat, Oliver."

"Yes, ma'am," he said meekly, mocking her bossiness. He turned away from her and went back to the motel room. He would have gone back anyway, even if she hadn't left the hat behind, which was probably why she'd left it in the room to begin with. She knew him well enough to know that he would make one last check of the closet and bureau drawers anyway, one last search behind the shower curtain and in the medicine cabinet and under each pillow. JoLynn, who never gave a thought to leaving anything behind, never ever left anything behind. But Oliver had to look for himself anyway or he would spend the entire trip home to San Francisco worrying.

He heard the Subaru door shut with a tight, solid clunk and hurried his pace. JoLynn was already in the car, as impatient as he to get on the road. They had so much to tell everyone when they got home. Not that they would ever be able to convey the very special excitements they'd found. Not that that would stop them from trying. Oliver made his last, obligatory run-through of the empty room, then remembered only as he was heading for the door again that his tourist cap was still on top of the bureau. He grabbed it and put it on and hurried out to the car.

TWO

JIM LEFT THE ENGINE RUNNING and the heater fan blowing. He set the parking brake and climbed stiffly out of the cab of the old truck. JayJay was already outside. Jim pushed the door closed behind him, the sound of it thin and tinny. It would be a struggle to get the half-shot latch open again—the old Chevy had seen better days—but he didn't want to lose the heat that had built up inside since their last stop.

Jim's eyes began to tear almost as soon as he was out of the truck. The cold wind sweeping down off the dry deserts of Oregon was mind-numbingly bitter. It stung his cheeks and curled down inside his shirt and made his eyes weep. He pulled the collar of the down-filled vest high around his neck and wished all over again that he'd thought to bring heavier gloves than these unlined everyday muleskins. But then, the sun had been bright and the air still when they left home this morning. The wind had come up since, and in this country it was the wind, not the temperature, that determined a man's comfort.

"With you in a minute, Jim."

"Don't bother."

JayJay was standing on the downwind side of the truck taking a leak. From where he stood, Jim couldn't see the activity, but could hear the splash on frozen ground and JayJay's grunt of satisfaction as he zipped his jeans.

Jim walked to the back of the truck, the brittle grasses crunching underfoot, and reached into the bed to drag first one dull brown protein block and then another onto the tailgate. Two should be enough here, he decided. The beeves hadn't quite finished the blocks they'd put out last time.

He skidded one to the edge of the rust-flecked tailgate and gave it a tug, dumping it off the truck and onto the ground. The cube-shaped protein block hit with a thump and rolled wildly away. Jim was careful to watch his feet. Boots or no boots, a tumbling fifty-pound block can give a man a helluva sore shin if one bounces the wrong direction. He dumped the second block off the tailgate and hurried back to the warm comfort of the truck cab. JayJay was already there.

JayJay grinned at him, exposing yellowed stumps and empty gum where most of his teeth should have been. Jim Beale probably didn't know half a dozen grown men who had all their own teeth. JayJay Lawrence likely didn't know as many as Jim did.

"You think them sons o' bitches appreciate all we do for 'em?" the hired man asked.

Jim snorted and grinned back at him.

"Yeah, ain't it the truth," JayJay observed. He reached inside his vest and pulled out a hard-box pack of Marlboros, offered one to Jim and lighted one for himself.

Jim released the parking brake and managed to get the old truck into first without grinding any metal off the gears. That was a feat that required a certain amount of delicacy. It also helped if you held your mouth right and had a bit of luck.

The Chevy lurched forward, the transfer case whining in four-wheel drive, and JayJay whooped and bounced on the sagging seat springs. "Grab leather, boys, he's at it again," he hollered.

Jim ignored him, cranked the wheel hard right and slowed to power through a depression in the ground that one of these days would develop into a gully. The truck crawled out the other side, and Jim mashed down on the accelerator just in time to send a back wheel crashing over a stub of half buried rock. He was pleased to note that the crown of JayJay's hat was flattened against the roof from the resulting jolt. JayJay laughed and braced himself with his feet hard against the firewall. That took the fun out of it, so Jim slowed down again.

"We ain't going to Wahoo?" JayJay asked. Wahoo Spring would normally be their next stop dropping protein blocks out for the beeves to find.

"Yeah. Thought I'd take the long way round."

"Hokay." JayJay pulled his hat off and stuffed a fist inside it to pop the crown out, then carefully reshaped it to his liking. The elderly Resistol had lost its color years ago to an accumulation of sweat and filth, but JayJay was meticulous about its shape anyway.

The atmosphere inside the cab was becoming hot and smoky. Jim opened a window wing to let some of the smoke out and cold in.

"Never satisfied," JayJay accused.

"Oh, I dunno. I think I was once. Course I was drunk at the time. But my friends tell me I was satisfied that night."

"You got friends? I'll be damn."

"Yeah, I've always heard that you would be."

"Wake me when we get to Wahoo." JayJay popped his hat back onto his head and tugged the brim low over his eyes.

"I'll do that," Jim said. And immediately began looking for another rock to bounce the truck over.

THEY STAYED INSIDE the cab of the truck. The wind beyond the thin sheets of glass and steel was too cold to face without reason. But that did nothing to detract from the pleasures of the moment.

JayJay made no comment when Jim reached forward and twisted the ignition key, killing the tired engine and letting the silence settle around them.

But then, JayJay had come to appreciate this almost as much as Jim did.

The two men sat quietly, looking out across the vast sweep of white and tan before them.

Tan of winter-dry grass on the great, rolling basin. White of sun-crusted snowdrifts scattered in pencil-thin lines like white-capped waves on a sere and solid ocean surface.

To left and right of the basin were rugged, ragged lumps of white-capped rock. Snow-peaked mountains so distant it would take a man and horse a day to reach them.

Closer in were a few dark and solid shapes, red and black and maroon. Too far to be recognizable, but cattle. Definitely cattle, not horses. A man could always tell the difference no matter how far away or indistinct they might seem to a city-trained eye. Distant beeves have an appearance that is square in shape. A horse's appearance is rounded. Jim or JayJay either one would have been mystified if told that someone might not be able to tell the difference. It never would have occurred to either of them to think otherwise.

"Mighty fine," JayJay observed softly.

"Yeah."

It was true and it was enough. It was what Jim had driven up here to see. Land, almost boundless land, land enough that it was counted not in acres but in sections, square miles. Land the Beales had ranched for generations. Seeing it like this, at any season of the year, was always enough to stir Jim Beale. It pleased him to think that JayJay responded to it too, even though he wasn't family. Jim grunted with satisfaction and reached into his shirt pocket for a Chesterfield.

The interior of the Chevy was becoming cool now without the heater, but Jim was in no hurry. He was enjoying seeing the land spread out before and below, enjoying hearing the whine and whistle of the wind that curled round the cab of the truck. He came to the top of Buttercup Hill every now and then just for this purpose.

Jim smiled softly to himself, thinking about the name of the actually nameless little hill.

Buttercup Hill wasn't a designation that appeared on any map. In fact, as far as Jim knew, the hill itself might not appear on any map. Certainly not on any map he'd ever seen. The hill was only one of countless lumps on the uneven surface of the high-desert basin, a little taller than most, situated, though, so that it provided an ideal view of the Beale holdings. That was what brought Jim here. And probably Bill too, although they'd never talked about it.

Buttercup Hill. The name had nothing to do with flowers. This wasn't country much given to any kind of flowers. The name was a contraction Jim and Bill settled on when they were boys. Bill had been eleven that year, if Jim remembered correctly. That would've made Jim . . . he had to think about it a moment . . . fourteen. Older and wiser and experienced in matters of the heart. Jim hid his smile behind a drag on the Chesterfield. Bill'd had his heart broken by Beth Danker. The experience had been a first and therefore was perhaps the worst such pain. Bill had saddled a horse and disappeared so long, their mother sent Jim to find him and fetch him home. Bill'd been up here assuaging his pain with a full bag of Roooo'o Peanut Butter Cups that he'd swiped out of the pantry. He'd eaten every damned one of them by the time Jim found him. And afterward the both of them referred to the no-name hill as Peanut Butter Cup Hill and, eventually, simply as Buttercup Hill.

That Danker girl had married a townie from Winnemucca and lived in Reno or some such place now, Jim thought. Probably had three kids and was fat. Jim wondered if Bill ever thought about her anymore. Probably not. No more than Jim ever thought about . . . hell, he couldn't remember the name of the girl who'd broken his own heart the first time. Funny how he'd remembered Beth Danker.

"Gettin' late," JayJay said. "Gotta hit Wahoo an' Cider Spring 'fore we head home."

"Yeah." They hadn't been here long, but it was enough. Jim reached for the key again, twisted it, fired the engine and crunched the transmission into first. They needed the heater going again anyhow after just that little bit of time. Damn, it was cold out. At Wahoo he'd let JayJay get out and drop the blocks off the truck.

He let the clutch out and the Chevy rolled down the north slope of Buttercup, popping and spitting and backfiring as he held it slow with engine compression instead of using up the brakes.

JIM WINKED AT HIS BROTHER and reached for another of the longneck Bud bottles. It was becoming difficult to tell the full ones from the empties. They'd have to do something about that pretty soon. Shuck those empties and get some full ones. That would work. He looked across the crowded, noisy room and chuckled.

"Gettin' that look in his eye," Bill agreed happily.

"Won't be worth a damn tomorrow."

"Tomorrow, hell. Will he be worth anything come Monday?" Bill Beale laughed and clinked his brown bottle against Jim's.

Saturday nights, Jim reflected, were a lot more relaxed when a man was married. Not more fun, necessarily, but a whole lot more relaxed.

JayJay Lawrence, John Joseph if anyone wanted to be formal about it, was on the "dance floor," which really was only a space where there weren't any tables to get in the way, jumping and quivering to the hard-rock beat of a song that had country western words and plenty of boom-boom drum. If the music wasn't much good, it at least was loud, and all a man needed to know to dance to it was that you stomped your boot whenever the drummer stomped his. Live entertainment by the Purple Sage every Saturday night, yahoo. Jim smiled and took a pull at the Bud.

It wasn't JayJay's dancing that the Beale boys found so amusing, it was his every-Saturday-night crouch. Along about this time of the evening every Saturday, old JayJay would start to hunch over when he danced. Get all loose in the legs and rigid in the middle and commence to breathe heavy. Which wasn't such a good idea if it was carried too far, because all the ladies who showed up at Talley's Corner were married or otherwise spoken for.

Here directly, Jim knew, JayJay would saunter over with his fancy Satur-day hat pushed to the back of his head. He'd make a point of saying how he was gonna head back early tonight—he did that for the benefit of Gloria and Maureen even though the two Mrs. Beales knew where he was off to as good as anyone—and then head the thirty miles into Win-nemucca to spend the rest of his Saturday night. It hardly ever failed. And the few times it didn't happen that way weren't so much fun as they used to be. The few exceptions were when JayJay went too far with some little ol' gal and got himself and the Beales involved in a fight. A fight at Talley's Corner wasn't so interesting these days as it used to be when they were all younger, Jim had noticed.

Jim glanced over at his younger brother. Even Bill was commencing to show his age nowadays. The kid had some gray in his hair. Well, he was past forty now and likely entitled to some gray. At least Bill had hair. Couple more years and Jim figured he could sell his comb.

Bill was looking across the room to where Maureen and Gloria were busy catching up on the past week's gossip, them and Nan Hanratty and Bess Arnold and some other ladies bent over their own collection of beer bottles, all of them with their mouths going at once so it was a wonder anybody could make out anything that was being said. Just like with the men, once the women got to a certain age, there was less dancing done here and more talk.

Still some dancing too, though, bless 'em. That wouldn't change. Not completely. Old Harve Waters and his bride of damn near fifty years were out on the dance floor right now showing the young buckaroos how to do it and not doing such a bad job of it at that. Jim decided he'd have another beer in celebration of Harve and Harriet Waters.

"Where you goin'?" he asked as Bill stood up.

"Heedin' the call of the wild geese."

"Bring back some more beers when you're done."

"I can do that." Bill flashed a grin and then was gone, winding his way through the tables and around the fringes of the dancers. Jim watched him go. Bill was a scrawny, scrappy little SOB. Looked like the buckaroo he was with his handlebar mustache and bushy sideburns and jeans slung low and fancy, Saturday night John Wayne shirt with the two rows of buttons on the front. Looked, in fact, a whole lot like his big brother Jim except that Jim's mustache was longer and nicer-curled. Bill looked like he would take on anything that had hair on it, human or otherwise. And so he would. Jim grunted and smiled.

Bill danced first with Jim's wife, Gloria, then lucked into a slow one when he danced with his own Maureen. That Maureen, she was all right. About as good a girl as Gloria, and that was high praise indeed. The Beale boys had done just fine.

Over to the side of the room where the kids always yarded up together, Jim could see Jimmy—the boy was named for Bill and Jim's dad, not for his uncle—and Tod snicker and giggle as they watched their folks cuddle and sway out on the dance floor. Just a few more years, Jim figured, and Jimmy would change his tune and be wanting to do some of that public cuddling his own self. That time wouldn't be far off now, the way those boys were growing.

Jim drained off the flat, tepid Bud and stood, weaving only a little bit. He'd make a stop in the men's room, he figured, then maybe grab Gloria off that chair and cut a caper himself. Show Bill he wasn't the only one in the family who could still raise some dust. Jim tipped his head back and let out a whoop that was lost amid all the rest of the noise, upset his balance for a moment and grabbed Anse Demont's shoulder to steady himself by, then gave Anse and Louise a wink as he passed by them. Saturday night. Hell, yes.

THREE

OLIVER LOOKED UP, winked and sent a soundless kissing expression toward JoLynn. She saw that he was on the telephone and substituted a smile and an airborne kiss for the cheery greeting she usually called out when she got home.

JoLynn disappeared into the bedroom to change. She was a secretary in a staid and stuffy law office and had to wear heels and hose during the day. Her first priority on getting home was to get into comfortable clothing.

"I agree," Oliver said into the telephone. "Of course you're right." He made a sour face. "But you see, this research isn't only to protect people like that. Think about all the innocent people, children some of them, who need transfusions. Can you imagine how you would feel if your own child was injured in a car accident and needed blood? Can you imagine how terrible you would feel if your child was infected with AIDS through no fault of his own? That's why we have to find a cure for the disease, Mrs. Bramley. It's a danger to all of us." He paused, listened. "No, ma'am, I'm not. But I do care. I do feel a genuine concern for the victims regardless of their personal, um, activities. And I'm sure you're a good and caring person too, Mrs. Bramley. That's why we're asking you to contribute to this . . . ma'am? Yes, ma'am. Volunteer. No, ma'am, not a penny. I'm doing this because I care, not because I'm paid." He paused again. "More than ninety percent, ma'am."

JoLynn came out of the bedroom barefoot and wearing a caftan. Oliver looked at her and rolled his eyes, motioning toward the telephone as he did so. She smiled and went into the kitchen to see how their supper was progressing. Oliver was home every day a good two hours earlier than she and nearly always had something in the oven by the time she arrived.

"Yes, ma'am," Oliver said. "As much as you care to give, of course, but a pledge of twenty dollars would do *so* much good." He paused. "No, ma'am, I'm afraid not, no premiums or prizes."

JoLynn drifted back into view. She was licking something off a fingertip.

"Twenty-five dollars would be wonderful, Mrs. Bramley. Thank you. Yes, ma'am, we'll mail you a confirmation, and of course it is tax deductible. Thank you, Mrs. Bramley. Thank you very much."

Oliver broke the telephone connection with the ball of his thumb but kept the receiver to his ear while he marked down the Bramley pledge on an index card and referred to the list for the next number he would call.

JoLynn padded over behind him and bent to kiss the back of his neck. He smiled. "Hi there."

"Hi there yourself."

He felt the warmth of her body close behind him and the cool fabric of the caftan, could smell the delicate fragrance she always wore to the office. "I could take a break here if you like," he suggested.

"How many more?"

He made a face and pointed. The list was endless. There would always be at least one more call that could be made. Before this list was completed, another would be provided and another after that.

"Later," JoLynn said. "I'll finish supper while you make some more calls. We'll discuss the alternatives afterward, buddy-boy."

Oliver winked at her again, glanced down at the next number on his list and began tapping the telephone's push buttons. Brant was the name this time, he reminded himself as the telephone on the other end began to ring. Oliver cleared his throat and prepared himself to go into the spiel.

OLIVER WRITHED AND SQUIRMED. Stretched. Groaned. He flopped from one side to the other and curled his knees high. Flopped back again to his original position and wadded the pillow under his ear.

It wasn't any good. He wasn't going to be able to go back to sleep now.

He sat up, blinking, and began to smile as he realized what it was that had wakened him. He could hear a rattling of dishware in the kitchen and the muted hiss and gurgle of the Braun brewing Sanka.

He lay back down again and stretched, enjoying it this time, as he realized this was Sunday morning and JoLynn's turn to make a lazy, lie-abed breakfast.

Weekdays they were up and away early to their jobs. Saturdays they ran, played tennis or racquetball, devoted the afternoons and most evenings to environmental issues. But Sundays were private. No telephone solicitations, no meetings, no rallies, rarely so much as a party.

They alternated the chores of the Sunday breakfast making as they alternated everything else—Oliver still despised cleaning toilets when it was his turn for that, but he knew that JoLynn disliked the indisputably necessary task every bit as much—and today it was JoLynn's turn to prepare the meal and bring in the Sunday newspaper.

He considered staying where he was until she came in barefoot and smiling with the tray, knew he couldn't hold out that long and left the bed to go to the bathroom. He washed, pulled on a bathrobe and wandered out into the kitchen to join her.

"What can I do to help?"

She smiled and blew him a kiss and pointed to the cabinet where the breakfast tray was kept. "Good morning, dear."

JoLynn frowned in concentration as she arranged finger slices of cantaloupe and kiwifruit in a chrysanthemum pattern on the plate. She always liked things to be presented nicely and was as intense about this as she was with virtually everything she did.

The toaster clattered, popping up half an oat bran bagel for each of them, but JoLynn continued placing the fruit until everything met her satisfaction. Only then did she take the bagel out of the toaster and place the pieces on two separate small plates. She poured four ounces of orange juice, nonreconstituted, for each, then got out the carafe just as the Braun finished making the coffee.

By then Oliver had the tray ready with napkins and vitamin tablets in place. JoLynn loaded the tray and looked around.

"The newspaper," he reminded her.

"Oops." She pulled her ancient and tatty but much-loved bathrobe together at the throat and went to collect the *Chronicle* from the doorstep —if the carrier who serviced the apartment building ever quit delivering door to door, JoLynn was going to be in trouble; a robe like hers should be seen only by the most intimate friends or relatives—while Oliver carried the heavy tray into the bedroom. She trailed behind him with the paper and carafe.

Oliver loved Sunday mornings.

FOUR

GOD, JIM BEALE hated Sunday mornings. Damn things followed Saturday nights just as sure as drought followed plenty. He sat up, rubbed the sleep out of his eyes and wondered what kind of creature had crapped in his mouth while he wasn't looking.

He got up, the springs of the old bed creaking, and went to the bathroom to brush his teeth quick before his tongue festered. Gloria was still sleeping when he came out and he let her be. With luck she'd sleep till noon today and for a change not drag him off all the way to town for services. He sent a hopeful squint toward the clock, although he knew good and well he'd wakened at the break of day like he always did. If Gloria would just keep on snoring until seven-thirty, eight o'clock at the very latest, it would be too late for them to get spruced up and make the drive. Jim prayed she'd sleep on this morning.

He stumbled bleary-eyed and shaky down to the kitchen and put coffee on for himself, sat shivering and miserable in his drawers while he waited for it to make.

Lordy, a man oughta know better than to do such things to himself.

Well, he did know better, of course. The only problem was trying to get himself to take all that good advice he was capable of giving.

No point in turning the radio on this morning. There weren't any market reports on Sunday mornings, and he'd had enough music last night to last at least till next Saturday.

He stood up again and went over to the window. There wasn't any frost to clear off it this morning. That was a good sign. The weather was breaking early this year. There'd been snow enough to seep down into the roots of the grass, and now it looked like they'd have an early spring.

He looked across to Bill's house, thought about getting dressed and walking over there to visit and take coffee with them. Maureen wasn't so insistent on having company when she went off to church Sunday mornings, so it wouldn't matter if she was awake or not. He knew Bill'd be up, of course, just the same as Jim was. There hadn't been a day either of them could remember that they hadn't been up with the dawn. The only thing holding Jim back was the question of whether the boys would be awake already. Bill's boys were wonderful kids and Jim loved them, but they were a bit much to take early on a Sunday morning. If they were awake, they'd have the satellite dish tuned to some cartoon show and the TV blasting.

He thought about it, heard the percolator give one last rumble before it fell silent, and decided to stay at home this Sunday morning.

He turned away from the window and reached a mug down from the cabinet.

JIM WAITED while Bill pulled his coat on. "You sure you won't come with us?"

"No thanks," Jimmy said, not turning his eyes away from the TV screen. Tod acted like he hadn't even heard. Both boys were lost in the antics of a bunch of cartoon monsters that Jim couldn't tell apart. If they'd been watching the Road Runner, he might have paid some attention himself. At least those were cute. But these roaring monster things and zoom-zoom space creatures he couldn't make head nor tail of. He wondered if he'd have been so taken in by them if there had been such entertainments when he and Bill were that age. Probably, he conceded.

"If mama gets back before we do, tell her we won't be long," Bill told them.

"We will, Dad."

"Which truck do you want to take?" Bill asked.

"The Sierra. No need to drag horses along with us today, and I don't want to mess with that hitch on the Chevy. It's too much fuss when we'd just have to turn around and hook the trailer on again."

"All right." Bill opened the hall closet and pulled out a Ruger No. 1 rifle that was a pet possession. The single-shot rifle had a heavy, varmint-weight barrel in .25-06 caliber and 10X Burris scope on it.

"You ain't hunting coyotes, are you?" Jimmy shouted over the noise of the TV.

"Nope," Bill assured him. "Not unless one is feeling suicidal."

"Okay, then." The youngsters would have been clamoring to go along if they'd thought there was any chance they might get to shoot their dad's .25-06.

Bill gave his brother a wink, and they stepped outside into the mid-morning chill.

It wasn't bad for this time of year, though. Nippy but not biting. Call it the high twenties to low thirties, Jim figured. By afternoon it might warm into the forties.

They walked over to the equipment shed, and Bill placed the rifle with care onto the prongs of the window rack behind the seat of the nearly new GMC. They carried a couple Ruger Mini-14s in the window of the old work truck as a matter of course, but if they were taking the good truck, Bill would be taking his good rifle too. It was something on the order of wearing one's best hat and boots on Saturday night.

Bill crawled into the passenger side of the cab, every bit as duded up and comfortable as Maureen's Buick sedan, and Jim opened the driver's side door. He paused there for a moment to reach for his cigarettes.

"Hurry up an' get that heater to working, will you?"

"Gimme a minute here." Jim fired up his Chesterfield, then cocked his head.

"You hear something?"

"Yeah, somebody's coming. I hear a motor."

Bill got out of the truck and both men walked out into the yard so they could look down the graded track that led to the road some five miles off.

They wouldn't have any trouble seeing what was coming. The Beale ranch was a cluster of buildings that was the only man-tall obstruction in sight from one mountain range to the next. Although a ranch headquarters generally involves enough structures to be mistaken for a small town by someone who doesn't know what he is looking at.

The Beale place had started with a sod house—it still stood, although it had long since been turned into a root cellar—and had been busy growing for four generations and now into a fifth. There was the old house where Jim and Gloria now lived, the newer house that Bill and Maureen had built, the good house trailer that JayJay occupied as their foreman and only year-round hand—that one used to be Jim and Gloria's until Jim's father died and they moved into the big house—the smaller trailers that served as seasonal bunkhouses, barns, sheds, tumbledown ricks and a maze of corrals and loading chutes that it would take a newcomer a map to work out.

"I'll be damn," Bill said.

"And it's not even midnight," Jim agreed.

JayJay's green Ford pickup rattled toward them at the head of a plume of dust that lifted into the cold air and hung there.

"What's he doing home at this hour?"

They stood and waited for him. JayJay pulled into the yard, stopped beside the equipment shed where the vehicles were kept under cover and got out with a grin.

"We sure didn't expect t' see you today."

"Aw, I'm raring to go." He slammed the Ford's door shut and came over to join them. "You boys working today?"

"Looking, not working."

JayJay shook a Marlboro out of his pack and lighted it.

"You look mighty smug today."

"I am," JayJay admitted.

"You seen Linda last night, didn't you?"

JayJay didn't say anything, but his grin said Jim'd been right. Last night JayJay went into Winnemucca to see the bright lights. This morning it looked like it had agreed with him.

The Beale brothers were both well aware of the tongue-tied fixation JayJay had on a certain blond lady in town there. She was a divorcée who ran an office supply store in Winnemucca and was undeniably attractive. JayJay, who probably hadn't written three postcards in his lifetime, had been known to stock up heavy on pens, pencils, notepads and envelopes, all purchased at the office supply. He'd waltz in there full of brag and bluster, then turn shy and not say a word when he made his purchases. The up side of it was that he kept Bill's boys handsomely supplied with the paper and stuff they needed at school.

"So what happened?" Bill demanded.

"Aw, not much." JayJay rocked back on his heels and peered down toward his boots.

"Where'd you go?"

"Elks."

"And she was there?"

"Kinda."

"Did you dance with her?"

"Naw, nothin' like that."

Jim guessed JayJay hadn't so much as spoken to her. Sure must have looked her over good, though. Apparently that was enough.

"You want to ride with us?"

"D'you need me?"

"No, we're just going to look around some."

"Reckon I'll go to the house then." Likely, Jim figured, he would sit in there and moon about Mrs. Haversal. There wasn't much else for him to do in the trailer. JayJay wasn't one for sleeping in the daytime and didn't own a television.

"We'll honk when we get back. You can come over an' take dinner with us."

"I'll do that, thanks."

The brothers waited until they were in the cab of the Sierra and JayJay was nearly to his trailer door before they started to laugh.

JIM DROVE THROUGH THE GATE and swung the truck not left toward the vast pastures of the Beale holdings but right onto the graded driveway toward the road. Beside him Bill raised an eyebrow.

"Thought we'd check the condition o' the grass on the public ground," Jim explained.

Bill nodded, satisfied, and slouched in a corner of the cab while his brother guided the softly sprung GMC around the worst of the potholes. Before long they would have to have a mechanic come out from town and convince the damn bulldozer to run again so they could scrape the drive. There was no point to that, though, until the chance of wet spring storms and consequent mud was past.

"Something bothering you?" Bill asked after they were on the public road and rolling north at a better pace.

"Nope." Jim fished another Chesterfield out of his shirt pocket and lighted it. Bill rolled his window down several inches to let the smoke out. Bill enjoyed a little snouse now and then but never had gotten the habit of smoking.

"You been thinking too much the last couple weeks," Bill accused. "I been seeing it come on you."

Jim grinned and shook his head. "You know me."

"Uh-huh. An' you been thinking too much."

"Just fretful. You know."

"It's all right," Bill told him. "It's gonna be all right."

"If you say so."

As the older of the brothers, Jim had always carried their burdens more heavily than Bill ever did. That was probably strange, considering that Jim had no kids of his own to pass things along to, while Bill was the one with boys who could be expected to take over someday. But that was the way Jim had always been.

"It's all right this year," Bill said. "We've had a good winter. Enough moisture. No winterkill to speak of. Looks like a good spring coming. So what the hell d'you want?"

Jim looked at him and didn't answer.

Bill shrugged and subsided into his corner of the cab. Jimmy got like this every year without fail. Worrying, always worrying. There wasn't going to be enough grass; there'd be a late norther during the birthing and they'd lose half their calf crop; their lease allotments would be cut and they wouldn't have graze enough to carry all their beeves. Hell, there was always something a man could worry about if he really wanted to. Jimmy always wanted to.

Bill was glad now that JayJay hadn't wanted to ride along today. Jimmy never was willing to let his hair down, what of it he had left, when there was anybody but family about. After a dozen years—God, could it've been that long now? closer to fifteen once Bill worked it out—JayJay thought of himself as family. But of course he wasn't. He only acted that way. The difference didn't matter all that much to Bill, but it did to Jimmy.

The truck reached a Y in the faint two-track that passed for a road this far up. Jimmy bore to the left, drove on another couple miles and veered off the visible road onto a track made over the years by the tires of the few vehicles that ever came this way.

Bill didn't need to pay attention to Jim's driving to figure out where they were going. He'd known that much ever since they turned right instead of left at the gate back home. He concentrated on looking around instead.

"Stop the truck," Bill snapped.

Jim's boot was pushing on the brake pedal before he ever bothered asking why.

Bill was pointing. The pickup had just breasted a faint rise, and they could see across the short, brown grass to one of the many lumpy hillocks that dotted the basin.

Jim began to grin. He reached down and switched the ignition off, surrounding them in silence.

Bill rolled his window down so they could listen even though the herd was impossibly distant. There was no chance they would hear the drumbeat from this far away.

"Damn, they're pretty."

The horses were half a mile off and had been resting in the midday sun, most of the small herd idly browsing, lipping the stem-cured sprigs of native grasses, some of them lying down. Now they came to their feet at this sign of intrusion, even the foals springing upright and standing poised to run if the soundless alarm flashed through them so quick that it sometimes seemed a whole herd had one brain among them.

"Eighteen, I make it, and the brown," Jim said.

"He's picked up two more mares someplace this winter," Bill agreed. "You recognize 'em?"

Jim shook his head. "Never seen those ones before."

The brown stallion stood alone just to the east of his band of eighteen mares and their handful of suckling foals.

The brown was not beautiful. Not in the ways any moon-eyed suburban dweller would think of as beautiful. The horse was stocky and close-coupled, with a head shaped like a hammer and a coat that was scarred and torn from his years as master of a wild band. His tail and mane had never been thinned, and his forelock was a tangled knot of ancient burrs.

There was something about him, though. Some presence. Some force of character. Innate and unreconstructed defiance was the heart of it.

The heavy-bodied brown stood with his head high and ears forward, staring at the truck across the distance as if in challenge. The stallion dropped his muzzle for a moment and pawed at the earth. The Beales didn't have to be close enough to hear to know that the brown was snorting, blowing snot and annoyance. And probably wondering what was taking the mare so long to make up her mind.

"Watch the mare," Jim said.

"I am."

The stallion was the master and the protector of the herd, but the real leader of the band was a mare, a thin-shanked and ugly thing that was even older and more scarred than the stallion was. The herd wouldn't bolt until she decided they should, and when they did they would go wherever she took them.

The mare stood on stiffened forelegs and extended her muzzle toward the truck. Shook her head, her ratty mane shivering, and pinned her ears flat against her skull.

"She's pissed," Bill observed.

"With herself, I bet. The sound didn't reach her to tell her the truck was coming. Wind must be against us."

Jim rolled his window down and lighted another cigarette. He grinned.

Far ahead of them the stallion stamped a forehoof impatiently.

"Telling the old girl t' make up her mind," Bill suggested.

The young ones in the band were getting curious now. One of the babies dropped its nose toward the dirt and began a stiff, stilt-legged approach toward the truck. Another, of a more placid nature, forgot the whole thing in the absence of any alarm and turned away to find its dam and bump its way under her belly to suck.

"You wanta see 'em run?"

"In a minute."

All it would take would be some motion at the truck and the herd would explode into flight. An opened door. A waved arm. A glint of light. Anything might set them off. But for now the lead mare was studying them, and the others, even the stallion, were accepting the presence of the truck as being without particular threat. The stallion tossed its head, took a few steps and dropped its muzzle to crop at the grass. The mare shook her head again and let her ears rise away from the flat shape that conveyed anger. She was still paying attention to the truck but didn't seem alarmed by it now.

Jim chuckled.

"They're breeding up good," Bill said. "Better than when we were kids."

"Uh-huh."

It was true, too. When Jim and Bill Beale were Jimmy's and Tod's ages, the wild bands were heavily hunted. The best of the breed were captured and broken for use. Whatever else was caught was sold for slaughter. Generations of such treatment led to a reversal of the normal rules that say the best and the fittest will survive. For those generations the best were captured and removed from the breeding pool. The wild horses became bands of ugly, misshapen creatures that had little value except for pet food and leather. Then the government, prodded into reluctant action by environmentalists, placed the wild horses on the endangered species lists and put them under legal protection. Ranchers could no longer capture wild horses for breaking and could no longer round up and sell the remainder for slaughter. In less than twenty years the Beales could see a marked improvement in the conformation, and in the simple beauty, of the wild horses that ran the public lands here. The rules of natural selection were once more in force. The process worked.

"Let's see 'em run," Jim said.

"Okay."

Bill sat where he was, thoroughly enjoying watching this band. Jim opened the truck door on his side. He didn't have time to step out of the cab before the herd was in motion.

As swiftly as if the group had become a single entity, the horses' heads swung away to the north. Powerful haunches bunched and drove. The wild horses raced away across the short grass, even the smallest foals keeping up for that first burst of speed before inevitably they began to lag behind their dams. The reddish brown mare ran in the lead. The brown stallion brought up the rear, nipping orders at the flanks of the slowest.

Jim whooped and laughed. Bill grinned and reached for his can of snouse.

"Did you see her? Did you see her do it?"

"You know better."

In all the years they'd been observing the wild bands, neither of them had ever seen a lead mare give a signal that was visible to a human eye nor heard one that could be detected by a human ear. When a wild herd panicked and took flight, they did it in one motion, and neither brother could decide what the signal was. Not for sure, no matter how many theories on the subject each proposed.

"Damn, but they're pretty."

The horses were a good mile away now, their tail-high response to panic subsiding. They were settling into a smoother, steadier run, slow enough now for the foals to keep up with the others. The stallion had quit forcing his charges into speed with his quick teeth and angry grunting, and the lead mare was running easy and head high at the front.

Bill laughed and slapped at his knee in pleasure at the sight of the wild horse band retreating across the basin.

Jim, smiling quietly now, stood outside the truck and watched the horses for another three quarters of a mile before he sighed and climbed back into the Sierra beside Bill.

"Feel better now?" Bill asked.

Jim interrupted his reach for the ignition key to pause and look at his brother. "Yeah. Maybe I do at that."

Bill nodded and twisted the lid off his can of Copenhagen. "Good. Then let's go look at some grass."

FIVE

OLIVER TWISTED the legs off a chilled shrimp, peeled the shell back and dipped the pink meat into a cup of spicy cocktail sauce. Shrimp were among the many reasons he would never have been able to survive as a vegetarian.

He deposited half a paper plate of shells into a plastic-lined trash can and went back to the buffet table for more shrimp. He saw JoLynn catch him at it from across the crowded room and winked at her. She used to accuse him, he thought in jest, of eating more in shrimp than he donated to the sponsoring causes at these fund-raisers. Tonight's function was devoted to animal rights. Fifteen dollars per couple plus pledge. Oliver would have wanted to give anyway. The buffet of shrimp and cold cuts and Almaden wines in disposable plastic glasses was a bonus of sorts.

"Oliver. So nice to see you here."

He nodded. Smiled. "John, Rhys, you're looking well."

"We're doing all right, Oliver," John said. But then John was not the one who had tested positive for AIDS. Rhys had. Rhys looked drawn but determined to enjoy himself this evening. Oliver thought of John as being courageous to stay with him but felt twinges of discomfort when Rhys was present. That was, he knew, absurdly illogical. And nonetheless true.

"Excuse me, please. I want to see what JoLynn is up to."

"Of course, Ollie," Rhys said. Oliver managed to keep from cringing. Probably that was what he found most uncomfortable about Rhys; it wasn't really the AIDS infection at all. Oliver hated to be called Ollie. As a boy he'd suffered through every Laurel and Hardy joke imaginable. It had been perhaps even worse a few years ago when Ollie North was in the headlines.

Most of the people he passed were people he was familiar with, even if he did not actually know them all by name. Most of them he at least recognized from other cocktail parties, other buffets, other benefit performances and demonstrations and parades.

And the one here whom he knew the very best of all.

He smiled, catching a glimpse of her with her back turned, unaware that he was near.

It was at an affair very much like this that he had first seen JoLynn Weaver. Raising money to provide a sanctuary for the seals, if he remembered correctly.

Incredible that he hadn't been attracted to her then. But of course, he had been with Elaine that evening. Oliver and Elaine were still together then. And JoLynn had been unattached at the time. Thank goodness. Oliver couldn't imagine now, certainly didn't want to imagine, what his life might have been like if it hadn't been for JoLynn.

He paused where he was and nibbled a shrimp and enjoyed watching her while she chatted, both of them so serious and solemn, with Carla Morris about the whale-watching trip this past winter. JoLynn was wearing the long-sleeved black cocktail dress he'd bought her for her last birthday. The dress suited her so well. Severe and seemingly plain but hinting of so much that was beneath the surface. Probably that was why he liked it so when she chose to wear it.

Carla said something and nodded in Oliver's direction and JoLynn turned to beckon Oliver to join them. She linked her arm into his when he did so, a reminder possibly to Carla or perhaps to Oliver. Not that she ever would have had to worry. Carla was sleek and glossy and seductively pretty but she had none of JoLynn's depth.

Oliver smiled and made an effort to catch up on the conversation.

"OH MY GOD!"

Oliver looked up with alarm, the Sunday funnies dropping into his lap. "What . . . ?"

"Look at this." JoLynn folded the newspaper section and thrust it at him.

"Oh."

"It makes me sick, Oliver. Positively sick."

He nodded mutely.

"Whoever could do such a thing?"

"Animals. No, dammit, worse than animals. Animals wouldn't treat each other like that."

The article was bad enough, he was sure, but he wished they hadn't printed the photographs to go with it.

The pictures were . . . awful.

Dead horses. Dead, decaying, desiccated carcasses littering a grassy hillside. Half a dozen of them in the large picture. One of them shown in stark and ugly close-up in an accompanying photo. The smaller picture showed a horse skull, shreds of dry, crusty hide clinging to it, teeth and lower jaw bared to the elements in a ghastly caricature of a grin. It was macabre. And frightening.

"It makes me sick," JoLynn repeated.

Oliver could feel it too. The dull, mindless horror of it. The helplessness and hopelessness of it. The sheer waste of it.

So very many.

Wild horses, of course. The headline said the death toll now was in excess of six hundred animals that had been found wantonly slaughtered and left to rot on government land over a period of several years. The photo caption said there were forty-seven in this latest discovery of bodies.

Six hundred. Oliver couldn't visualize how many magnificent animals six hundred would be. Simply could not imagine them standing all together in one place alive and free. The forty-seven most recently found were almost as difficult for him to visualize.

They were dead now. Good Lord. Six hundred.

He started to read the article, but JoLynn pulled it back away from him.

Oliver moved the breakfast tray aside and slid over next to her so he could read beside her shoulder. He had no taste now for the mundane amusements offered by "Peanuts" or "Garfield." JoLynn held the newspaper between them so he could see, and the two of them read with horror about these ugly finds in the Nevada desert.

OLIVER DIPPED THE LADLE into a steaming red mess that he hoped was a ragout. Perry's instructions had been imprecise but interesting. He stirred the mixture, bent over it to inhale the aroma and finally lifted a minuscule amount of it to his mouth, careful to blow on it thoroughly before he tried tasting it. Not bad. Not as good as it had sounded, perhaps, but not bad. He improvised by adding a dash of cayenne, a little more oregano and some onion salt, then stirred before he set the ladle aside and replaced the lid so it could simmer.

He thought he heard the apartment door, but there was no cheery call. He turned to the chopping board and began dicing some onion to go in with the summer squash. Yellow squash, he supposed it should be called nowadays. This certainly was not summer but there was squash in the markets, probably imported from Peru or Chile or wherever.

He jumped, startled, when he heard the scrape of chair legs at the table, and JoLynn sat down. She was frowning.

"Are you all right?"

She nodded.

"You don't look good."

She sighed.

"What is it?" he insisted. This wasn't at all like her. Usually she came home in a wonderful humor. Always she helped him with whatever dinner preparations still had to be done. Tonight she sat at the small table in a state of obvious dejection or worse.

"I can't stop thinking about those poor horses, Oliver," she said.

"Me neither." It was almost true.

"The article said they expect more will be killed this year."

Oliver nodded. He had read the same article.

"When those ranchers bring their cattle onto the public land, Oliver."

He nodded again.

"I can't stop thinking about that, Oliver. That land *belongs* to those horses. It is *public* land, Oliver. It belongs to *us*. And to those horses. Nobody seems to be protecting them. Someone in Washington passed a law. Is that supposed to be enough? Pass a law and it's automatically done? That hasn't been enough, Oliver. Those horses *aren't* protected, Oliver. They are being killed, and no one cares." JoLynn looked as if she were going to cry. Her eyes were large and moist and filled with the pain her empathy for those mute animals brought her.

"I know, dear."

"I want to do something about them, Oliver. I really do."

"I know."

"And I don't mean just lobby for another damned law either or put five dollars into a collection box. I want to *do* something, Oliver. Something . . . real. Oh, I don't know what I want." She bolted off her chair and out of the room.

He could hear the slam of the bedroom door and the softer, muted bump as she threw herself onto the bed they shared.

Oliver thought about going to her at once, then reconsidered. He would give her a few minutes to herself before he went in to try and comfort her. She would be crying now. She wouldn't want him to see, God knew why. It wasn't as though she minded him knowing, of course he knew, but JoLynn retained a certain measure of privacy—not aloofness, exactly, but certainly a sense of privacy—when it came to her emotions. Even with him she would prefer to have a little while alone. Then he could go in to her and she could cry again, this time in his arms, and it would be all right.

Oliver shook his head in shared sympathy with JoLynn's pain and turned back to the stove. He dialed the burner under the ragout to a lower setting and slowly, desultorily resumed chopping the onion. He wouldn't put the squash on to cook yet, though. Not until he knew they would soon be ready to eat. You don't want to overcook yellow squash.

"I want to go there, Oliver."

He didn't have to ask where she meant. It was Thursday evening, and JoLynn had been thinking about very little but those dead horses ever since she read the article in Sunday's newspaper.

"I really do," she insisted, although he hadn't said anything to try to dissuade her from it.

Oliver looked up from the text he'd been reading. It was a volume on computer programming theory and slow going, even at his level of expertise.

"I've thought about this, Oliver. And I want to go over there. It isn't so far. Just the other side of the mountains, practically. I called the Highway Patrol this afternoon. They say the passes are all open. It wouldn't take so terribly long to drive."

"What do you want to do once you get there, honey?" He thought it a reasonable enough question. Whatever *could* be done?

"I don't know. Not exactly. But I want to experience it for myself, Oliver. Like we did with the whales, I suppose. I want to go and see those horses. And if there is anything I can do to stop those men from shooting them . . ."

"There isn't. There couldn't be. What are we supposed to do, honey? Jump in front of the guns? I mean, it isn't like Greenpeace. We wouldn't have a boat to run in front of the trawlers to save dolphins from the nets or something. And those people are crazy. They'd have to be."

"Oh, I don't mean we should run around in front of crazy people with guns, Oliver. That would be stupid. But I want to do *some*thing, dear."

He rubbed his eyes and thought about it. "I have that camera," he suggested. "If we could get pictures—the newspapers say there isn't any proof of who is shooting the horses—if we could get pictures of the men with their guns, well, that would be proof, wouldn't it?"

JoLynn's face brightened with a smile. "Of course it would be. We could get pictures. We could testify in court if we had to. Then someone would have to do something about those people."

"You know, of course, that it's damned unlikely we would see a wild horse, much less someone trying to shoot one."

"I know, Oliver. But I want to try. I can't stand the thought of sitting at home in comfort here and not at least trying to do something."

He pursed his lips. He would have to get a telephoto lens for the camera. He didn't own one. Rarely found a use for the camera at all, actually. He'd bought it on a whim, and now it sat on a closet shelf gathering dust nearly all the time. But there was no reason why he couldn't buy a long-range lens for it and get someone at a camera store to show him how to operate it.

And he did have a week's vacation due. More than a week if he really needed it and wanted to use sick time. He hadn't taken a day of sick leave since he started the job, and that had been more than five years ago. They certainly owed him some time if he wanted to use it. He never would have considered the possibility of allowing JoLynn to go off to the desert without him. "Can you get off?"

She nodded. "I already asked." JoLynn's employers were stuffy and rigid when it came to law or finance but not when it came down to matters of activism and social awareness. They were very careful not to be. "I can have a week, Oliver."

He grunted, still trying to think this through. Crossing the mountains, they would risk encountering spring storms. But the Subaru had four-wheel drive. That would serve them well once they reached the desert too. They wouldn't be confined to pavement and easy going. The Baja trip had proven that about the little car. And they already had camping equipment. If it wasn't too cold in Nevada—how cold does a desert get in spring, anyway?—the trip might actually be fun. They could spend a week camping under the stars. Oliver could think of worse things than that. And JoLynn would feel better having tried to do something constructive.

He looked at her and smiled. "We promised to spend this weekend on the telephone campaign. How about Saturday a week from now?"

JoLynn looked like he had just presented her with a rare and valuable gift. And perhaps he had, except that this gift was of understanding and compassion, rarer by far than material possession.

She left her chair and came over to his. She knelt there and laid her cheek on his knee. "Thank you, dear, for not pooh-poohing me."

"Pooh," he said cheerfully.

SIX

TINY GEAR WHEELS whirred and clattered. Bells rang. Electronic thingamajigs beeped and tinkled and buzzed. Hell, it was like a slot machine. Except at least with the slots you had some chance of a payback.

Jim tried to close his mind if not his ears to the noise and continued unloading the grocery cart. Powdered milk that Gloria would use for cooking. Lone gallon of whole milk that they would use while it was still fresh enough. They didn't drive to town to shop often enough to try to keep fresh milk in the fridge all the time. Spuds in twenty-five-pound bags—damn store didn't stock the fifty- and hundred-pound sacks anymore. Rice. Which Jim didn't much care for but Gloria did. Dried beans of just about every variety that grew. Only two dozen eggs this time. Gloria worried about his cholesterol and was cutting back on how many eggs she would fix for him. Wheaties, Oreos, taco shells, two jumbo-sized bottles of picante sauce, at least a hundredweight of canned stuff. Four cartons of Chesterfields and five of Marlboros. Sheesh.

At least they'd come away with only two carts of stuff this time. Bill and Maureen were checking through the next aisle, and they had three carts full and all of those mounded so high it was a wonder everything fit. The difference was that they had the boys to feed too. Jim and Gloria shopped for JayJay on these expeditions. Bill and Maureen shopped for themselves and the boys. It worked out.

Sue Deaman worked fast and furious to get it all rung up while Jim unloaded things onto the black rubber conveyer belt and some long-haired kid Jim never saw before packed it all untidily into boxes. Everything would have to be repacked once they got it out to the truck anyway. The perishable things and frozen foods would go into the big ice chests. Jim could see to it then that things were arranged so they wouldn't get broken by the bumping and thumping on the way home.

He got the last of their purchases out of the cart with a sense of relief and rolled the empty cart to the front of the checkout counter, then ambled back around to where Bill was still piling stuff onto the belt.

"Fun, ain't it?" Jim observed.

"Ain't it just," Bill agreed.

Neither of them liked shopping. What the grocery stores oughta do, Jim had long since decided, was set aside one or two days a month when the ranchers could come in and undergo the pain all together. Clear the aisles of the day-by-day buyers and rip through there with scoop shovels and front loaders to drag stuff out to the pickup trucks. Better yet skip the nuisance of having to stock everything on shelves. Just drive the semis into the parking lot and dump cases of things straight from the big trucks into the little ones. Seemed a helluva notion. He pulled a Chesterfield out of his pocket and fished around in there a second time looking for his lighter.

"There's a sign, you know. No smoking nowadays," Bill reminded him.

"Yeah, I know." Jim found the lighter and fired up his cigarette. It tasted extra good, as it always did. He made an effort to keep from smoking while they were going through the aisles, but knowing that he couldn't smoke always made him want to all the more. It wasn't a matter of simple perversity but a fear of deprivation. He'd figured that out a long time ago, but knowing it didn't make him want to smoke the least bit less whenever he couldn't.

"You gonna make that phone call?"

"Unless you want to."

"You go ahead," Bill said. Jim had known he would. Bill liked talking on a telephone even less than Jim did. The only reason either one of them bothered with having one of the things around was so the girls could talk to their cronies from one end of the county to the next.

This call, though, wasn't one either of them wanted to make on a party line when somebody outside the family might be listening. This was better done from in town, where they had private telephone lines.

"I'll help Glory get your stuff loaded if you want to go now," Bill offered.

"Okay, I'll, uh, see you later. Over at Stargill's?"

"Yeah, that'd be fine."

They always made a point of doing the grocery shopping first thing when they came to town, just in case a storm came up and they had to roll out in a hurry to race it for home. Then Gloria and Maureen would go off and do whatever it was they did when they were together, and Jim and Bill would have a drink or two at Stargill's. The girls would meet them there whenever, and if the weather was holding, they'd all have a bite of somebody else's cooking before they started back over seventy-odd miles of bad, sad road for home.

Jim hitched up his britches and went outside to find a pay telephone.

BILL PICKED UP THE PAIR of longnecks in front of him and swiveled around on the bar stool. Jim had just come in, his coat collar turned high against the breeze outside. Bill stood and handed one of the Buds to his brother, then both of them wandered away from the bar to stand behind the row of gaudy, blinking slot machines.

"Well?" Bill asked.

"We got time," Jim said. He shoved a hand deep into the right front pocket of his jeans and found some quarters. Idly he plugged one into the bandit and pulled the lever. The wheels spun noisily round and round and stopped with solid-sounding clunks. Lemon, plum, cherry. A bell chirped briefly, and two quarters clattered loudly into the steel pan. Jim retrieved them and put them both back into the machine. Bar, cherry, bar. No pay. Oh, well.

"So what did he say?" Bill asked.

"They'll open our permit the middle of June, and we can use it through September."

"But what about our count? They haven't set it?"

"Not yet. The boys here are pretty busy. You can guess why."

Bill nodded. The Bureau of Land Management people had been going nuts around Winnemucca ever since those dead horses were found. The BLM wasn't exactly overstaffed to begin with, and the added burdens of publicity and howling politicians hadn't done anything to reduce their work load. Word was there were letters of protest coming from as far away as England ever since those news stories went out.

"Jack said there'd be some guy come over from the Battle Mountain regional office in two, maybe three weeks to take an inventory. Then they'll set the count for us."

"Two weeks," Bill repeated.

"At least two. More likely three."

"All right, then. Good deal."

It was too soon for either of them to feel relieved, of course. The BLM guy from Battle Mountain could turn out to be a nitwit. And the permit level was critical.

Very few ranches in arid or semiarid country were actually owned by their owners.

Typically a ranch consisted of so many square miles of deeded land, land that was actually owned outright by the people or the corporation that operated the enterprise, plus additional acreage, often several times as much, that was owned by the Bureau of Land Management but grazed by the rancher's livestock under lease permits. Lease rights were for all practical purposes "owned" by right of heredity or purchase. But the BLM determined how many head of stock could be placed onto BLM land and how long those animals could remain on the public land. The rancher had the right to graze the property but could not otherwise control it. Anyone else could enter the BLM lands to hunt, camp, fish, prospect for minerals or simply sit in the middle of it all and loaf. The rancher could not restrict public access to the public lands, but only he had the right to graze livestock on that property.

For the Beales and for virtually every other rancher who depended on BLM lease permits for a significant portion of their annual livestock feeding needs, the head count allowed under their permit essentially established their maximum income for the year to come. Because of natural phenomena like cold or drought, they might produce less beef, wool or lamb than the permits would allow. But they were capable of producing no more than the limits imposed by the permitted head count.

The BLM determined the number of permitted head by assessing the ability of the land in question to support both wild and domestic stock. Ranchers were not allowed to overgraze public lands. And a portion of the available graze must by both law and regulation provide for the maintenance of wild animals as well as domestic.

The available graze was stated in terms of "cow units," one unit being equivalent to one mother cow with calf . . . or five sheep, five deer, seven antelope . . . or slightly less than one wild horse.

Jim and Bill Beale both loved the independence and the beauty of the free roaming wild horses that competed with their cattle for graze on the public lands.

But neither wanted to pay for that beauty to the detriment of their beeves and, only slightly less directly, of their families.

"Two weeks," Bill said again.

"Ayuh. We got that long to worry about it." Jim dropped another quarter into the slot. He pulled the lever, and the symbols blurred and rattled.

JIM LET THE CHEVY SLOW without bothering to apply the brakes. He kicked the clutch in and let the truck come to a stop, then put it into neutral and reached down to wrestle with the transfer lever.

"Want me to do it?" Bill asked. Bill was wedged into the middle of the bench seat, his legs straddling the transmission hump, with JayJay on the passenger side. The arrangement had begun because both Jim and JayJay liked to be able to flip their cigarette ashes out the vent windows. Now it was a habit.

"I can get it. Just a minute here." Jim pushed and tugged at the lever. Damn thing was sticking again. He would have to remember to crawl underneath soon and clean out the mud that built up on the mechanism.

The lever finally moved, and he shifted the transfer case into four-wheel high. This time of year there were soft spots in the borrow ditches, and it was generally easier to put the truck in four-wheel drive when it wasn't really needed than have to count on being able to do it later.

"Got it," he announced.

JayJay coughed and shivered. He wasn't fully awake yet, although they'd been driving for the better part of an hour. The sun was just now lifting above the mountains to the east of the basin.

Jim put the truck in reverse and cranked the wheel hard. Times like this he wished the power-steering pump hadn't gone out. He backed slowly, keeping track of where he was in the side mirrors, and the long stock trailer swung off the graded road surface with a bang they could feel through the hitch. There was a snort of protest from back there and a clatter of hoofs on steel.

"That's your boy," Jim said. Bill's favorite big-swing horse was a kicker and didn't like the trailer to begin with.

Bill grinned. He was the only human that'd ever been able to abide the homely ap. The creature was undeniably ugly and had a disposition to match its looks. Worse, it was scared of cows and hated to work close to them. It was also all-day tough and couldn't hardly be worn out. Bill had no particular affection for it, but it was invariably the horse he brought when they were going to be covering country.

JayJay sat upright and yawned, then shook himself like an old dog shedding rainwater while Jim guided the trailer up against the spoil bank beside the road. JayJay reached for a cigarette, making a sour face and shuddering as the taste of the smoke clashed with whatever else he was tasting this morning.

Jim felt the back end of the trailer nudge into something solid, slipped the truck into neutral again and killed the engine. The three of them crawled out into the early morning chill, and Jim left the keys hanging in the ignition. The truck was parked halfway onto the roadbed. If somebody came along wanting past while they were gone, he'd be able to move it out of the way.

Jim stopped, shivering, to take a leak against the trailer tires while Bill and JayJay unhooked the back of the stock trailer and eased it down onto the dirt. The horses inside began to shuffle and move, knowing it was time for them to go to work now.

Bill caught Jim's red dun by the reins as it tiptoed down the ramp and held both it and his own ap until Jim got there. JayJay was already hauling his cinches tight.

The brothers flipped their stirrups up and snugged their saddles, then mounted. Bill grunted when the seat of his jeans hit the cold leather. He reached down to scratch his leg and wobbled unsteadily when the horse shook itself and humped its back a little. The ap was a kicker, not a morning bucker, though. Bill ignored the movement and continued to scratch himself, then stood and adjusted the legs of his britches. There wasn't anything much more miserable than a lump or a crease between butt and seat leather.

Jim lighted a Chesterfield and let it dangle off his lip while he sorted his reins into a just-right lie between his gloved fingers.

"Shit, I forgot to bring another pack of smokes," JayJay complained.

"You wanta run home and get some?" Bill said with a grin.

"I brought plenty," Jim told him.

JayJay made a face again but didn't say anything. Normally he didn't want anything to do with Jim's unfiltered cigarettes, but if the choice lay between a barefoot smoke or no smoke at all . . .

They'd each packed their own sandwiches or whatever for lunch and usually a couple beers to wash the midday meal down with. Today the beers might actually still be cool by the time they got around to them. The lunches were carried behind their cantles along with an assortment of tools and trash that remained in the saddlebags all the time. Rusty fence tools, loose horseshoe nails, a bottle of Cut-Heal medicine that was sticky with brown gum, a little of this and a little of that. Whatever might be needed while they were covering ground. It was a helluva long way back to the toolshed if they wanted anything else.

"You want to start bunching them up yet?" JayJay asked. The beeves were loosely scattered over the west end of the Beale ranch. They would have to be brought together into a compact group before they could be driven off the Beale land to BLM ground. At that time, too, the herd would be culled of whatever animals had to be sold—in case the permit limit required it—and any necessary doctoring done. Branding and ear marking wouldn't be done until fall, when all the late calves would be on the ground. Spring and fall, though, the Beales had to hire in some seasonal part-time hands, buckaroos in this country no matter what they might be called elsewhere, to help with the work. Most of the year the brothers and JayJay could handle everything that was needed.

"I don't think so," Jim said. "Too early. If we see any too far to the south we might drift 'em up a little, but I don't want to start them herding yet. Don't have all that much graze left."

Jim looked at Bill for confirmation, but that was only a courtesy, as was Bill's nod in answer. Bill was content to let Jim call the shots for both of them when it came to managing the grass. Bill's forte was the breeding end of it, nowadays using a computer program to keep track of bloodlines and produce. Jim wouldn't have argued with Bill about that any more than Bill was going to argue with him now.

"I figure we'll take a swing down below the Cedar Hill tank, then north along the west line. After dinner I want to cut up to the BLM and see how the grass looks on that end. Get an idea what we can expect when they write down our numbers. We haven't got as much late snow as I'd've liked."

"Whatever you say, white man." That last referred to an ancient joke having to do with Tonto and the Lone Ranger. JayJay looked wide awake now that he was on horseback. "Race you to the water tank," he challenged. He bounced up and down on his saddle and flopped his boots in and out in the stirrups but was careful to not touch the sides of his brown with his spurs.

The three men squeezed their horses into a sedate walk to let the animals warm up, then bumped them into an easy jog that would cover the miles without causing stress or strain on horse or rider. Old movies aside, horses and cattle were worked with much more deliberation than speed.

"You know what I'd like to do this weekend?" JayJay mused around a mouthful of corned beef sandwich.

"Hell yes, we know what you'd like to do this weekend."

"No, I mean *besides* Linda," he said with a grin.

Jim opened his mouth to say something more, but they were interrupted by a loud squeal and a dull thump. Bill's damned appaloosa had its ears pinned flat against its skull and was trying its best to commit mayhem on JayJay's brown. From the sounds, it must have connected at least once.

"Settle down, dammit," Bill roared. The horses settled down—no one believed Bill's grumbling had anything to do with that—and went back to cropping at the short grasses that grew on the hillside below where the men were seated on some flat rocks with their lunches spread out around them.

"You're gonna have to start hobbling him at the ass end," Jim said.

"If I do that, damn him, he'll hippety-hop a mile and a half before I can get a sandwich ate." Bill took a bite off a pickled sausage and washed it down with a swallow of lukewarm Bud. "So anyway, JayJay, what is it you're wanting t' do this weekend? Aside from jump that pretty lady's bones, I mean?"

"I was thinking we oughta go up in them hills and run some horses. You know. Take the boys along and show them how it used to be. Stay out overnight an' have the kids back in time for school Monday. Hell, they're old enough. And even if they wasn't, it's been a long time since I done anything like that."

Jim smiled, remembering too, just as JayJay probably was. Remembering back to their dad taking him and Bill up onto the hills to chase the wild ones.

Of course, it had been different then. Then there'd been a reason for it. When there got to be too many wild horses eating grass on the flats, you'd want to go clean them out some. Set up the tall canvas fences—flimsy but the horses didn't know that, and high enough that they couldn't see over; a horse won't jump something when he can't see what he's jumping into

—and drive the wild herds inside. Keep anything that looked worth having and sell the rest. That wasn't legal now, though. Not since the wild herds got protected.

It was a helluva sport the government ruined with that law.

Lordy, that'd been fun.

You didn't drive wild horses slow and easy. You ran 'em for all you were worth and then some. Leap and twist. Jump gullies and crash through brush. Go like hell with the wind in your face and the bugs in your teeth 'cause you couldn't stop grinning. Whoop and holler and hope your damn horse didn't bust something if it tumbled. And that you didn't neither. Clyde Brandt got himself killed running wild ones that way. So did Pete Laycock's father. Jim tried to remember old man Laycock's name and couldn't now. It bothered him that he couldn't call Pete's dad's name to mind.

But damn, that used to be fun. Sometimes they'd get a whole bunch of riders together. Fellows in from all over the basin. They'd take off during the summer when things were easy and all ride up into the mountains. Meet at Spring Canyon or some such and set up a big camp. All stay up there and run horses for a week sometimes. Jim had got his first taste of hard liquor beside a campfire one of those nights. Just a bottle cap full of it slipped to him by old Brandt. Four Roses, it had been. Jim could remember that just as clear as if it was yesterday. Could practically still taste it. He hadn't tasted Four Roses in . . . he couldn't remember how long. Hell, he didn't know if they even made it still. He smiled.

Those big runs were over and done with, but it was still all right to go up in the hills and run the horses just for the sheer fun of it. Not catch anything, though. Jim doubted he could find a canvas fence left anywhere in the basin by now. There hadn't been any use for them in years. Their own canvas panels got used to cover hay with a long time ago. He sighed.

"You know, Bill, that's something we are gonna have to teach those boys of yours. Something they oughtn't to be left out of."

JayJay grinned.

"Not this weekend, though," Jim added. "The way they're so hot about dead horses right now, I don't want some weekend warrior in a fighter plane seeing us run horses and get the wrong idea. One of them boys see us playing, he'd be on his radio right now. Anything we want to do with them horses . . . anything at all . . . we'd best keep it to the middle of the week. But this summer, yeah, I think we oughta take the kids up there and let 'em have some fun. I think that's a good idea, JayJay." Jim took a bite of his own corned beef sandwich—aside from preferences, there was often a lot in common between Jim's groceries and JayJay's, what with Gloria doing the shopping for both—and considered with pleasure the idea of teaching Bill's boys how things used to be when the country was freer and not so bound up by regulations and eyeballs. Nowadays a man couldn't take a squat without having to look up and wonder if there was a spy satellite looking back at him.

JayJay brushed his hands off and popped the top on a can of Mountain Dew. "Y'know, Jim, I kinda wish Gloria wouldn't keep on buying beef outa Argentina to put in our lunches."

"Makes you wonder, don't it. We're setting here eating beef from way the hell down there, an' in Tokyo there's some squint-eyed Jap right now eating a piece of meat we grew."

"Does that mean you're going to buy a Toyota next truck you get?" Bill asked playfully.

"Shit."

Bill laughed. "That's your problem, Jim. No sense of gratitude."

"Hurry up, girls, or it's gonna be midnight before we get home tonight."

"Yes, mother."

They stood and began picking up after themselves, then ambled down the slope toward the waiting horses. It was warm enough in the sunshine by now that they could shed their coats and ride the rest of the afternoon wearing nothing heavier than vests. By the time they got back to the truck and trailer, though, they would be grateful enough to have the coats along.

Jim blew his nose and lighted a cigarette, then reached for the cinch straps to snug his saddle tight again. He grimaced a little as he swung onto the seat. Little aches and nagging pains. If this kept up, he was going to have to conclude that maybe he wasn't as young now as he used to be.

SEVEN

"OUCH!" Oliver snatched his finger away and shook it.

"Are you all right?" JoLynn sounded concerned. Then she saw that the pinch was only a minor one and smiled. "Mister mechanical strikes again."

He crossed his eyes and stuck his tongue out at her. Although it was perfectly true, of course. He wasn't mechanically inclined in the slightest. This time he'd been playing with the Fiberglas poles for the tent and managed to get the pad of his index finger caught when the shock cord–loaded joint snapped the two ends together. He was trying to familiarize himself with the tent again. It was some time since they'd had occasion to use it, and it was better to figure it out on the living room floor than at night in the middle of a rainstorm. Assuming such a thing was possible on a desert. Oliver didn't know but didn't want to take any chances on it.

This afternoon they had washed out the Igloo and the cooking kit. JoLynn had cleaned the stove and the lantern globe—managing to destroy the delicate ash mantle while she was at it—and Oliver had spread out the sleeping bags on the sofa to air. There were two of the big flannel-lined bags, but they zipped together to make one bag large enough for two people.

Except for doing the grocery shopping and buying some fuel for the stove and the pressurized lantern, they were fairly well set. Oliver had already found a telephoto lens for his camera. It was three hundred milli-meters long and mated with the auto-exposure gadgets on the camera. Thank goodness. The photo store had longer lenses to sell, but those cost three times as much. He was sure this one would do nicely. It certainly brought in images from across the street close enough. He could admire the Nagel prints on the walls over there as well as if he were in the room with them. Mildly envy them too. He and JoLynn had a fair collection of Nagels in the bedroom but only the garden-variety poster prints that weren't limited. The neighbor across the way had three of the limited edition serigraphs.

"Are you ready to make out the shopping list?" JoLynn was seated on the armchair with a pad and pen on her lap. She was wearing shorts, and Oliver's attention was not really on food at the moment.

"Sure. Filet mignon. Eggs Benedict. A little foie gras, I think. And of course some caviar. By all means, caviar."

"Whatever you say, dear," she said seriously. She began to write it down.

"Fruitcake," he accused.

"I'm not sure I can find any this time of year, but I'll try." She wrote that down too.

"Nut," he told her.

"Pea or cashew?" She wasn't able to contain her smile any longer.

"Seriously, whatever you think."

"Dried or canned?"

"We won't be hiking very far away from the car, I shouldn't think. Let's get canned. That's a lot cheaper. Easier to fix too."

"By all means, dear, let's go for something easy to fix."

"We'll just keep it simple," he said. "Whatever looks good in the store."

"We should have a list, Oliver. I know how you are. You'll clean the store out if we don't have a list."

"Okay, we'll make a list." He stuffed the wad of thin blue nylon and bundle of Fiberglas wands back into the bag they'd come out of and shoved them out of the way, then crawled the few feet to the armchair and leaned against JoLynn's legs. "You're bony, you know that?"

"Complain, complain, complain."

"I thought we were making out a list now."

"We are. Just tell me what you want on it."

He grinned and stroked her ankle while he thought about what foods they should pack for the trip.

OLIVER FROWNED. Damned noses. Their placement was terrible, always in the way. He craned his neck to push his chin high—as if that would do any good; it wouldn't—and made a face as he used his free hand to shove the tip of his nose aside. It was right there on the upper lip that was always difficult. He coughed and scowled and drew the buzzing, rasping shaver through the soft fur of his beard.

Tiny clippings sprayed over the back of the bathroom sink, collecting everywhere so that he would never be able to clean them all up afterward. JoLynn invariably fussed every time Oliver trimmed his beard, but what was a fellow to do? He liked a tidy, well-groomed appearance and this was the price he had to pay to keep it.

He paused for a moment to clean out an accumulation of longer hairs from between the plastic teeth of the depth guide clipped onto the head of the shaver and then attacked his left cheek. That part was much easier. It was only under his nose that he had trouble maintaining the right cutting angle.

The shaver itself was a source of small amusement to him. "Doggy Trim" was written on the silver label glued to the black plastic barrel of the electric device. The shaver was identical to the ones marketed in home haircutting kits, but the pet accessory cost little more than half what the people version did. And they threw in a canine toenail trimmer.

Oliver chuckled and finished his trim. It hadn't been necessary again quite yet, but he hadn't wanted to wait until they got back from Nevada. Another week and a half, two weeks would have been too long.

He turned the noisy shaver off and used a brush to remove the bits of loose hair from what was left of his facial fur, then dampened a washcloth and tried to wipe away all traces of his mess. He unplugged the shaver and packed it and the depth guide back into the appropriate depressions in the styrene carrier. The boxed Doggy Trim went back under the sink where it belonged.

Oliver made a face into the mirror while he checked to make sure there were no long hairs straying, then brushed his teeth and gargled.

Tomorrow, he was thinking, he would have to take the Subaru by the Lube Stop for a quick oil change and lube job. Oliver was meticulous about the car, and the Nevada trip would run him over the recommended mileage if he waited until they got back before taking it in for the routine service.

He was beginning to feel a growing excitement about the trip now.

JoLynn's idea had taken root and was blossoming. It was going to be nice to get away, just the two of them. He could already imagine it. Crisp nights and starlight and campfires. It was going to be great.

If they could accomplish something by going, well, so much the better.

He already had three 36-exposure rolls of color film in the camera bag and most of a 24-exposure roll still left in the camera.

If they got any photos of wild horses, Oliver had decided, any good pictures, that is, they would have some blowups made of the best one or two. Something really impressive. Sixteen-by-twenty-inch prints, perhaps. They could frame them and put them on the living room wall next to the whale picture JoLynn snapped when they were in Mexico.

Oliver smiled, spat into the sink and wiped his mouth with the hand towel. He dried his toothbrush and placed it back in the holder.

He really did hope they could at least get a good look at the wild horses.

"MMM, LET'S SEE NOW. You wanted pâté, didn't you. Oh, yes. And the caviar. Can't forget the caviar." JoLynn took down four cans of tuna in water and tumbled them into the steel shopping cart.

Oliver refused to rise to the bait. He was peering at the canned bay shrimp on the shelf above the tuna. He did love shrimp. But canned shrimp were dreadfully expensive, besides not tasting nearly so good as the fresh or the frozen.

Anyway, they were going to rough it, weren't they? He took his eyes off the shrimp and reminded himself to be serious now.

"Chili?" JoLynn asked.

"By all means, chili," he agreed. It was apt to be cool in the evenings. Bowls of steaming hot chili con carne would be welcome.

JoLynn added several cans of chili with beans to their cart.

"Corned beef?"

"Why not?"

Two cans of corned beef joined the rest of the items.

"Pork and beans?"

Oliver made a face.

"No pork and beans," JoLynn mumbled. She consulted the list in her hand—she carried it faithfully but referred to it seldom—and moved on toward the next aisle, Oliver trailing a pace behind her with the cart.

Why is it, he sometimes wondered, that all shopping carts come equipped with sticking wheels? One of the minor puzzlements of civilized society comparable to but of much more immediate interest than the age-old chicken/egg dilemma.

"Bread. We need bread, Oliver."

"Did you put rye on the list?"

"I just wrote down bread."

"Well, we need rye. Whole wheat too. And no sourdough this time, all right?"

"No sourdough," she agreed.

"Maybe some sweet rolls," he suggested.

"I put down pecan."

"That's fine. Some cinnamon too, though."

"I swear I don't know why I ever bother to make out these lists. You never pay any attention to them."

"You're a list person, what can I say?"

She gave him a look that he couldn't quite interpret, then sniffed loudly and moved off again. Oliver trudged dutifully behind, pushing the shopping cart with its one dragging wheel.

EIGHT

JIM BEALE smiled his thanks at Anne for the coffee refill, then reached for Gloria's cup to pull it toward the front of the booth to make it easier for Anne to reach.

"No more for me."

"Me either," Maureen added.

"We have too much to do this afternoon to sit around lollygagging with you gentlemen of leisure."

There was time enough if they wanted to take it, of course, but Jim and Bill both knew what the truth was. The girls didn't want to waste a minute that could be spent in a store gawking at the colors and feeling the fabrics and weighing this bargain against that one.

Not that either of them was a big spender. They'd come in to town today because Jimmy and Tod needed shirts and socks and underwear and Gloria said there were some things, unspecified, that she wanted to pick up too. Entirely mundane stuff. But that wouldn't stop the ladies from examining every item in every store they entered. Jim never had figured out how they could get such a kick out of looking at things they weren't ever going to buy, but they did. Every time.

"How 'bout you, Billy?" the waitress asked.

"I'll take another cup, you bet."

Anne poured it for him and carried the pot back toward the kitchen. She had gone to school with Bill and never did quit using the nickname that he'd tried to leave behind in junior high.

"You can let me out now, please," Gloria said.

Jim had to lever himself out from behind the big table in the small booth so Gloria could slide out beside him. He bumped his head on a hanging plant, then stood there to receive the peck on the cheek Gloria gave him.

On the other side of the booth Bill was doing pretty much the same.

"We'll meet you at the truck later, okay?"

"What time?"

She grinned and shrugged.

"Okay. See you then." He gave her another brief kiss, and the girls ankled off toward the street by way of the restrooms. Jim and Bill resumed their hunched posture in the booth with the steaming coffee cups under their noses.

"Anything you need t' do?" Bill asked.

"Not really. You?"

"Naw."

"Might stop over to Carruthers' later."

Bill nodded.

Jim took a sip of the coffee. It tasted slightly acid to him now, telling him that he'd had enough for the time being. His belly was already filled and warmed by the huge platter of enchiladas and refried beans he'd just finished. His salad sat untouched beside the greasy dinner plate.

"Whose turn t' pay?" Bill asked.

"Yours." Jim reached for a Chesterfield. He winked and added, "Of course."

"Then you leave the tip." Bill shifted aside to be out of the stream of pale smoke that curled off the tip of Jim's cigarette. "You think we need another bale of rope yet?"

"It can wait," Jim said. "If we got too much setting there in plain sight, those boys will make themselves new catch ropes whether they need 'em or not." That was something you could count on with the seasonal bucka-roos. They'd waste stuff if they thought there was plenty. "No need to buy any till fall, I don't think."

"All right. You already put the word out when we'll hire?" Bill asked.

"Some. We'll spread it around some more this afternoon."

Bill nodded. "What about the other?"

"Next week, I think," Jim said. "Not too much time left, but we got to wait until the weekend's over. Early next week."

Bill's expression was solemn, but he didn't offer any actual objection. Jim had known he wouldn't. That sort of thing Bill always left up to Jim to work out. And JayJay just didn't care. He'd do whatever Jim said too.

"Finish that coffee," Jim said. "We'll walk over to Carruthers'. See if he's got anything in that we can't live without."

"All right." Bill picked up his cup, holding it in both hands as if to warm them, even though the inside of the restaurant was plenty warm already. Jim thought he looked worried, but if he was he didn't say so.

The two men stood, and Bill reached for the check. Jim dropped a dollar bill onto the table for Anne Masters, and the brothers headed for the front door.

WALT CARRUTHERS' GUN SHOP was small, reasonably well stocked and friendly. Walt was two years older than Jim and had been a standout running back on the high school football team. There had been a time when Walt Carruthers was Jim Beale's idol. A twisted knee in his senior year cost him a college scholarship. Walt had settled for gunsmithing school in Denver and picked up taxidermy skills afterward. He made out.

As always, he was perched on a backless stool. Walt probably weighed three hundred pounds now and found it difficult to stand for any length of time. Nowadays it was hard to spot the cut-and-slash running back in Walt Carruthers. "Got something you might like here, Bill."

Jim took no offense at the fact that Walt was friendlier now with Bill than he was with Jim. That only stood to reason. Both the Beales had been raised with rifles as part of their everyday experience, but only Bill really cared about them as precise, even beautiful instruments. To Jim a rifle was just another tool, not all that much different from a rope or a hammer or a fence stretcher. Of the two, Bill was the one who might buy another rifle just to possess the thing. Jim was more likely to spend that same money on a saddle or a gadget for his pickup truck. If either of them had money to spend, that is. And that sure remained to be seen, didn't it?

Jim hooked his thumbs behind his belt and wandered around the display area while Bill went over to see what new wonder Walt had got in.

"It's the Mark Five," Walt was saying. "Look at the grain in that wood, will you? You can't hardly find wood like that any more. And the fit? Can't hardly slide a piece of paper between the barrel and the stock there."

Jim glanced over his shoulder toward the two of them. Bill took the Weatherby—it was a handsome scutter, no doubt about it—from Walt and put it to his shoulder. The dark, slim rifle had no sights on it yet; that choice would be made by the buyer to his own tastes later.

"Feels good," Bill admitted.

"Hell, it's a Weatherby, ain't it?"

Bill took it down from his shoulder and gave it an admiring inspection. "Awful glossy," he noted aloud. "Sunlight catch on that, there wouldn't be anything in the county couldn't see where you was."

"If you want the gun, Bill, I can take the gloss off it for you. Buff it out with some jeweler's paste and it won't shine. I wouldn't want to take off too much finish, though. It's there to protect the wood more'n to look pretty."

Bill turned the rifle in his hands, holding it down at arm's length while he tried to make out the writing impressed in the steel near the receiver. Bill, too, was experiencing the awkwardness of having trouble reading things close up.

"Twenty-five-caliber Weatherby magnum," Walt supplied for him. "Plenty faster than that twenty-five-ought-six you got now. This'un comes with bases and rings. I could move that Burris of yours over onto the Weatherby here and take your Ruger in trade on it." Walt knew perfectly good and well what Bill's pet rifle was; Walt had sold it to him.

Bill grunted.

"Try that action. It's slick as glass."

Bill raised the rifle to his shoulder again. He paused for a moment, sighting out the window at something across the street, then slapped the bolt action up and back, then swiftly forward and down.

He grunted again and frowned, then repeated the sequence of rapid motions.

Jim smiled to himself. He knew Bill wasn't satisfied, and he knew why. When the two of them were boys, their father'd given them the use of a battered old .30-40 Krag made by Springfield for the army. The old gun hadn't been pretty—nor particularly accurate, for that matter—but it'd had the slickest, smoothest bolt action ever manufactured, and it nearly a hundred years old. That old gun set a standard nothing made in this century could compare to and was the reason Bill didn't own a bolt action rifle today. And wouldn't be buying any fancy Weatherby even if he could afford it. Walt might not realize that yet, but Jim did.

Bill frowned and handed the pretty thing back to Walt.

"You don't like it?"

"Huh-uh."

Walt shrugged and set the Weatherby back into the rack. Bill pushed his hands into his back pockets and idled along the wall racks, admiring what he saw there.

Jim turned away and went back to looking for what he'd come here to find.

Over there in the corner they were. Wooden crates filled with clear plastic Ziploc bags of jumbled, tarnished, discolored cartridges. Each bag had been written on with a black marker to show the caliber of the

government surplus ammunition it contained. Some of the ammo in obscure foreign calibers was probably older than either of the Beale brothers.

The U.S.-made 5.56 millimeter was what Jim wanted. That government cartridge was the same as the commercial .223 caliber and fit the
rugged Ruger carbines they carried in the pickup. Walt bought the army
surplus ammunition in quantity, bagged it into small lots and sold it
cheaper than what it cost a fellow to buy the cartridge components and
reload his own ammo.

"You wouldn't give a fella a break on the price if he bought, oh, a
couple hundred rounds o' this stuff, would you, Walt?" Jim asked from
across the room.

"I suppose I would, Jim. You got a lot of shooting to do?"

"Time we think about teaching Bill's boys," Jim said. "Let them get in
some plinking, you know. Maybe bring in some coyote pelts come fall."

"What size are you wanting?"

Jim told him.

He thought it over, then nodded and named a price. "That's per hundred."

"Throw me about four hundred rounds into a box, would you? Just
loose would be fine. I don't need all these plastic bags."

"Hell, I got cases of the stuff in the back. Give me a minute, and I'll
break one for you. You wouldn't want a whole case, would you? Thousand
rounds in the case, the way I buy 'em. Give you an even better price that
way."

A thousand rounds was serious money. Jim looked at Bill, who shook his
head.

"Naw, four hundred is enough," Jim told him.

"Whatever you say, boys. Wait right here. This won't take me long."

"We're in no hurry," Jim assured him.

Bill looked unhappy, but he didn't say anything. This sort of decision he
always left up to Jim.

"MAYBE THIS YEAR we oughta lay off. I mean, I don't think—" Bill began.

"Good," Jim snapped. "Keep it that way." He was feeling testy now.

"What?"

"Don't think, Bill. Jeez!"

"But—"

"Dammit, we don't have any choice. Now do we? Do we?" Jim's voice
was sharp, demanding. The look in his eyes was even angrier.

Bill couldn't meet his brother's gaze. He dropped his eyes away from

Jim's and concentrated instead on the dark brown longneck that rested between his forearms. The girls were still off shopping somewhere. The Beale boys were hunched over a pair of Buds.

"Look," Jim said in a softer, more conciliatory tone, "it's okay. You know? It's gonna be okay. Beef prices are gonna go up. They have to. A couple good years, and we won't have to worry about it."

They had been giving and receiving assurances like that with each other for as long as either could remember. They'd heard very much the same from their father before them.

The silly fact was that anyone who wasn't in the business would naturally assume that a rancher was a man in high cotton.

Between deeded land and leases, the Beale boys controlled over a hundred square miles of land, didn't they? Of course they were rich. Weren't they?

In point of fact, they were not. The holding was large. So were the expenses. Some years the Beale ranch showed a net loss. A corporate ranch could use those losses to advantage for tax purposes. A family outfit could not. A family operation like the one Jim and Bill Beale ran could only tighten its belt and hang on in the years when the costs of producing beef exceeded the price its marketed product brought in.

Ten yearling calves fed out to market weight and sold at a profit could make the difference between a good year and a bad one. Ten calves sold early at a loss could put them in the hole for another year.

And twenty calves? Fifty? There could be that much difference involved when the grazing allotments were established. Because, of course, it is the market crop that has to be trimmed first if cuts must be made. A man can't sell off his mother cows; they are the source of his crop. He can't sell his replacement heifers, because they are his future. He certainly can't discard his bulls; without them his cows are a useless liability. The only leeway he has lies in the calf crop. And that is where he makes his profit. Or doesn't.

Either Jim or Bill Beale would prefer to be caught on the horns of an angry steer than on the horns of that particular dilemma.

"Whatever you say," Bill said without sounding like he meant it.

"It's gonna be all right," Jim assured him. He took a pull on his Bud, picked up the loose change from the counter—Bill's change, actually—and walked over to a bank of slot machines. Maybe this was his lucky day.

NINE

OLIVER LOWERED THE TAIL LID of the Subaru, pressed on it until he heard the latch click shut, then pulled out his key ring and carefully locked it. He checked each door as well to see that all were locked, then briskly rubbed his hands together. As soon as JoLynn got home, they could be on their way.

Oliver's excitement had been growing. Now he was probably even more eager than JoLynn.

He glanced at his wristwatch. Hardly any change since the last time he looked. JoLynn wasn't really due for another forty-five minutes, but he was hoping she could break away early today. Friday evening traffic was going to be a bitch, at least until they were clear of Sacramento. Not that Oliver minded. He really didn't. But the first part of the trip *could* have been much easier. Interstate 80 went all the way from the Bay to Winnemucca. The normal way to get there would be across the Golden Gate, slide over to Vallejo, then up to Sacramento and roll it right along. As it was, though, JoLynn was terrified of crossing the bridges, even the Golden Gate, ever since the quake of '89. She could manage as a passenger, except maybe on the Bay Bridge—he doubted she could handle that yet—if she absolutely had to but paid for the convenience with cold sweats and white knuckles. Too heavy a price to pay, Oliver believed. They would start north by first driving south. Loop around through San Jose, take 580 across and go up I-5 through Stockton to reach 80. It was a long way around, but what the heck. Oliver wasn't so much anxious to finish the trip as to start it. Once they were on the road he would be quite content to take his time about getting there.

He sent another glance toward the crammed interior of the station wagon. He was reluctant to leave all their things piled there in plain sight even if the car was locked. Still . . . He went back up to their apartment for one last inspection. Just in case he'd forgotten something.

He was still there, prowling nervously from bedroom to bathroom and back again, when he heard the front door.

"Is that you, honey?"

"No, silly, it's the burglar. I thought you'd left already."

He smiled and gave her a quick kiss, then hustled her in the direction of the bed, carefully made up with fresh sheets, where her camping clothes were laid out waiting.

She kicked away her high heels and stripped off the conservative suit, shimmied out of her slip and bra and pantyhose so that she wore only a pair of white nylon panties. She was a dark knife blade, lean and resilient and lovely to look at. No time for that, though. The traffic was going to be bad enough without waiting for it to get any worse.

She pulled on thick socks and a pair of jeans, dragged a long-sleeved rugby jersey over her head and fished her pigtail out of the back of the neck, then perched on the side of the bed to step into her hiking boots and quickly lace and tie them. While she was doing that, Oliver was hanging her suit up and gathering everything else to dump into the laundry hamper. He gave her shoes a soccer kick into the closet. He closed the closet door. By then JoLynn had her boots laced and was reaching for the down-filled vest that was the last garment remaining on the bed.

"All set?" he asked.

"Did you remember the camera bag?"

"Of course I remembered the camera bag." It had been in the pile of things they'd laid out in the living room over the past several days waiting to be loaded.

"The traveler's checks?"

He patted his hip pocket. "Right here."

"My purse. I forgot to lay out a purse. I can't carry this one. What purse should I . . . ?"

"Good grief, woman. What difference does it make? It doesn't matter what purse you have."

Her brow squeezed into a small frown, then she shrugged. "I suppose you're right. I can carry this one." She picked up the purse she'd carried to work that day. "All right, Oliver. I'm waiting on you."

He shook his head in a show of pretended annoyance and trailed her out of the apartment, pausing at the door to make sure it was locked.

OLIVER FELT HIS LIPS FLUTTER. It was a gentle, tingling sensation and not at all unpleasant. Then the meaning of it struck him. Good Lord, he didn't snore, did he? JoLynn sometimes teased him that he did, when he was particularly tired for instance, but he hadn't really believed her. Did this mean that he'd actually been snoring?

He came fully awake, although his eyes remained closed. How awful.

Worse, snoring wasn't the sort of unpleasant personal habit that someone could exercise conscious control over. It wasn't like smoking or neglecting to bathe or becoming fat. One snored. Or one did not. One did not choose either way.

Oliver felt his ears burn with a flush of acute embarrassment. He remained carefully still so JoLynn would not notice.

The gentle, rhythmic bumps and swayings of the car continued, but there was no question that he could go back to sleep now.

Even so, he pretended to sleep. If he sat up now, JoLynn would tease him, and he wasn't really in a mood for that at the moment.

Oliver had driven through the night, getting them safely away from the traffic of the Bay Area, safely past Sacramento, safely through the Sierras and down into Nevada.

It was just as well that part of the trip had been completed in the dark. If it had been daylight, Oliver would have wanted to leave the interstate and loop down to Tahoe. He loved Lake Tahoe.

As it was, the drive had been uneventful, the roads dry and the skies clear despite his early fears that the four-wheel drive would be necessary in the mountains. In truth there had been fewer road hazards than they would have found in summer. There had been much less traffic on the road than Oliver had ever seen here before.

While Oliver had driven, JoLynn had slept in the reclined passenger seat of the little station wagon. Then at a service station outside Reno they had changed positions, and JoLynn was taking them the rest of the way up to Winnemucca.

Oliver coughed a little and wiggled. The pillow he was using in the car was JoLynn's. It was softer than Oliver's and after a full night and much of a day of use felt lumpy and sweaty and carried the scent of her cologne and his aftershave mixed into one fairly nauseous brew.

The inside of his mouth was dry and tasted sourly stale. His stomach was in rebellion after a night munching banana chips and sesame sticks washed down with warm cola.

All in all, this seemed a fairly unpleasant way to travel.

He sat up, tugged the lever to bring the seatback upright from its reclined position, and shoved the sleep-soiled pillow over the headrest to drop behind the seats.

"Sleeping Beauty awakens," JoLynn said pleasantly.

"Ugh." Oliver smacked his lips loudly and made a face.

She laughed. "Want some breakfast?"

"Is there anyplace to stop?"

"Look around you, dear."

They were off the highway and on a two-lane road with houses and fields and not far ahead a long string of commercial buildings. Off to the left the road was paralleled by railroad tracks.

"Where are we?"

"Winnemucca. Just coming into it."

Oliver ran a hand over his face and rubbed at his eyes. That was one nice thing about wearing a beard, he reflected. You could spend a hard night and not look grubby with stubble the next morning.

Not that that changed the taste in his mouth, though. He bit back a yawn, his teeth chattering lightly, and nodded. "I would like some breakfast, yes please."

"There's a Wendy's sign up there."

"Do they serve breakfast?"

"Nobody will be serving breakfast at this time of day, dear."

"Hamburgers for breakfast?"

"If it breaks your fast, then a hamburger is breakfast. Q.E.D., yes?"

"I'd much rather have oatmeal than logic right now if it's all the same to you, madame."

"But you'll settle for a hamburger?"

"But I will settle for a hamburger, true."

JoLynn grinned and took her foot off the accelerator. The droning sounds of the Subaru's progress lessened as the car began to coast and slow.

JoLynn chose a corner table as far as possible from a family with three noisy children, and Oliver followed behind with their tray. Neither, it turned out, had felt up to facing hamburgers for breakfast. Decaffeinated coffee, the salad bar and, for Oliver, a small Frosty sounded much better.

"Is this all right?"

He nodded and set the tray down. They took the disposable platters and both attacked the salad bar. Oliver particularly liked the blue cheese dressing at Wendy's. Skinny as she was, really in need of more weight rather than less, JoLynn always took the low-cal Italian.

When they were back at the table, JoLynn began to chuckle. He looked at JoLynn and raised an eyebrow.

"I was just remembering something I meant to tell you when you woke up. In fact, dear, I almost woke you so you could see the signs along the interstate advertising Winnemucca. I love them."

"You're kidding."

"No, I mean it. 'Free Admission. Winnemucca.' I mean, does that make you eager, or what? 'No Caves, No Sea Lions, No Mystery Houses. Winnemucca.' "

Oliver smiled.

" 'Open 24 Hours. Winnemucca,' " she went on.

"You're pulling my leg, right?"

"I swear I'm not. You want to hear the best one?"

"I think I'm willing."

She giggled. " 'City of Paved Streets. Winnemucca.' "

Oliver laughed.

"I was seeing those signs for the past two hours. It was all I could do to keep from waking you every time I saw another one coming up."

"You could have shaken me. I would've hit you, of course, but you could've done it."

"Tough guy," she accused.

"That's me."

He stabbed a bite of salad, took a sip of the coffee. Having something to eat was nearly as mouth-cleansing as brushing his teeth would have been. Quite an improvement. "Where do we go from here?" he asked.

JoLynn gave him a blank look.

They were in Winnemucca. City of Paved Streets. And wild horse notoriety.

Neither of them had the faintest idea where to go now that they'd come this far.

THIS WASN'T QUITE what Oliver had expected.

He didn't know exactly what it was that he'd expected. Certainly not something out of an old B western. Not cowboys with Mexican-bandit mustaches and six-guns or false-front stores and hitching posts. He hadn't actually expected to see that sort of thing here.

He knew for sure, though, that Winnemucca wasn't at all what he'd expected to see in an area where wild horses were inhumanely slaughtered.

Winnemucca was . . . a *nice* town.

Small. Cheerful. Friendly. Clean.

They drove around the streets awhile gawking and staring. The houses were compact and tidy and perfectly groomed. Many of the people they saw watering lawns or riding bicycles in the residential neighborhoods looked like retirees.

Tourists dismounted in droves from charter buses downtown, the buses carrying license tags from Idaho and Oregon mostly, and flocked chattering into the small casinos. Day-trippers down to laugh and gamble and play, obviously.

Oliver rather liked casinos himself. There was a certain lively excitement to them that he enjoyed. A sense that lightning just might strike despite the odds. Before he met JoLynn, he used to enjoy visiting Reno or the glittering, glitzy gaming halls on the Nevada side of Lake Tahoe. JoLynn, though, disapproved of gambling. Oliver certainly did not like casinos well enough to prefer them to JoLynn. He did not suggest that they visit one now.

Instead they wove back and forth through the shaded streets and past the manicured lawns of Winnemucca and wondered what any of this had to do with the kind of person who could destroy a beautiful wild horse.

Now that they were here, the whole idea seemed preposterous.

"We need to get a Nevada map," Oliver said, pointing out the obvious. "I mean, our atlas won't show the little roads we need to find. And we can't expect to see wild horses in the middle of town, can we?"

"Pull over for a minute, please, Oliver."

"Sure." They were in the business district again, a few blocks away from the tiny downtown casinos. Pedestrians ambled in and out of the stores. No one seemed in a great hurry. People smiled and frequently stopped to chat with others they passed on the sidewalk.

"Have you noticed something about the men here?" JoLynn asked.

He shrugged. "They seem friendly."

"Yes, but that isn't what I meant."

"What then?"

"Look at them. So many of them are limping. Just the men, though. And the younger men at that. The old men seem all right."

"No." But he turned and looked. Of seven men in sight who were middle-aged or younger, three of them were limping. "Isn't that weird."

"I wonder why," JoLynn mused.

"Darned if I know."

She laughed. "You don't think . . ."

"What?"

"It's springtime. Do you think maybe a lot of them ride horses? Like maybe if most of the horses hadn't been ridden during the winter and now they are and a lot of these men are being thrown off or something and that's why they limp now?"

"I suppose that makes as much sense as anything," Oliver conceded.

If JoLynn's theory was true, well, maybe this part of the country really was foreign enough to be home to the kind of man who would shoot down a free and beautiful wild horse. Just maybe that was possible after all.

Even if everyone did look normal and nice here.

He put the car back into gear, checked the rearview mirror and pulled out into the light flow of traffic.

"There's a highway marker up ahead. Some road that goes up into Idaho. We'll drive out of town a way and see if that looks like what we came here to see."

"All right." JoLynn shivered and hugged her arms tight over her chest at the reminder of their mission.

Oliver, too, was suddenly conscious of the long telephoto lens in his camera bag. For just a moment there he felt almost like a spy entering a strange country with a forged passport. Or at least what he thought such a spy ought to feel like.

TEN

JIM LET HIMSELF IN without knocking—it never would have occurred to either him or Bill to stand outside like some idiot waiting for permission to enter his own brother's house—and called out a hello to let them know he was there.

Maureen heard him and looked up from her sewing. It was a wonder she'd been able to hear him speak. The boys were watching the Saturday morning cartoons and had the TV volume turned near as high as it would go. Maureen didn't seem to mind. She grinned a welcome and pointed toward the office to tell him that's where Bill was. Jim gave her a circled thumb and forefinger and headed in that direction.

The room Bill used for the ranch office was called a den-slash-study on the house plans. It was small and out of the way and Bill had been using it as his office ever since the house was finished. Their father'd had his office in a ground-floor side room of the old house, but Bill hadn't liked having to come over there every time he wanted to get to a list or a file or a semen catalog. Now their father's office was cluttered with piles of old newspapers and paper bags full of dusty Christmas decorations and the like. Bill no longer used it and Jim never had.

"Howdy, podner." Jim stood behind the doorjamb with his head poking into the opening.

Bill looked up from his computer screen and smiled.

"Busy?"

"Naw, nothing serious." He punched a button on the keyboard in front of him—a device of deep mystery so far as Jim was concerned—and leaned back in the huge wooden swivel chair that their dad always used to sit in and his father before him. The chair was the only piece of furniture Bill had taken out of the family house. "Just trying to run a model. See what kinda feed conversion we can expect if we bring in some o' that Simental blood."

"How the hell can a electric gadget tell you a thing like that?"

"You really want me to explain it to you?" Bill challenged.

"Not really. I wouldn't understand it anyhow." Jim pushed a thin stack of magazines off the seat of a straight chair and slouched onto it. He reached for a Chesterfield, remembering only after he'd lighted it that he was going to need an ashtray. Bill found one under some papers on a nearby shelf and handed it to him. "Thanks. So about these Simentals, how does it look?" The tried-and-true bloodlines they used now were basically a deep Angus cross with a touch of longhorn that'd backdoored its way into the herd. They used longhorn on their heifers because the calves were small and easily birthed and so got the young mothers off to an easy start on the business of producing calves.

"Maybe not as good as the Santa Gertrudis would," Bill admitted.

"Back to them again," Jim said.

"Back to them again," Bill agreed.

"This country ain't right for Santa Gertrudis," Jim insisted. It was an old argument.

"I still think our herd is right for them. I want to try some. I don't mean t' buy no new bull. Just pen up some cows and bring in some semen for a test. Just ten cows, that's all."

"Then somebody's got to feed the sons o' bitches . . ."

"The boys can handle that. They need more chores anyhow."

". . . and watch 'em for their estrous cycle," Jim went on as if Bill hadn't said anything. "Using semen's a pain in the ass."

"It's also good business if it builds us some better beef."

"I know. I'm just lazy, that's all." Jim grinned. They both knew that if Bill really wanted to try some Santa Gertrudis breeding in their herd, he was going to. Bill and his computer knew more about that end of the business than Jim ever would want to. But Jim still thought he was wrong about it.

"So what'd you come over for?"

"I'm makin' up a mail order. Stockman's Supply. Steroid implants an' like that. You need anything?"

"Ear tags. Might as well get 'em now if you're sending an order anyhow."

"What d'you fancy for this year's color?"

"Purple might be nice." The ear tags every cow, steer or calf on the place carried were color-coded to show age as well as being numbered and recorded on the computer so Bill could keep track of the genealogy lines and the production that resulted from the different matings.

"Purple it is," Jim said with a straight face.

"Pink polka dots for the heifer calves, please."

"I think they're havin' a special on the ones with polka dots," Jim agreed. "I'll get you plenty. If there's leftovers, you can use 'em to make up earrings for the ladies and sell 'em on a street corner."

"Shit, them tourists would prob'ly buy 'em too. Tourists'll buy anything."

"See there? I might just've found a way to make our fortune."

"Good thing you've done it in time so I can enjoy spending it all as a young man. You, on the other hand . . ."

Jim chuckled and crossed his legs. "Going to Talley's tonight?"

"Does a chicken have lips?"

"No, but it has a pecker," both of them said in unison.

"We can drive in together. Gloria and me will spring for supper if you wanta go in early enough."

"All right."

"Might be a good idea if JayJay was to ride with us t'night too," Jim said.

"Oh?"

"I want him nice an' steady on Monday."

"Monday," Bill repeated. The laughter left his expression, and for a moment he appeared to be sad. Jim didn't have to ask what that was about. Shit, he didn't like it neither. But it was something that had to be done. A man can't make out if all he ever does are the easy things.

Bill's frown was pushed aside almost as quickly as it had appeared. He knew how things were just as good as Jim did. He forced a smile—Jim could see clear as glass that that's what he was doing—and slapped his leg.

"If you're buying the steak, Jimmy, you can count on me to be first in line. Five o'clock?"

"Yeah, that sounds about right."

"You tell JayJay. And hell, I'll contribute. I'll get the kids to wash the car this afternoon. How's that grab you?"

"Five o'clock," Jim said. He stubbed his cigarette out and stood, his knee joints creaking, to go back to the house and tell Gloria she should start getting ready early. They were gonna have a fine time tonight. He could just tell.

JIM SAT on the foot of the bed. He hooked the arch of his right boot behind the heel of his left and pushed, levering the tightly fitted Saturday boot off, then used his left foot to pry the right boot loose. He owned probably a dozen bootjacks in grades from plain to extra fancy—he even had an original of the famous Naked Lady jacks—yet the only way he ever took his boots off was with his own feet.

He expelled a sigh of relief when the left boot popped off and dropped to the floor with a clunk. He wriggled his toes and sat there for a moment relishing the sense of relief and freedom. Everybody liked to wear boots tight, but Jim was thinking maybe he'd overdone it this time. Just a leetle.

Gloria came to the bathroom door and looked in on him. White foamy toothpaste residue rimmed her mouth where lipstick had been just a little while ago, and she'd taken her party duds off. She was wearing pantyhose and a slip and bra but nothing else. Her belly sagged over the waistband of the slip some, and even with the support of a brassiere her front wasn't so perky and pointed as it used to be, but Glory was still a fine figure of a woman. Jim winked at her.

She ignored the suggestion and asked, "Is Billy all right?"

"What d'you mean, babe?"

"He was awfully quiet tonight."

"Did you think so?"

"That isn't an answer," she pointed out. Correctly.

Jim shrugged and yanked at his shirtfront, popping the pearl-covered snaps open to the waist. He stood and began peeling, tossing his clothes in the direction of a chair in the corner. "I didn't think he was so quiet." He grinned. "Not when he was having that little discussion with Parker, I wouldn't say." Bill had damn near turned Clement Parker's face inside out tonight. Jim had no idea what that'd been about, and likely neither of them could remember now. Before the night was over, Billy and Clement had been bent over the bar side by side until somebody might think they were the brothers and not Bill and Jim.

"You really didn't notice anything?" Gloria persisted.

"Nothin' serious," Jim told her.

Glory gave it up and padded back into the bathroom. Jim could hear the water run and the sounds of her spitting as she finished brushing her teeth.

Jim shucked his underdrawers and let them lie on the floor beside the bed. He pulled the covers back on his side and crawled in. The wooziness he'd had earlier was cleared and gone now, and he was feeling fine. Just fine.

He thought about Gloria in the bathroom there and for a moment visualized, could see in his mind just clear as clear could be, the slim, bumping, hip-shaking, belly-grinding shape of Audrey Conyers on the dance floor tonight. Shee-oot, but that heifer was prime cut, old Audrey was. Not that Jim Beale was a strayer. Never had been and wasn't fixing to start. But it never hurt to *think*, did it?

"Glory! You 'bout done in there?"

"You dirty old man."

He laughed. "That's me," he called out. He could hear the sound of her laughter too.

The toilet gurgled as it flushed and then he heard the laundry hamper lid drop shut. Gloria said, "Don't start without me, I'm on my way." She was naked and smiling when she came out and reached for the light switch.

Yeah, by damn, his Glory was still a fine figure of a woman, all right.

JIM CAME OUT FIRST. Gloria was still inside primping. He started the Buick and backed it out of the shed and around closer to the house, then got out and left the engine idling so the heater would be warm by the time she got in. Days you'd think it was summer instead of springtime, but the mornings were still on the cool side. Besides, here lately Gloria was funny about temperatures. She'd complain about being cold in the middle of the afternoon or swear she was burning up when it was just nice as it could be. Whichever way she was feeling this morning, the car would be ready for her.

Jim walked over to Bill and Maureen's place and let himself in. "Anybody up?" He kept his voice down just in case they were still sleeping.

"In here." Bill's voice came from the kitchen.

Maureen came out. She was up and ready just like she'd said she would be. She was wearing her blue dress and high heels and looked real nice. Jim told her so.

"Thanks." She gave him a peck on the cheek in passing. "Is Gloria out already?"

"Might be by now. The car's by the house. Don't know if she's made it that far yet, but I reckon she couldn't be much longer. She already looked like she was fixing to stand up for a portrait."

The girls had decided last night that they'd ride in to church together. Jim had begged off with the explanation that him and Bill and JayJay had work to do. Which they did.

"Boys!" Maureen called.

"Do we have to?"

Maureen didn't bother to answer. A moment later Tod and Jimmy came out into the living room, both of them looking like they'd been beat with sticks, and trudged out of the house. Maureen was busy giving her hair a fluffing out just like Gloria always did before she thought she was fit to be seen outdoors. "We won't be coming right back. We'll get something to eat in town and maybe press our noses against some store windows before we drive back."

"No hurry. We'll be gone till dark most likely."

"All right. 'Bye, Jimmy." She added, " 'Bye, honey," in a louder voice and then was gone.

Jim wandered into the kitchen and helped himself to a cup of coffee and a seat. Bill looked like hell warmed over. "Feelin' good this morning, are we?"

Bill grinned at him. "It's all your fault, y'know."

"Hell yes, it is. I oughta keep a tighter rein on you. Course it's my fault."

"My hand hurts."

"Your head ought to too."

"Well, it does."

"The wages o' sin, old son."

"You ain't gonna drive fast today, are you?"

"Not me." Jim grinned. "We'll float along like a cloud. Guarantee."

"You son of a bitch."

"Careful what you say about your own mama."

"You're gonna look for every rock and pothole, aren't you?"

"Never," Jim lied.

Bill groaned. Nope, he really wasn't looking so good this morning. There were breakfast dishes piled on the kitchen counter. Just three;

Jim counted. Enough for Maureen and the boys. "You better eat something before we go."

Bill made a face.

"I'll fix you some toast. Hell, you can hold a little toast down."

"All right." But he didn't sound happy about it.

Jim got up, found a loaf of bread in the refrigerator and dropped a couple slices into the toaster. There was butter, but Jim ignored that. Bill didn't need any grease in his belly right now. Jim helped himself to a snip of leftover ham off a plate and poured more coffee for both of them.

"Is JayJay around yet?" Bill asked.

"I ain't looked to see. He oughta be, though. He come home in better shape than you last night."

Bill groaned again, shook his head and looked like he regretted doing that about half an instant too late. "What d'you figure to do today?"

"Just drive around and see where the critters are using. We'll wait till after the weekend before we do anything."

"All right."

For just a moment there Jim was tempted to tell his little brother that he could stay home if he liked. For this whole next week if he liked.

But that would've been insulting. A hired man would quit if anybody implied that he wasn't up to pulling his share of whatever needed doing. And be right to do it, too. It'd be all the worse to suggest that of Billy.

Jim kept his mouth closed except for sipping at the coffee.

ELEVEN

FOR A CAMPING TRIP this wasn't half bad. They had a king-sized bed and cable television. And room service if they wanted it. Oliver chuckled and slipped his wristwatch on. A quarter past nine. They probably should have left a wake-up call.

JoLynn came out of the bathroom and picked up her duffel bag.

"We might as well leave everything here until after we have breakfast," Oliver suggested.

"You want to eat here?"

"Why not? It's just like with the room, honey. We'll pay half the price here that we would in a regular restaurant. Honestly."

She set the duffel onto the bed, but he thought she looked doubtful. Last evening he'd had an awful time convincing her to stay at the casino instead of looking for a motel room. But the rooms and the meals really were cheaper here than anywhere else available. After all, the casinos expected to make theirs off the guests' gambling losses. Everything else came cheap as a come-on to get people in and keep them under the casino roof.

And of course it worked just the way the casino people wanted it to. JoLynn hadn't been willing to play, but Oliver hadn't been able to resist. He'd played keno and the slots and inevitably lost a little. Not too much. The point was, he'd enjoyed himself doing it.

"We have to get serious today, Oliver," JoLynn said.

"I know. Don't worry. We'll buy a map today."

Yesterday they'd spent the afternoon driving along the paved highways that radiated out from Winnemucca. Not only had they failed to see any horses that looked wild, they hadn't seen any likely camping sites. By dusk they'd concluded that they would have to come back to town, to the City of Paved Streets, and take a room for the night. Today they could get a fresh start and hopefully accomplish something this time.

"Come on. We'll grab some breakfast and be on our way in no time."

ONE NICE THING. At least around here no one was giving them strange looks because of the way they were dressed or the camping gear in the back of the Subaru. Even at the casino with all its mirrors and chrome and sparkling lights, no one seemed to think it the least bit odd that a pair of crudely dressed people carrying duffel bags instead of luggage wanted to check in for a night. Boots and camping clothes seemed quite acceptable.

"I think we should see if there is a Bureau of Land Management office," JoLynn suggested.

"It'd be closed on Sundays."

"Oh. Of course it would be." She shook her head in annoyance with herself for having so quickly forgotten what day of the week this was. But then, they were on vacation, weren't they?

Oliver stroked her elbow affectionately and put the gas cap back on. The tank hadn't been particularly low but he wanted to keep it topped off since they might be, better be, heading into rough country today. "Last chance if you want a sit-down potty," he reminded.

"Don't forget that map," JoLynn reminded him in turn.

"I won't."

They both walked toward the station, JoLynn veering off to the right, in the direction the white signboard said the rest rooms would be, while Oliver went inside and reached for his wallet.

"I owe you four dollars and thirty cents for the gas. And I need a map. A good one."

The dark haired young man behind the counter, probably not yet out of high school, pointed toward a rack suspended on the wall near a door that led into the service bays. "The maps are over there, mister. Dollar and a quarter apiece."

Oliver looked them over. They were standard highway maps, the sort of thing that gasoline companies used to give away free. The rack mostly held maps of Nevada but there were a few others showing the roads in Idaho and Oregon and Utah as well. One, very grimy, was of California. Another showed Wyoming and Colorado combined.

"This isn't what I need. We're, uh, wanting to go camping. On public land? I was looking for something like hunters might use. I don't know what you'd call them."

"Sure, I know what you mean. Sectionals. Forest Service, BLM, like that."

"You don't sell those?"

"No, sir. Not much call for them in a gas station. You know?"

Oliver nodded glumly.

"Mr. Carruthers sells them at his gun shop," the boy said. "But he'd be closed Sunday. Same thing with the BLM. Was there something in particular you wanted?"

"We were hoping to see some wild horses while we were here," Oliver said.

"Maybe I can help you, then. My dad and me saw a bunch of them last fall when we went deer hunting."

Oliver's interest quickened. "Could you tell me where?"

"Easy." The boy left his counter and came around to take down one of the Nevada maps. "This thing won't show much, but I can kinda give you an idea where to go." He spread the highway map open and pointed.

"Here's Winnemucca. And the interstate and up here Highway 95. That's just a couple blocks down. If you look you can see the sign from here. See it?"

Oliver nodded.

"You just go up there like you're headed for Boise. That's what the signs say, Boise, but you don't even get outa town before you turn off. Just past the railroad tracks there's a sign pointing west, that's to your left, mister, on a road that goes to Jungo and Sulphur. They don't show on this map, but that's where the road goes. But you don't take it that far anyhow. You drive out . . . that a pretty tough little car, mister? The road, it ain't much once you get out past town."

"It's four-wheel drive."

"All right, then. You drive out, oh, twenty, thirty miles, something like that, and you come to this little hoot an' holler joint. I forget what they call it, but it's a little crossroads bar and dance hall sort of place. I think they got a gas pump too and sell peanuts and pop and hunting licenses. Stuff like that. Anyhow, you drive out till you see this place . . . you can't miss it; except for some ranch houses away off the road, it's about the first thing you come to once you've left the city behind . . ."

Oliver was mildly amused to hear the boy refer to Winnemucca as a city.

". . . and you turn north, that'd be right, on a dirt road there. Nothing from there, I mean *nothing* from there north except a couple more ranch houses until I guess you're halfway across Oregon and heading for Washington State."

"And that's where you saw the wild horses?"

"We sure did. A lot of that land, most of it once you get another twenty miles or so north of that crossroads, a lot of it is government land. My dad has a proper map to show what's government and what's private, but most of it's public. I remember that much from looking at our map when we were up there hunting."

"And you actually saw wild horses?"

"Sure." The boy sounded like that was the most normal and natural thing possible. He laughed and made a rueful face. "What we didn't see was deer. We were after deer, and all we saw was those horses and some antelope that were too far off to go after. We neither one of us got a deer last year." He grinned. "But I got one fall before last. When I was sixteen. We went to a hunting camp up in the mountains with some fellas my uncle knows, and I got me a three-pointer. My dad put his horns up on the wall and a picture of me with him."

Oliver smiled and made the obligatory noises of approval and appreciation even though he thought hunting an exercise in cruelty conducted for reasons of machismo and masculine bonding. But he did not expect everyone to understand that. That was what education was all about, and education was one of the reasons he contributed to some of the antihunting movements. People needed to understand that what they were doing to innocent wildlife was wrong. They could not be expected to change until they themselves believed that hunting was wrong.

"But up here, you say . . ." He pointed toward the large expanse of empty white space, completely devoid of roads or map markings, where the boy indicated there should be wild horses.

"Right. That's where my dad and me went last year. And we sure did see horses." He shrugged. "They looked about like any other horses to me. Heck, I wouldn't have known they were wild except my dad said so. Then we put the glasses on them, and I could see what he meant. They had real long tails. That's because they weren't ever trimmed. And burrs and junk in the long hair on their heads. Kinda pretty except for that. But like I said, they really looked about like any other horses. They were just standing around grazing like any old horse behind a pasture fence."

"And this land is public up where you and your father were?"

"That's right. You get a little ways up there and it's nearly all government. Anybody's allowed to hunt on it or camp or anything you want."

Oliver smiled. "You've been a big help. Thanks."

"Any time."

"Thanks a *lot*," Oliver enthused.

"You're welcome, mister."

Oliver grinned and clapped his hands together. This was all right. Now they knew where to go, and . . . He turned and started out toward the Subaru in a hurry.

"Mister!"

He stopped at the doorway. "Yes?"

"You wanta pay for that gas now, please?"

Oliver felt his cheeks burn as he grabbed for his wallet.

"MY GOD, OLIVER, LOOK." JoLynn's voice was a whisper even though the horses were at least a mile away. When she took his hand he could feel her trembling. Not that he blamed her. The excitement of the moment had captivated him too.

They sat in the Subaru staring out across the dull brown prairie and both marveled at the beauty of the wild horses.

"It's just like that boy at the service station said. They're just standing there."

There were five horses in the band, one gray horse and four dark-colored ones in various shades of brown. JoLynn's hand tightened on Oliver's.

She released her grip on him and swiveled around to kneel in her seat and rummage in the back for the binoculars. "Why didn't we pack these where we could grab them in a hurry?" she complained.

"Who ever would have thought . . ."

"I have them. I have them, Oliver." JoLynn fumbled the snap open on the black imitation-leather case and turned in her seat again to face the distant horses. She got the binoculars out and handed them to Oliver.

"No, you go ahead. You spotted them."

He didn't have to say it a second time. JoLynn lifted the binoculars to her eyes. She dialed the thick, knurled wheel to focus them, and he heard a faint gasp as the breath caught in her throat. "Oh . . . Oliver!" She was whispering again.

JoLynn peered at the horses only for a few moments before she relinquished the Tasco binoculars to him.

Oliver felt the same surge of excitement that must have gripped JoLynn as the lenses brought the herd of horses seven times nearer in his vision.

They were . . . magnificent.

That was all there was to say about them. The horses were simply magnificent.

JoLynn squealed softly with pleasure and wriggled on the seat beside him.

"They don't mind at *all* that we're here," she exclaimed.

"They're ignoring us."

"Surely they can see us, can't they?"

"They can see the car, certainly, but they can't see any people. Maybe that's it. The car isn't a threat to them. I bet they'd run if we got out."

"Don't get out," JoLynn said quickly.

Oliver shook his head. He would like to see the horses in motion, true, but he certainly was not going to run them off just for that. He was having too much fun just being able to watch them stand wild and free where they were.

He handed the binoculars back to JoLynn and turned to find his camera bag in the back. It was easier to reach than the binoculars had been. He opened the case and brought out the camera, the telephoto lens already attached. He began rolling the window down.

"Oliver!" JoLynn warned.

"I'll just put it partway down. I won't open the door."

JoLynn was watching the horses through the binoculars. Oliver discovered that the telephoto lens brought the image of the herd almost as close. The image of the horses was shadowed and grainy on the ground-glass focusing plane of the single-lens reflex camera.

"We really need to be closer," he said. He rested the heavy barrel of the telephoto on the top of the partially lowered window glass, took a moment to steady his breathing and snapped a picture. The camera clunked and whirred as the shutter was triggered and a new frame of film was automatically transported into place. He shot another picture and then a third even though the horses were really much too far away for a good shot.

"I wonder if they sell film at that funny little place back there. Talley's, was it?"

"I brought plenty," he assured her. "If we do run out, well, it's only a few hours back to town. We could drive in and be back in half a day."

Out across the prairie the five horses shuffled a few feet forward, grazing their way ahead. Oliver took another picture of them.

"Do you think we could camp somewhere around here, Oliver? I mean, since we know there are wild horses in this area."

"I don't see why not." He laughed. "Pick a spot, any spot."

JoLynn laughed too and squeezed his hand.

It seemed unreal that there could be this much bare, empty, open ground stretched out for miles and miles in every direction.

The country was vast and virtually barren. Nothing but grass and sky. And a few distant mountain tops stark against the horizon to east and west. They had passed the last hints of civilization more than an hour ago. And that had been only a turning of one dirt road off the other with the roofs of some buildings barely visible to the west of the one-lane dirt track that passed for a road here.

Here the land was as flat as it was barren. To the north there were a few knobby undulations in the ground, but right here the land was a platter of short grass and pale soil.

There were no signs to indicate where the private land had ended or where the public began, but surely by now they were on the government land. They hadn't passed a fence line for miles. And no gates whatsoever. Practically since they left the crossroads with the honky-tonk called Talley's, they had been in open country.

Every few miles at first there had been a fence line to pass through, the barbed wire fences stretching out of sight to east and west, but even then there had been no gates, only the rumbling steel strips of cattle guards to slow down for and drive over. They hadn't crossed one of those in so long now that surely they had reached the public land.

"It isn't too early to make camp, is it?" JoLynn asked. "After all, there are wild horses here. Surely we could make camp off the road here and no one would mind."

"We might scare them off."

"We could drive off the road a little way. Not toward them, though. And if we keep the car between the horses and us, maybe it won't bother them. I'd really like to stay where we can watch them if possible."

Oliver nodded. "We can try it, can't we?"

JoLynn smiled. He could see that she was still excited.

And across the grass the horses continued to graze as if they were completely unconcerned by the intrusion of man on their natural domain.

TWELVE

THE OLD TRUCK slowed nearly to a halt, then rolled up and forward as Jim balanced clutch and accelerator to help it over the lip of the borrow ditch. Bar ditch, some called it. Not that any kind of a ditch was needed this year. There wasn't any runoff to have to worry about. The promising early snows had stopped cold and weren't replaced with spring rains. The grass was as dry as these dirt tracks, dammit. June might bring fresh growth in abundance but by then it would be too late; by then the grazing allotments would already be set, based on the condition of the grass as it was no later than the end of next week. Even if it rained this evening—fat chance—there wouldn't be enough improvement seen in that time to make a difference.

"Dammit," Jim mumbled aloud.

"Huh?"

"Nothing."

"You said something."

"I didn't say nothing, dammit."

"You don't have t' shout."

Bill tugged his hat brim down and hunched his shoulders in a sulk. JayJay pretended not to have heard. He was staring out the passenger-side window.

"Dammit," Jim repeated to himself. This time no one responded.

There was a loud squeal from under the hood as the Chevy crawled out of the shallow ditch, the front half-axles being drawn in opposite directions by the abruptly uneven terrain. The truck had been making that noise for years but nothing seemed to bust because of it. Bill's theory was that it was the transfer case howling. Jim thought it sounded more like something rubbing against something else.

"Tomorrow," Jim said. "We'll go out tomorrow morning early."

Neither Bill nor JayJay looked at him, but they'd heard, all right.

Well, the simple truth was that he'd been hoping for something different too. He didn't like this shit. But then he didn't have to. All he had to do was do it: There wasn't anything written down to say he had to enjoy it too.

He fished underneath the flap on his shirt pocket and pulled out a smoke and his lighter, lit the cigarette and dropped the lighter back into his pocket. Warm as it was this afternoon—and dry too—they were riding with the windows already down. The smoke was pulled out of the cab by the hint of breeze that flowed through.

Jim stopped the Chevy and put the shifter in neutral so he could lean down and wrestle the transfer lever out of the off-road locked position to the normal driving range. The lever was balking again, so he grunted and forced it. He really was going to have to remember to clean the mud off that case soon.

Bill waited until the truck was in gear and moving again, then reached for the Pepsi can that was hanging in a cup holder on the dashboard. He spat a squirt of brown juice into the can and replaced it in the gimballed holder, where it bobbed and swayed with the motions of the truck. You could hear the cold spit and tobacco juice sloshing around inside the can.

Jim turned his head away and sucked on his cigarette. People bitched about smoking and smokers nowadays, he reflected, but the ones that said all those things about smokers didn't know what a nasty tobacco habit really was. Snuff, now that was nasty.

"Hey!" JayJay straightened up in the seat, unusual for him, and added, "What th' hell is all that?"

"What?"

JayJay pointed.

"Shee-it," Jim said.

"Early in the season for crazy people," Bill observed. He gave the floorboards a shove to push himself into an upright position too now. The hikers and naturalists and high-desert campers who sometimes showed up in summer were all regarded as crazy people by those who knew better. The tourists who came in to lose sleep in the casinos in the towns were all right; at least they were doing something halfway sensible with themselves. The ones who showed up out here, having so-called fun by deliberately making themselves uncomfortable, they were just plain crazy.

"Reckon we better have a word with 'em," Jim said.

He spun the steering wheel hard to the right, and the old truck jolted off the track and through the shallow ditch. JayJay grinned and grabbed hold of his hat, and Jim gunned the engine into a loud, roaring rush.

The Chevy bore down fast on the tiny campsite and palomino-colored Jap station wagon beside it.

At the last moment Jim stomped on the brake pedal. All four wheels locked up, and the truck slewed sideways and slid to a dust-raising, gravel-throwing stop not ten feet from the blue-and-white dome tent that had sprouted in the Beale pasture sometime since they went past this morning. The tent looked like a stemless psychedelic mushroom, its bright and gaudy coloring out of place in this setting.

"Let's see what we done found here," Jim said as he snatched the truck door open and stepped out.

THE SOUND of the truck skidding to a stop and flinging bits of dirt and gravel onto the clean, tight, hardly-been-used fabric of the tent brought 'em outside, all right. Right quick. They looked apprehensive, both of them, and the man like he was ready to get huffy in defense of his woman. Except of course he wouldn't. Jim could see the way the man's eyes kept cutting over to the other side of the truck where JayJay and Bill were stepping out now. This thin, city-looking fella wasn't going to take on any three grown humans, though he might snort and paw the ground some to keep the woman from seeing how scared he was.

"Howdy." Jim nodded and added a smile to show the guy that there wasn't any need for him to get fussed up. He dropped his smoke onto the ground and took his time about grinding it under the sole of his boot, keeping his head cocked a bit and his eyes squinted so he could look the pair over while he was busy with the butt.

Tourist types, that was his impression. The man was trim and seemed fit enough but was pale behind his beard and likely was softer than the surface showed.

The woman, she looked almost Indian. Dark and skinny and plain. No boobs, no ass and no makeup. She looked like a librarian, or at least like a librarian is supposed to look but almost never does. She only lacked the funny little round eyeglasses to complete the picture.

"Hello." The man acted like he didn't know whether to smile or not so soon after coming out of that tent half set to fight. A hint of a smile flickered on and off and settled for staying on. He turned and helped the woman off her knees and onto her feet as she crawled out of the low, zippered door of the tent. After she got to her feet—she was at least as tall as the man was, Jim saw now—she edged behind the man and fiddled with the front of the jeans she was wearing. It occurred to Jim that maybe the roaring arrival of the pickup truck could've been better timed. Not that it was the sort of thing a fella could come right out and apologize for. But still . . .

Jim coughed into his fist and spent a moment examining the camp these two had set up here.

It was a summer-people rig, all right. Ducky little propane cooking stove set up on wire legs. Ducky little folding table nearby. Folding stools. Paper grocery sacks on the tailgate of the foreign station wagon.

Strange as hell place to pick for a campsite, though. There wasn't a lick of shade or water, either one, not for miles. The views weren't much from here neither. If the guy'd been so horny he couldn't wait another few miles, he wouldn't have gone to the trouble of dragging out the stove and table, surely.

"You, uh, break down or something, did you?" Jim asked. Bill and JayJay were leaning against the front of the truck, just kinda listening in and keeping an eye on things. Not that there was anything to worry about from a couple like this.

"No, no trouble," the man said. The woman had got her pants together and was standing beside him now. "We wanted to photograph the wild horses."

The woman turned and looked off to the southwest. She took her husband's arm and smiled. She didn't look so plain when she smiled. Almost pretty, in fact. "I was afraid your truck would have frightened them away," she said. Nice voice, Jim thought. "I see it didn't."

"Ma'am?"

"The wild horses." She raised an arm and pointed. She sure had long fingers and bony hands.

Jim looked to see what she was pointing at, and it was about all he could do to keep his face straight. Over at the front of the truck Bill was covering his mouth with a hand now, and JayJay was turned all the way around, his shoulders shaking like he'd gotten a case of the shivers.

"Ma'am, I reckon you folks are welcome t' photograph them horses all you want," Jim said solemnly.

"We'll make it easier for you if you like," Bill offered. He tilted his head back and fitted his tongue to his teeth and let out a shrill, piercing whistle.

There wasn't any wind for the sound to fight against, and across the pasture the heads came up and the ears tipped forward. Almost immediately the horses swung into a quick trot, heading for the truck and the promise of feed.

"Oh, hell," the man said, a sheepish look on him now.

"They aren't . . . ," the woman began lamely.

"No, ma'am," Jim said gently. "Just some o' our ponies that we haven't gathered up yet."

The two looked at each other and laughed. The joke was on them, but they didn't seem to mind.

"This is public land, isn't it?" the man asked.

Jim grinned and scratched under his chin. "I sure hate t' be such a all-around disappointment to you folks. But as a matter o' fact, it ain't. There's another fence line 'bout four miles up that way there." He pointed to show them. "BLM ground picks up there an' runs pretty far."

"We're on your private land?"

"Uh-huh. The Beale Ranch. You passed the houses eight, nine miles back."

"We really didn't . . ."

"Hey, it's all right. No harm been done. Stay right here if that's what you want."

"But those aren't . . ."

Jim grinned again. "Huh-uh."

The man groaned and rolled his eyes and looked at his woman, the both of them chuckling now.

The horses came up, old Boy Blue in the lead, eager as always to get to the groceries first in line, and trotted through the city people's camp to reach the truck. It was the back end of the truck they were interested in, not the people. The city couple looked nervous about being so close to a few horses. The woman kept eyeing them like she expected to get bit or kicked or something. Which of course she just might, so Jim didn't offer any false reassurances.

"We got anything in the back o' the truck, JayJay?" Jim asked.

JayJay took his boot heel off the bumper of the Chevy and walked around to take a look.

If they'd brought the horse trailer with them today, there would have been some sweet feed in the tack compartment, but the trailer was back home. Jim hated to call a horse and then not give it some tidbit at the least. Lie to them like that and they wouldn't be so quick to come next time. And someday you might need that horse to come, like if you were laying hurt on the ground.

"Got a couple chunks of busted protein block back here," JayJay said.

"That'll do," Jim told him.

JayJay gathered some of the bits and pieces and carried them off away from the camp where their dust and commotion wouldn't be a bother. The horses crowded close behind him with their ears pinned flat as they jockeyed for position nearest to the man with the treat.

"I'm really sorry . . . ," the man started in again.

"No harm done." Jim smiled at them. "You say you're out here looking to see some wild 'uns?"

"We were told there were wild horses out this way."

"Too damn—excuse me, ma'am—too darn many of them, that's the truth."

"Would you like us to tell you where you might see some?" Bill offered.

"Would you?" The man and the woman both perked up just as eager as a pair of pups.

"Sure. But it'd mean you'd have to move your camp. Go up onto the BLM and do some driving off the road. You think that little thing can handle it?"

"We have four-wheel drive."

"You can get there easy," Bill said. He glanced over at Jim and said, "Salt Spring?"

"You bet," Jim agreed.

"Got a map?" Bill asked.

The man shook his head.

"That's no problem. We'll tell you how to go. You can't miss it." He grinned when he added that part. So did the man with the California plates on his station wagon.

"C'mon, Jimmy. Give me a hand with this." Bill took a few steps forward to split the difference between where he was and where the California couple was standing. He hunkered down and used the edge of his hand to smooth a place on the ground where he could draw in the dirt. The people came over to him, and the man knelt beside Bill. Jim and the woman stood over them so they could see the map Bill was sketching now.

"Now where we are, see, is right here. To get to Salt Spring you'll want to go. . . ."

"I BET THAT OLD BOY isn't gonna be able to get it up again for another week, maybe longer," JayJay said, going into another fit of laughter. He was slumped in the corner of the cab practically helpless from it as Jim guided the Chevy fast down the road, a rooster tail of dust rising behind them as they headed it home.

"I got to admit," Bill agreed, "it'd take the edge off." He grinned and poked an elbow into Jim's ribs. "You oughta know better'n to do a thing like that."

"Aw, if I'd known, boys, I woulda snuck up on 'em slow and easy. We coulda peeked in and watched."

"Then I'm glad you went in so loud," Bill said. "JayJay get one look at that woman nekkid and he'd be useless this whole week long."

"Hell, I practically did see her nekkid. She wasn't wearing no braziere."

"Leave it to ol' JayJay to spot that right off."

"Not that she needed one. No tits, hardly. And skinny? Lordy, a fella'd get all bruised an' bumped around wallowing on top o' that."

"You're saying you wouldn't if you got the chance? Is that what you're telling us, JayJay?"

"Now that ain't *exactly* what I'm telling you," JayJay said with a snicker.

"Shit, you know JayJay. He'd hump a snake if he could get somebody to hold its head."

"He'd jump a bonfire if somebody threw a snake into it."

"And a long-haired woman with a pretty smile? Well, I reckon."

"What the hell is this, boys? Pick on JayJay week?" JayJay tried to look offended but couldn't manage to bring it off. He was laughing too much to appear wounded.

"Crazy Californians," Jim said.

"Got them some pitchers of wild horses though, didn't they?"

"Yessir, they got them some pictures o' wild horses."

The three of them whooped and hollered some more at the thought of anyone mistaking those stodgy old geldings for a wild bunch.

"I seen that Lonesome George horse get wild one time," JayJay claimed, speaking of the thin chestnut with white saddle-gall scars that had been part of the "wild" band back there. "You remember that one-balled hermaphrodite stag Harry Thaller used to ride? Damn thing tried t' get amorous with Lonesome George once. George got wild that time, all right. Like to kick that stag's head off an' Harry still setting on the thing at the time."

"I remember that. Harry, he was on crutches for a month after he come off that horse."

"Sold the sonuvabitch too, first phone call he made after Leona got him home from the emergency room. Dog meat. But that horse, it shoulda been made into dog meat the day it was born. D'you remember . . . ?"

The couple from California were forgotten for the moment as the conversation shifted to the bad horses each of them had known and then, inevitably, to the good ones. There were more good ones than bad, really. But the bad horses made for better stories.

JIM PROPPED A BOOT on the lowest rail of the old corral and crossed his arms on the top rail. It was chilly at this time of evening and he hadn't put a coat on when he left the house, but he didn't mind so much. He'd spend another few minutes and then go back inside. Most nights he came out just to take a walk-around and see that everything was all right. More often than not he'd stand here for a few minutes. Not doing much of anything. Just breathing deep of the air that came in from across the grass. There was no cloud cover tonight. The stars overhead were bright and steady on a background of black velvet.

He heard footsteps coming up behind him but didn't bother to turn his head. " 'Lo, Bill."

" 'Lo, Jimmy." There was no need for him to ask his brother how he'd known who it was. Bill would have known too.

"Saw me walk out, did you?"

"Uh-huh." Supper was over and done with. At home Gloria was washing up the dishes. Probably Maureen was doing the same in their place. The boys would be belly down on the floor in front of the TV doing homework when the commercials were on. Bill hooked a boot onto the rail and leaned against the fence beside him.

"Funny, those Californians," Bill said.

"Yeah." Jim smiled, remembering how nervous the man'd been to start with and then how apologetic and finally how grateful for the help. "Salt Spring, huh?"

"You don't mind?"

"It's where I'd've sent them myself if I'd thought of it. Not too far away. And we won't be anywhere around Salt. They won't bother us none up there."

"That's kinda what I had in mind."

"You did good, little brother."

Bill grinned. "Little?"

"Still whip your ass any day o' the week."

"I dunno, Jimmy. Been a long time since that point's been proved."

"Be a while longer, too," Jim agreed. He reached into his pocket for a smoke. There was no breeze tonight but from habit he cupped his hands close around the flame when he clicked the lighter afire.

Bill lifted his face toward the sky and drew in a long breath. "God, I love this place. I can't imagine living in a city someplace drawing wages."

"People make out."

"People don't know."

"Ain't that the truth." Jim grinned. "Don't tell 'em any different, right?"

"We'd be overrun with Californians."

"Have to go to a damn city just to find some privacy."

Black shapes moved in the darkness in front of them. There was the wet, fluttering sound of a horse blowing snot and a muffled stamping of shod feet but no squealing or fighting.

"Getting cold," Jim said.

"Time t' go in," Bill agreed.

Neither of them moved to leave or spoke again for quite a while.

THIRTEEN

"GOD, THIS IS BEAUTIFUL." JoLynn's voice was a soft, husky whisper in the night. She sat with her back to him, face lifted toward the stars. They were so bright and so many. More than Oliver had ever known was possible. The sky was a carpet of bright, pinpoint lights, the Milky Way startling in its distant, dense clarity.

"You don't want to go in?"

"Do you?"

"No." It was cold. But not that cold. Oliver was enjoying the unaccustomed night sky much too much to want to go into the tent now.

And the silence. Lord, the silence. It was complete. Now that the evening breeze had died away, there wasn't even a sound of rustling grass. Nothing. Nothing at all. They had turned off the lantern as much to be relieved of the faint sounds of its hissing gas flow as for any other reason. There certainly was no need for privacy here. As far as either of them knew, there wasn't another living creature, not so much as a bird, within miles and miles. By now even the clicking, groaning, knocking ticks of the Subaru's cooling engine had died, and there was no intrusion on the solitude from any source.

He leaned forward, lifted the long, cool, satiny weight of her hair into his palm and stroked through it with the brush. It felt like liquid in his hand, the slight drag of it syrupy and slow against the stiff bristles of the familiar brush. God, he loved JoLynn's hair. There was nothing in life that could give him more peace or pleasure than this nightly ritual.

He drew the brush down to and through the trailing ends below the level of her waist, then lifted it and started again.

Every so often he would push the dark cascade to the side a bit and lean closer. He enjoyed the smell of her hair and of her flesh. The soft, tender skin at the nape of her neck delighted and stirred him. Rarely could the sight, the touch, the taste of her there fail to arouse him. Tonight certainly was no exception.

"Again?"

"Mmm." He stroked her back and nibbled the side of her neck.

She laughed and leaned back against him.

Oliver knew what she was thinking. Those cowboys in the pickup truck this afternoon had very nearly interrupted something. Not that the interruption had been of a permanent nature. They'd taken care of that just as soon as the camp was moved and this new one set up.

"Tell me, Oliver, do you think they were for real? Or did Central Casting send them out for local color?"

He chuckled and pulled the brush through her hair again. "Central Casting," he decided.

"I thought so."

They'd certainly looked the part. Rugged jaws and worn-down cowboy boots and everything. Definitely not drugstore cowboys. One look at those Nevadans had been enough to prove that.

Oliver wouldn't have said anything to JoLynn about it, but for a few moments there he'd thought the cowboys scary. They'd seemed as uncivilized as this wild, empty country they lived in.

But of course they hadn't been. They'd been polite and helpful and nice as could be.

Although for just a moment there . . .

"Do you know what I forgot?" he asked.

She shook her head, the motion causing her hair to flow and gather on his hand.

"I forgot to get a close-up picture of those wild horses when I had the chance."

JoLynn laughed and swatted at his knee.

"Ouch."

"I didn't hurt you."

"No. But you might have."

"Keep it up, buddy, and I'll show you hurt."

"Huh. Just try it. I can feel myself reverting, woman. I'm going primitive. Mess with me and I'll find a club and whop you one over the head. Drag you back to my cave and ravish you."

"As long as it's a promise about that ravish part, all right. Just don't be so insulting about my Italian ancestry. That slur was uncalled for, sir."

"Say what?"

"I distinctly heard you call me a wop. Something about my head."

"What I said was that I would whop you. Though now that you mention it, I've always heard that skinny Italian women do give the best head."

"Care to experiment, mister?"

"I don't have any cigarettes or chocolate bars to give you."

"That's all right. I take Visa, Mastercard, American Express. For you, Joe, a discount."

"I love you, idiot."

"It works out nicely, doesn't it, because I love you too."

"Come along, woman. A thousand and one delights await. And we even have a tent to do them in."

"You'll whop me if I don't come?"

"Careful what you say. Some of my best friends are Italian."

JoLynn stood, and Oliver laid the hairbrush aside. He was glad they'd come on this trip. Whether or not they got to see some genuine wild horses.

OLIVER HELD HIS PALMS OUT, fingers splayed, to the heat of the propane stove. A campfire would have been more appropriate to the circumstances, a heck of a lot more aesthetically pleasing too, but there were several rather good reasons why they would have no campfires here.

First and foremost among those reasons was that there wasn't anything to burn.

They hadn't, after all, thought to pack the car with firewood. Who would?

And here . . . Oliver's nose wrinkled as he looked around this Salt

Spring place now that they had some good daylight to see it by. It had been dusk when they found it yesterday and completely dark by the time they finished unloading and setting up the camp.

Dreary. That was the most charitable description he could give it.

Salt Spring turned out to be a lump of rock and dirt protruding from the ground like a canker. Easy enough to locate in this flat, arid country but otherwise unexceptional. There was a mud wallow. That, he supposed, was Salt Spring.

Wild horses and other desperately thirsty things might find the muddy water palatable. But the scene was hardly what one would call picturesque.

Besides, surely wild horses would shy away from the sights and the sounds of man. Here there was no good place for them to stay out of sight from anything approaching across the prairie.

The hillock that stood above the mud hole that was Salt Spring was barely large enough to park behind. A band of wild horses coming toward the water here would have to approach from a very specific, very narrow angle to avoid seeing the car. And weren't wild animals supposed to have a good sense of smell? The way the small hill loomed immediately over the water, Oliver and JoLynn and the Subaru too would have to be awfully close to the water source if they were to have any hope of hiding themselves from the horses.

Oliver frankly didn't think this campsite was going to work out particularly well.

Not that he intended to say anything to JoLynn about it. He was enjoying the experience of being here with her. Real-life wild horse observations and photo opportunities, well, that would be icing on his cake. If it ever happened.

He just hoped JoLynn wasn't going to be disappointed when nothing really came of their trip.

"Is it ready?"

"Not yet." He turned, took a look at her and couldn't help but smile at the look of resigned embarrassment on her face.

There wasn't any way they could hide from approaching wildlife nor from much of anything else that might be in the neighborhood. And there weren't any restroom facilities out here.

JoLynn had had to take a roll of toilet paper and a folding spade with her to tend to her morning needs. She had disappeared somewhere beyond the car. God knew how she'd felt, exposed on virtually all sides like that. Oliver knew for sure what his reaction had been to feeling the cold morning breeze on his backside. And he at least had the minor advantage of knowing that any people they might encounter out here would almost certainly be other males. JoLynn must have been awfully uncomfortable.

Deciding that was a subject best left alone, he lifted the lid on the big all-purpose pot and checked the water they were heating. It wasn't boiling yet but was beginning to steam. He held his hands close to the hissing flame and warmed them again. It was colder at dawn, he was sure, than when they'd gone to bed last night. Hopefully it would warm soon under the sun's influence. He checked the rotary knob, but the gas was already turned on as high as it would go.

While Oliver was busy at the stove, JoLynn got out a pair of plastic mugs and a matching plastic pot. She put three tea bags into the pot ready for Oliver to add the water, then found bowls, spoons, a plastic bag of honey-colored raw sugar and the paper packets of instant oatmeal.

"Apple and cinnamon?"

"Blueberry," he said.

"One pack?"

"Two, please." He was hungrier than usual this morning. Something to do with the rigors of the fresh air, he was sure. And, perhaps, the exertions of last night.

At least the bedding had been comfortable. With plenty of room to haul and store their equipment in the station wagon, they'd decided to bring foam rubber mattress pads instead of the smaller but unreliable air mattresses. The foam pads worked just fine.

"Did you mix the milk?"

He grunted. "I knew I forgot something."

"Never mind then, I'll get it." She opened a quart serving package of dried milk and dumped it into a plastic container with a tight-fitting snap-on lid. Oliver lifted the five-gallon water jug and poured for her. This early in the trip the container was much too heavy for her to easily manage by herself. They'd brought ten gallons, two containers, with them. If they ran out, well, they could always strike the camp and drive back to that cross-roads place for more. That would be, he guessed, fifty or sixty miles away now. Maybe more.

JoLynn stirred the milk by putting the lid onto the plastic container and shaking it, then set it aside. "Pour some more into this, please." She held out a small bowl. "We'll need some clean water to brush our teeth in. We can wash in whatever hot water is left from the tea and the oatmeal."

Oliver tipped the heavy water jug again, and JoLynn went to the car to get their toothpaste and brushes.

The water on the stove was beginning to boil now. Good. He was sure he would feel better about this campsite once he was warm and had his belly full. The thought of the oatmeal was enticing.

JoLynn was bent over, leaning into the back of the wagon in search of the toothbrushes. She looked so *serious*, he thought. But so dear.

On an impulse he picked up the camera and focused on her. Because of the long telephoto lens, her face in profile filled the frame. Dark, intense, tho thiok braid of blaok hair dioappoaring bohind hor ohouldor. Ho snapped the picture and knew even as he did so that it was a good one. The newly rising sun gave a golden rim of backlight, almost an aura, and the lines and textures of her face were captured now on film for him to keep and enjoy forever.

JoLynn heard the sound of the shutter. She looked at him and smiled, and all the severity in her features disappeared in a flash of instant radiance.

THEY SAT ON TOP of the hill overlooking Salt Spring. JoLynn had the binoculars, Oliver the camera with the long lens attached. Oliver, frankly, was bored. The sky was cloudless. The views beautiful only in the distance. And there wasn't so much as a bird to look at any nearer than those far-off mountains.

"Dear."

"Mmm?"

"I think we made a mistake."

He looked at her. "How do you mean?"

"I don't think this is a good place for us to see wild horses. I know those men meant well. But I don't think they sent us to a good place."

He laughed and took her hand and squeezed it.

"You've been thinking the same thing, haven't you?" she accused.

"Well. Maybe." He grinned at her.

"You could have said something sooner."

"I thought you were enjoying yourself."

"I thought you were."

He grinned again and kissed her. "So what do you want to do? Go all the way back to town? That Bureau of Land Management place would be open today. We could buy a map there."

"It would take us all day to get back to town."

"True."

"I was thinking, Oliver. If there is a spring at the bottom of this hill, well, maybe there are springs at the bottom of other hills too."

"Yes?"

"We could look, couldn't we?" She stood and motioned for him to join her. She handed him the binoculars. "See up there to the north? There's a hill up there. A bigger one than this one."

"It's awfully far away. No road to it that I can see."

"We don't need a road, do we?"

"Mmm, I suppose not."

They'd come to this Salt Spring place without any road for miles and miles back. And those cowboys had said it was all right to do that. This was wide open public land and anybody was allowed to come onto it. If they were allowed to drive here, well, they should be allowed to drive there too.

"I guess we could look."

"And if that hill doesn't have a spring at it, we could look for another."

Oliver shrugged. "Why not. As far as half a tank of gas will take us, anyway. When we hit a half tank we'll turn back regardless. Okay?"

JoLynn smiled. "Okay."

"Maybe even a bit below a half. After all, we can buy more gas at that crossroads place. That's a lot closer than town."

"It's a deal," she said. She sounded enthused and happy again. And that was all that really mattered to him anyway.

JoLynn brushed off the seat of her jeans and bounded down the hill ahead of him. By the time he reached the campsite, she was already dumping their things into boxes and duffels. While JoLynn took charge of the kitchen gear, Oliver began stripping out clothes and bedding so he could take the tent down.

"PERFECT!" JoLynn was bouncing now. Vibrant. "Perfect," she repeated.

Oliver had to agree. This place was much, *much* better than the other one had been.

Just as JoLynn had hoped, there was a water hole at the base of it. Except unlike poor, dreary Salt Spring, this one had a real water hole. A spring and a pond and cattails growing in the shallow fringes of the pool. The water wasn't clear and clean-looking enough that Oliver would want to drink out of it himself, but he certainly wouldn't have hesitated to drink from the spring that rose a dozen or so feet above it on the hillside. There was nothing within half a hundred miles here that could cause pollution.

And the hill itself was perfect too.

It was too small to be called a mountain. But surely it couldn't be thought to miss that by much. This hill was ten times the size of the lumpy little thing at Salt Spring.

He had driven the Subaru once around it, then around to the back side —the east actually, they considered the front to be the point where the spring and pond were—and right on up nearly to the top.

Up there the car and their camp would be completely out of sight if any wild horses came to drink.

Better yet, there was a rounded, almost flat area on the hillside above the spring. Oliver had no idea what a place like that should be called. Not a ridge, certainly. And it was too softly rounded to be what he would think of as a ledge. A more or less flat area, anyway. It was an ideal spot where they could sit and wait and watch for the horses with their camera and binoculars.

The ledge—so to speak—was quite a way above and back from the place where the horses might come. Oliver judged the distance to be roughly two football fields. Call it two hundred yards. He wished he had bought an even longer telephoto lens for the camera. Still, if they could get some pictures from up here, of a whole herd of wild horses, say . . . He smiled and nodded his agreement with JoLynn. This spring and hill were perfect for what they wanted.

"I love it," JoLynn exclaimed.

She stood with her face to the breeze and her arms held wide to the infinite, blue sky. "I love it," she said again.

"It would be hard not to."

Far out to the west they could see snow-capped mountains and, nearer, a line of lesser peaks. To the east, if they walked around to where the car was parked, there was a chain of smaller, lower mountains with dark slopes and bald gray-and-tan tops.

The prairie spread out at their feet was rolling and beautiful. Countless acres of grass gouged here and there with shallow gullies and lightly shadowed contours.

JoLynn gasped, and for a moment he thought she might have seen a snake or something. But when he looked at her, he saw that her expression was one of wonder and not fear.

"Oliver! Look. Why, I can't see anything, not anything, that has been touched by man. I mean . . . oh, I know people have been here before us. But there isn't a single mark left by man. Not a building. Not an electric line or telephone pole. Not a road or track. Not even an airplane contrail in the sky right now. I don't believe . . . I don't think I've ever, ever been anywhere before that there wasn't *some* sign of man. Here . . .

this is natural, Oliver. This is nature. This is just the way this country was made. Just the way it is supposed to be."

There was a sense of joy in her voice. And, he thought, a tiny hint of nervousness underlying it. She was not afraid. He was sure of that. But she was awed by this experience.

He stood beside her and shared it with her. And looked to see if he could disprove her claim that there was no hint of mankind to be seen in this world that was spread out below them.

He could not.

There were not even tire tracks to be seen on the soft grass below, although they had just driven completely around the hill before coming up here. The tires of the Subaru had left no lasting impression on the land. And he was glad they had not. He sighed and put an arm around JoLynn's waist. She shifted close against him and rested her head on his shoulder as for a time both of them peered out over the vast, empty space and drank in the virgin beauty of a countryside that had yet to be despoiled by man.

It was an experience that neither of them had ever had before. An experience that few people ever are privileged to know.

"God," Oliver said. The utterance was more prayer than it was exclamation.

They stood like that for quite a while before they turned away to go and begin unloading the Subaru and once again establish a camp. This time, though, there would not be a need to move again. This place was where they wanted to stay the entire time they had left.

FOURTEEN

"SO WHAT d'you think?"

"I think I don' know where the sons o' bitches have got to, that's what I think." Jim Beale squinted and tilted his head to one side trying to avoid a stream of cigarette smoke that was collecting under his hat brim.

"Supposed to be right here."

"Uh-huh. You reckon we can take 's'pose to be' t' the bank?"

A few feet away JayJay chuckled and yawned.

"Time for your nap, old fella?" Jim challenged.

"Damn right," JayJay said agreeably.

"So what do you boys think?" Bill asked again.

Jim grunted and scratched the back of his neck. He swayed gently on his saddle while the dun horse shifted position, stretching out its forelegs a bit and releasing a loud, splashing stream of urine onto the rock-studded hillside where the horsemen had paused.

"I just hope t' hell they ain't gone over to Salt Spring," JayJay put in.

"Wouldn't that be a helluva deal. Send those city people over there and the horses show up too," Bill said.

"Be just our damn luck," Jim complained.

"Aw, we'll find 'em." JayJay let his reins go slack. He pulled his right foot out of the stirrup and brought that leg up and over, hooking his knee behind the saddle horn. He locked his fingers together at his knee and leaned back a bit, the picture of a gentleman at leisure. More or less. Bill Beale winked at Jim and began fidgeting and fussing with the lid of his can of snuff. Every time he tugged at the lid, he also tugged as if by accident at the off rein of his appaloosa. Slowly the brown-and-white mottled ap began to shift position in response to the repeated small annoyances. The appaloosa, known to be a kicker, was brought around inch by inch so that its butt was pointed toward JayJay's seal-brown day horse.

"Hey!" JayJay saw the threat in time, grinned and gigged the brown a few steps downhill where it would be out of the line of fire if Bill's ap let go. JayJay didn't bother to change his precarious balance atop the saddle nor so much as pick up his reins to move the brown.

Bill and Jim both pretended not to know why JayJay had moved. Their expressions reflected no disappointment.

"They been trending north," Jim said.

"That means Salt Spring."

"If the wild herd went to Salt, then we're shit outa luck until those city people clear out. And if there's horses using that water for them people to see, there's no telling how long they'll stay an' take pictures."

"So we better hope they didn't head for Salt."

"We better assume they didn't. What I think we oughta do is loop on around an' ride wide of Salt. Go on up toward Coffee Hill an' see can we pick 'em up there."

"You want to go back for the truck?"

"Naw, that's half a day back."

"Half a day on to Coffee Hill from here too."

"Maureen promise you something special if you come home tonight, boy?"

Bill grunted and turned his head away to spit.

"Point is, I wanta ride a wide swing west of Salt. That way do we cross some tracks we can maybe get a idea where they're using. Could be we'd save more time'n we'd use."

"Yeah, an' it could be we'll be the next three days afore we get back to the truck an' trailer."

"If there's something you'd ruther do, Billy, you just turn around an' go do it. You hear?"

"I was just mentioning . . ."

"Well, don't."

"Yes, sir, Massa Beale, sir."

"Why'n't the both of you unpin them ears an' let your hackles smooth down," JayJay suggested.

Jim hunched his shoulders and pretended not to have heard. He examined the stub of the Chesterfield he'd been smoking, extinguished the coal against the heel of his boot and held the ash end tight between his fingertips for a moment to make sure no fire remained before he dropped the butt to the ground. "If anybody'd rather," he said, "we can go back an' get the truck. Start out fresh again tomorrow."

"What I think we oughta do," Bill said, "is stay with the horses and ride around west of Salt Spring. Stay outa the way of those Californians and see do we pick up any tracks between here and Coffee Hill."

"Sounds okay by me," Jim said of his own idea. "JayJay?"

"Whatever you fellas say."

"That's what we'll do, then," Jim announced.

JayJay dropped his leg off the horn and resumed a normal seat. He pulled out a cigarette and lighted it, then picked up his reins.

The three horsemen, Jim in the lead and JayJay riding next in line, came down off the small rise and moved at a smooth jog toward the northwest.

"SEE THERE? We're all right." The others could read the sign as easy as Jim could. The wild band—Jim was sure this bunch was the one with the blue roan stallion and a spooky bitch of a chestnut mare leading them—was for sure pointed toward Coffee Hill, although by a meandering, roundabout way.

"Lot o' colts on the ground this year," JayJay mumbled around the filter of his Marlboro.

"Damn things breed like rabbits are s'pose to," Bill complained.

"Ain't that the truth." Last fall there had been the stud horse and twenty-two mares or fillies in the bunch and a handful of half-grown horse colts that hadn't yet been driven off. This year there were at least eight, ten sets of tiny hoofprints mixed in with the bigger tracks.

"There didn't used to be so many of them survive."

"Well, think about it. The predators are all gone. Anything big enough to threaten a foal, it's been either trapped out or shot out. And now we can't control the herd sizes neither. The little guy ain't allowed to an' the government refuses to. So what else is there t' hold the numbers down? Bad winter is our only hope, an' we didn't have one of them this year. I guess it's no wonder there's getting to be so many of them."

Bill looked off toward the mountains, judging the time of day by the sun hanging low against them even though he was wearing a wristwatch he could have glanced at instead. "Be pushing it to get to Coffee before dark," he said.

"What I think I'd rather do if it's all right with you boys," Jim said, "is lay out away from the water tonight. Slip in real quiet before first light an' see what we see there."

"That sounds good to me."

"JayJay?"

"Sure. Whatever."

"Then that's what we'll do." Jim reined his dun horse to the east and set off at a steady clip, Bill and JayJay riding abreast of him now as they traveled and talked.

BILL WAS ACTING BROODY, sitting with his back to the fire and staring off into the night like one of those zombie monster creatures on the boys' Saturday morning TV shows. Jim didn't like to see his brother acting like that. He wished he'd thought to slip a jug into his saddlebags.

It was a wonder they had anything at all to get along with, much less liquor. But then, they always allowed for the possibility of staying out longer than expected when they came off on the long swings. A fella just never knew. So they had a little food along and could make do with saddle blankets instead of the sleeping bags and such they'd've brought along if they'd thought to drag a pack horse with them. No beer or soda pop, of course, but there was water aplenty in this country, despite what the land must look like to a city person. Nobody ever needed to stay thirsty here if he knew what he was doing.

Jim sure did wish he'd brought a pint of Jack Daniels or something, though. That would've gone down just about right.

"Did you hear something?" Jim asked, just to be making conversation.

"It was JayJay checking the horses," Bill said in a slow voice. JayJay'd taken off ten or fifteen minutes earlier with a roll of toilet paper and a purposeful stride. "He's looking at the hobbles. No, he's done now. On his way back."

Jim assumed Bill must be able to see JayJay moving out there. Jim was night-blinded himself, but then he'd been looking into the fire and Bill hadn't been.

"I figure we'll leave the horses where they are come morning and walk it over to the spring," Jim said once JayJay joined them at the fire.

Bill shrugged. JayJay made a face but didn't say anything. It was a mile over to Coffee Hill and by the time they walked clear around to the far side where the water was, well, that would be another half mile afoot, probably. Call it a mile and a half on their own hind legs. None of the three of them much cared for that, but there wasn't any way around it. Not unless they wanted their own saddle horses to spook the wild band and blow this whole deal.

They had set up their camp a mile east of Coffee, knowing the wild ones would be coming in from the west if they came in at all. Knowing they'd be coming in about dawn, too. Critters tend to drink evening and early morning if they're left be, deer or horse or coyote all the same.

"We'll leave outa here well before dawn," Jim said, "an' get in position 'fore the sun comes up. I figure I'll slide around south of the hill and find me a likely spot from that angle. JayJay, you're prob'ly the best shot of us." That was a bit of a lie, but a compliment never hurt anybody. "I'd like you t' take the other gun an' come around from the north side. Lay down a crossfire, like." They only had the pair of .223-caliber Ruger Ranch Rifles, tough and dependable little guns that could bounce around in the back of a pickup truck for months on end or slap and batter along at the side of a saddle and still come up accurate and reliable.

It wasn't bothering Jim any that they only had the two rifles with them so that somebody had to be left out of the shooting. Despite what Jim'd said there, Bill was hands down the best rifle shot of the three of them. But Bill was also the last one that oughta be doing the shooting, what with the way he seemed to be taking this.

"What d'you want me to do?" Bill asked.

Jim knew better than to ask him to stay in camp by himself. A suggestion like that would just get them to snapping at each other again. "I'd like you t' come with me and help me spot. Your eyes are a lot better than mine. 'Specially in the dark. JayJay, you can hold fire till we open up on the other side. Then you jump in too, y'see."

"That skittish old mare first?" JayJay asked.

"Damn right she goes down first. You take her if she's on your side; I'll nail her if she's over toward me. The other mares an' fillies next in line. Forget the stud horse."

JayJay nodded and reached for a Marlboro. He was unsurprised by the instruction. But then, JayJay knew wild horses about as good as the Beales did. People like those dewy-eyed, bleeding-heart Californians would likely think the herd stallion would be disposed of first, Jim knew. But that wasn't the way it really was.

The stud horse was the one that was romanticized in all the Bambi Visits Black Beauty bullshit about wild horses, but in truth the stud's importance to the herd mostly consisted of servicing the mares once a year and bragging on himself the rest of the time. It was the lead mare—there always was one in every herd, and when she died, another would step up to take her place—that was actually in charge of keeping watch for danger, deciding where the bunch was going and when they would go there, all that sort of thing.

Besides, if the idea, distasteful though it might be but necessary, was to thin out the wild herds, then the way to go about it was to reduce their ability to breed. And to do that you wanted to eliminate the mares. The stallions were just too easily replaceable to bother with. Get rid of the blue roan stud horse of this bunch and knock down every young male in the band too and before the day was out there'd be another stallion show up to take over and quick enough half a dozen more to challenge for the privilege of owning this harem. Shooting the males was mostly pointless. Shooting the mares would keep more generations of the horses from competing for the grass needed by mankind and his cattle.

Damn, but Jim did wish he'd brought a jug along. He leaned forward, picked up a chunk of dried cow flop and tossed it onto the fire. A dung fire doesn't make coals worth a damn but other than that is just fine, and a fellow never has to worry about running out of fuel.

Bill sat where he was, staring out into the dark. JayJay yawned and stretched and wandered over to the saddles. He picked up one of the Rugers and began checking it over for cleanliness.

Jim sighed and pulled a Chesterfield out of his shirt pocket. He plucked some grass stems and twisted them together, leaned forward again and held the tips in the pale flame of the cow-shit fire. When the grass flared, he used that to light his smoke and dropped the loose twist onto the fire when he was done.

He was already looking forward to getting back home tomorrow evening. He'd get Glory to cook him up a platter of eggs and bacon and fried potatoes. And afterward he thought he'd set in the front room and get himself thoroughly, happily buzzed. Hell, yes. He felt better just thinking about it.

FIFTEEN

"DO YOU have to do that?"

She looked at him, smiled, lifted her face to his and gave him a brief kiss. "No, dear, I do not have to. But I want to."

Oliver sighed and conceded defeat. He did love the way JoLynn looked when her hair was flowing soft and free. But she found it more comfortable to keep her braid regardless. Perhaps that had something to do with the way it tangled whenever it was down. It was so very long, after all. But so pretty. Oh, well. He sat on the aluminum and canvas camp stool and enjoyed watching her as she worked on her hair.

"We'll have to go around to the other side if we want to see the sun coming up," JoLynn said.

It was still dark, although the night was giving way now to shadings of pale gray off behind the low mountains to the east. Oliver couldn't believe they both were awake so early. Yet fresh and invigorated and quite ready to start the new day. On a nonworking day at home they would still be hours away from waking. Here it had seemed the most natural thing possible to get up before the dawn and breathe deep of the chill, clear, lively air. The desert air at this hour seemed as effervescent as Perrier. "I'll take the camera and photograph all this," he said. "Title it 'Desert Dawn,' mmm? We'll make prints and sell them. We'll retire rich and famous."

"We? And what is my contribution supposed to have been?"

"Inspiration, of course. Better yet, I'll use you for my model. 'Desert Dawn with Nude.'" Oliver felt the faint stirrings of an erection, and the silly bantering notion all of a sudden became quite seriously attractive.

It really would be something if he could get JoLynn posed nude on this hilltop with the desert and the mountains and the rising sun behind her, the planes and sweet textures of her backlighted in red and gold. Oh my, yes. In his mind's eye he could as good as see the exact composition of the photograph he would like to achieve.

"Actually . . ." He cleared his throat. "Actually . . . now that I think about it, dear. . . ." He told her what he had in mind.

JoLynn smiled and shrugged and said, "Sure, if that's what you would like to do, dear."

Oliver grinned and went to get the camera.

OLIVER WAS TREMBLING with excitement. This was good! If the prints, any one print of the many frames he was taking, if any single one of them came out half as good as he hoped and thought they were, why, he would have to have a monster blowup made and framed and placed on the bedroom wall.

There was just a thin, bright wedge of sun visible to the east.

Then the dark, stark, cardboard-cutout line of rugged mountaintops and, nearer, the purpled desert floor still in cold shadow.

And finally, nearest to the lens, JoLynn.

She was naked. Posed standing in three-quarter profile from behind. Outlined in shimmering red at throat and breast and indented hip. So sleek. Feline. Lithe and lovely.

Oliver was so entranced by the beauty of the photographs he was creating here that the sexual arousal he'd felt earlier was gone now.

"Turn just a little, please. Lift your head a bit? Now tilt it back. Yes, terrific. Like that. Now swing your shoulders. No, the left one back just a little. A little more. Now forward again, thanks. Hand on your hip? No, too high. Down. Down more. Mmm, that isn't working, forget it."

He clucked and grunted and concentrated. This was wonderful.

His fingers flew over the controls of the camera. Auto exposure. Push the button for backlighting. Flash off and then on again to try one shot with the flash fill-in. Off again and override the automatic exposure mode to try a frame with the lens one stop wider than the camera wanted to set for itself. Then another stopped down below the auto setting. Bracket the exposures and try every-dang-thing. If even one of these shots turned out the way he hoped and believed . . .

"You're gorgeous. Have I ever told you that?"

"Eye of the beholder, dear."

"Don't talk in clichés."

"How do you think a saying becomes cliché, Oliver? By being so valid that it is repeated to excess, of course. Think about it."

"The fact remains. You are gorgeous. And I love you." The shutter snapped and snapped again.

"You damned well better," JoLynn said lightly, "because I'm freezing my ass off over here."

"Wait until you see. This is worth it. And anyway, darling, I will personally warm those pretty buns for you just as quick as we're done here." He knelt seeking a fresh angle, duckwalked to one side and then the other, tilted the camera and refocused, snapped frame after frame.

The light was becoming too strong to shoot into as the sun lifted swiftly free of the mountaintops. Oliver moved over, abandoning the backlight in favor of harsh, strong side lighting. The reddish yellow light accentuated every muscle and contour, turned to gold every wisp of body hair on JoLynn's lean form. He moved in and began taking close-up exposures of her. Tilt of breast. Concavity of belly. Curve of ear and jawline. Mystery of shadowed pubis. Hip and rib cage. Dimpled cleft of her rump. Dimpled and, he saw now, goosefleshed too. She really was cold.

"Just let me finish this one more roll, okay? Then we'll get you warm."

"Okay."

He already had two exposed rolls in his jacket pocket and was working on the third. This was great.

He paused, peered, backed a few paces away wanting to get a shot of the way JoLynn's braid fell in the shadows between her shoulder blades.

He saw that she was shivering. Actually shivering now. And when he stopped what he was doing and paid close attention, he could hear her teeth chatter lightly.

"Oh, shit," he apologized. "You're really freezing, aren't you?"

"I thought I mentioned that already, dear."

"Yes, but . . . Jesus, I'm sorry, honey. I didn't mean for you to get this cold. Come on, let's go back to the tent."

She made no attempt to talk him out of the offer. She grabbed up her clothing and held it bundled tight against her chest while she loped awkwardly away, barefoot on the rocks and gravel, toward the tent that waited on the far side of the hilltop.

Oliver stayed behind to gather his camera bag and tripod and JoLynn's discarded boots and socks before he followed her. He glanced down the hillside. The countryside to the west of the hill was still shadowed, although there was light enough to see by. Oliver yawned and smiled again, thinking about the many ways it might be possible for him to warm JoLynn's marvelous body inside that tent. Why, they could . . .

He froze in place, and an electric thrill of excitement jolted through him.

No. Impossible. Wonderful. "JoLynn." His urgent whisper was barely audible to his own ears. "JoLynn!" He tried again and this time the sound came out in a tight, throaty croak. But at least it did come out. *"JoLynn!"*

He dropped to hands and knees and inched forward toward the gently angled slope where this ledge began to fall away toward the steeper hillside and the cattail-rimmed pond below.

"JoLynn. Come here, dammit. Right now."

"But aren't you—"

"Later. Now pull some clothes on and come over here right this instant. You aren't going to believe this."

He didn't want to take his eyes off the scene below him so that he could check and see if she was doing what he asked. But a moment later he heard the faint scuffle of fabrics and zippers and then JoLynn's approaching footsteps. Still without looking around, Oliver reached back and motioned her to get low to the ground before she joined him.

"Shhh," he cautioned, even though they were several hundred yards away and couldn't possibly overhear.

JoLynn's expression was rapt. Her eyes glistened with unshed tears as the emotions of the moment threatened to overcome her. Oliver understood that well enough. He too felt almost like weeping. The horses really were that beautiful.

The wild herd—there was no question, none, that this truly was a wild herd this time; just looking at them now he recognized a difference that was more felt than seen—was warily approaching the water hole in this first light of the new day.

A bony, tough-looking light brown horse—the herd stallion?—led the way. That one looked old but perhaps because of this wise. It certainly did not look like Oliver's idea of what a wild stud should be. It was much too small-bodied and lightly built for that. Still, there was no question that this was the horse that was in the lead, so it must be the stallion despite appearances.

Trailing behind all the others and staying slightly aloof from them, there was another horse that was more like his expectations of a wild stallion. That one was a dark, steely color, its coat lightly mottled and somewhere between gray and black in hue. It was magnificent with its streaming, never-trimmed long tail and mane, its erect carriage of head, small, pointed ears, arched neck. Oliver guessed that this one was or soon would be a challenger to the skinny chestnut-colored stallion's throne.

Between those two there were—he tried to count them but could only guess—two dozen or more grown horses and probably half that many babies.

The horses tiptoed out of the west toward the water, their muzzles held low to the ground and their nostrils flaring in search of danger even though they were following their leader and presumably should feel safe.

Oliver felt JoLynn's hand tighten on his forearm as the first of the horses reached the water and began to drink. Even from this far away they could see how the animals' ears jerked as they drank.

"It's like they're pumping the water with their ears," JoLynn giggled.

Oliver chuckled and nodded.

"They're gorgeous."

"Perfect," he agreed.

"The camera, Oliver. Where's your camera?"

How could he have forgotten that? Huh! How could he take his eyes off the horses to go get the camera? He lifted himself over JoLynn and wriggled belly down on the hard, graveled ground to reach the tripod. If he scared the horses off . . .

"Hurry," JoLynn whispered.

"I am." He'd had his regular lens on the camera so he could take pictures of JoLynn this morning. The telephoto was in the camera bag, and that was all the way back in the tent. No time to run get it. At least he didn't know that there would be time enough. He decided to shoot the rest of this roll of film with the short lens. Then if the horses were still at the water—please God they would be—he could get more film and the telephoto too.

The tripod wasn't really needed for pictures taken so far away with a normal lens. Oliver dismounted the camera body from the tripod and focused on the herd at the water hole. So far away. Too far. Still, it was better to get a poor picture than none. He set the camera for auto exposure and snapped a frame. If nothing else, they would have that much to look back at and remember.

They . . .

"Oh . . ."

A horse seemed to slip and fall. The thin, light brown herd leader. It dropped to its knees without any warning.

Down the slope to Oliver's left there was a sharp, short, ugly bark of noise.

And then off to the right more snapping, crackling noises.

Horses began to rear and tumble.

JoLynn clamped her hands to her face and sat up, her wide eyes reflecting sudden horror as down below them someone shot guns—that was, that had to be what those noises were—into the beautiful herd and the wild, free, gorgeous creatures began to die.

The guns spat—the sounds were smaller, duller, infinitely more ugly than the make-believe noises of gunfire in the movies or on television—and horses screamed.

Oliver hadn't known that horses could scream. The sounds made Oliver sick to his stomach.

There was blood now. On the soft ground at the water's edge and spilling into the water too.

Dying horses thrashed their legs in agony.

Others dashed frantically for safety. Wherever that was. Some ran into each other in their panic. Tripped and fell. Others were cut down by the bullets and fell without tripping.

"Jesus!"

Oliver was on his feet without having any idea how he had come to get up. The camera was still in his hand. He began using it, pointing it blindly downhill toward the carnage.

JoLynn was standing beside him. She was crying, nearly hysterical. He didn't have time to comfort her. Not right now. He wanted to record this on film.

Damn whoever would do something like this.

"Oliver. Over there." She grabbed his arm and pointed.

He could see men—two men—rising out of concealment. One of the men had a rifle in his hands. Oliver took their picture. The distance was impossibly far without his telephoto lens. He snapped the shot anyway. Maybe . . .

JoLynn, gasping, whimpering, pointed to the right, to where another man with another rifle was rising into view.

At the water hole there were only a few dead and dying horses now. Just that quickly the survivors of the horror had run away.

But there were . . . a dozen—at least that many—a dozen dead or dying horses spilling their blood onto the muddy bank of the water hole. The horses had come here for water to sustain life. The treachery of man took life from them.

"Those sons of bitches." JoLynn's voice was hard and cold and ugly. "Those miserable . . ." Speech failed her. There were not words to convey what she was feeling. Oliver knew because he felt exactly the same right now. There simply was not language to vilify these men adequately to the occasion.

JoLynn took a step forward. Toward the slope that would lead down to the water hole and the dead horses. And the men.

Oliver grabbed her arm to hold her back. "No, honey. People like that . . . you can't know what somebody like that might do."

"I think—"

"No." His voice was stern. JoLynn had a mind of her own. But not this time, dammit. He would not allow her to go down there and confront those men. It was simply too dangerous.

"Oliver, look."

She was pointing toward the slaughtered bodies at the far edge of the water hole. At first he couldn't see what she was trying to point out. Then he did.

There was movement there now as a horse—just a baby, a foal that couldn't be more than a few months old—dragged itself out from under the fallen body of a grown horse. Its mother? Oliver assumed so.

The little animal was a pale, pretty, reddish hue. Almost a red-gold color. Its wispy mane and tail were dark red, and a dark line ran down its backbone linking the dark mane and tail. The little creature was shaky on its legs and even from this far away pitiful in its terror and loneliness.

The baby horse tried to run, tripped and sprawled onto its side in the mud. It whinnied, its voice thin and plaintive and tried to rise.

"No! Dear God, no."

There was a sharp, ugly bark of noise again.

Just the one shot this time.

The baby's head jerked, and the tiny thing fell dead beside its mother.

"Damn you! Damn you to hell." JoLynn's voice was shrill and seemed very loud.

Oliver grabbed for her arm, but he was too late. She was already moving. Already rushing down the hill toward those sons of bitches with the guns.

"Damn you," she shrieked again as she ran.

SIXTEEN

BILL TOUCHED JIM'S ARM and pointed and Jim looked off in the direction his brother indicated. There, they were coming in. Just about where and when they'd figured. The light wasn't good yet and they were still pretty far away, but he thought this was the blue roan's band, and if it was, it would be that skittish old chestnut mare leading the way for them.

Jim badly wanted a smoke but wasn't about to risk lighting one. Not yet. The breeze, what little of it there was drifting slow through the basin, was coming down from the north, so any man-smell would be carried away from the horses. Still he wasn't going to take any chances. That old lead mare was a spooky thing. She wouldn't have to smell smoke to booger and wheel away like a puff of dust. If she no more than saw smoke where there shouldn't be any, or just guessed at a danger she couldn't actually sense, she would be gone.

Nervously Jim flicked the safety catch off and back on again.

The horses were much too far away to start the shooting yet, but when the time came, he wanted to be damned sure the Ruger was ready to fire.

Beside him Bill flattened himself tight to the ground, taking advantage of what little cover they had here. Jim stayed where he was. Bill didn't have the rifle and could stay out of sight if he wanted. Probably wouldn't want to watch anyhow. Shit, Jim couldn't blame him about that. This wasn't any kind of fun thing for a man to be doing.

From where him and Bill lay, they couldn't see JayJay off on the other side of the water hole. Jim could only take it on faith that JayJay would be where he was supposed to be and wouldn't move or smoke or do anything to give them away.

Jim moved the safety catch to the fire position and then back to safe.

The horses were coming in now. It was the blue stud's bunch, all right, for right there was that chestnut. Jim remembered the mare from back before there were laws protecting the wild ones. She was that old. She never would have survived this long if she hadn't been protected. Being that old, too, she was poorly bred. All the really old ones were, the horses that were bred when the best of the herds were being trapped and taken off the range and only the culls were left behind to reproduce. Now the natural selection processes were working again and the quality of the wild horses was actually pretty good. This old mare was proof of how poor they used to be.

She was a smart old thing, though, even if she wasn't much otherwise. Jim remembered her, all right. Him and Bill and their father and old Charlie—that was long before JayJay came to be the year-round hired man—they'd had this same mare penned once but she got loose. If she hadn't managed to get loose, she'd have been canned Fido food a long time back, for she sure hadn't been worth breaking and keeping for anything, though she'd been young then. Hell, they'd all been young then.

Jeez. Memories. Good ones. From a whole long time. So now it was time the mare gave it up. Well, she'd had twenty years more than she'd been entitled to anyhow. That was one way to look at it.

He took the Ruger off safe and put it back on again. Took his hand off the small of the grip and ran his palm over his jeans just to make sure there wasn't any sweat to make his aim slip.

Not that they were so far away as to have to worry. Sixty yards on this side. JayJay was likely as close on the north side. And JayJay was a good shot. No need for anything but the iron sights at this distance. Easy. Only way to miss, hardly, would be to work at it. Aim and fire, that would be the ticket. Pop, pop, pop, quick as you please, because once the shooting started, there wouldn't be time to mess with any fanciness. Each gun had a thirty-round magazine, and there wouldn't be time to reload. Just up an' do it and keep pulling the trigger till you run out of targets or ammunition, whichever come first.

Except for that first shot, of course. Had to put the lead mare down first thing because that would confuse the rest of them and keep them in range a few seconds longer while they stood there leaderless trying to figure out what to do.

Jim flipped the safety off and on. Wiped his hand again. Took the safety off and this time left it off. The horses were at the water now. No way to make sure JayJay was ready to shoot once Jim started it. Take that on faith. But hey, JayJay was always ready for whatever was needed.

What was needed now was a clear shot at the chestnut mare.

There she was. The horses behind her were already at the water, but she was standing at the edge of the cattails with her head up and ears pointed, her nostrils flaring in search of any warning scents.

Jim and Bill's dad had laid eyes on this same old mare back when she was just a filly. Jesus, wasn't that a strange thought. If he was alive today, Jim could go home and ask him did he remember, and he would. He'd remembered damn near every horse he'd ever known and a good many cows too. Jeez.

Jim wiped his hand one more time, felt to make sure the safety was off and laid his cheek nice and tight against the stock of the Ruger just the way he'd been taught all those many years ago.

He aimed for a spot just back of the mare's eye so the tiny, hard-jacketed bullet would make a clean, killing brain shot. He didn't want to hurt the old mare. It was enough, dammit, that he had to kill her. He wouldn't stand for hurting her too.

He took a breath, let half of it out and then allowed his finger to squeeze, slow and soft on the trigger so that he wasn't supposed to know his own self just exactly when the gun would fire.

Ah, God. Jeez! There were horses rearing and squealing and running every which way.

Jim was on his knees, Ruger at his shoulder, the little gun snapping and nudging at him with its polite, mild-mannered recoil.

Over to his right JayJay was firing too, hard and fast as he could.

Between them there was hell to pay.

Horses falling. Horses running. Horses dying. Shit!

No time to pick out which was the mares or fillies and which the adolescent males. Shooting the males was a waste but what the hell were you supposed to do? Couldn't take time to try and sort them through. There were only a few seconds to work with and then they'd all be gone except for the ones that wouldn't be gobbling up the grass any more.

The Ruger spat quick, quick, quick, and the spent cartridges cases flew and tumbled and clinked and clattered as they hit the ground.

He closed his ears to the sounds and concentrated on what needed doing.

Bap, bap, bap, and a brown about two years old went down. Bap, and a dun dropped out of sight behind a scampering, kicking bay. Bap, bap.

JayJay was shooting. Jim was shooting. It would be a damned wonder if any horse survived.

Jim's breath was coming ragged in his chest now, and his aim wasn't worth a flip. Point and shoot, point and shoot, quick, quick, no time to aim anyhow, just point and shoot.

"Whoa, Jimmy."

"Huh?"

"They're gone, Jimmy. They took off on you."

He blinked, feeling shaky and oddly disoriented for the moment. "Oh."

"You okay, Jimmy?"

"Shit, yes." He took the gun down from his shoulder, glanced at it and pushed the safety on.

There was still a little movement over by the water hole as dying horses flailed their legs and tried to prolong the pain of life.

Jim frowned and spat and took a few steps forward. He reached for a Chesterfield. The smoke was dry and rasping in his throat. He sucked on it greedily, wanting the calming influence of the nicotine or whatever the hell it was about a cigarette that is so wonderfully soothing to a man.

JayJay was up too now, moving forward just like they were.

"Damn," Bill said.

"What's the matter?"

Bill inclined his head, and Jim's attention swiveled back toward the water hole.

There was a foal struggling to its legs. A pretty little red dun horse colt. Pretty enough to catch and keep if a man thought he could get away with it and the damn government not find out.

Except the poor little SOB had a busted foreleg that was skewed at an ugly angle. It hurt to look at, damn it.

"A shame, ain't it."

"Yeah. Jeez."

Jim took the Ruger off safe, raised the gun and sighted carefully. The little horse was already suffering enough. He sure didn't want to cause it anymore.

The colt tried to run on that busted leg and fell, taking it out of his sights. Jim winced and swallowed. It tried to get up and couldn't hardly manage. Jeez.

Quickly he aimed again and fired, putting the little thing out of its pain.

"Damn," he muttered.

Over to the right JayJay'd been about to do the same thing. He nodded his approval for Jim shooting first, then reached for a Marlboro.

"Daaaaammmmmmn yyyyoooooooou!!!"

"What the . . ."

All four of them turned to stare up toward the top of Coffee Hill to where the noise was coming from.

"It's those ████████ Californians. What're they doing here?"

"Oh, shit." Jim felt a queasy emptiness in his belly. Those dumb bastards had seen. Jesus, God, those juice-and-tofu California shits could turn them in and then where would they be?

Prosecution, sure. Hell with that. Jim didn't mind prosecution if that's what it came to. Some court lay a fine against them, okay. Even some time in jail if he had to. Bill could see to things without him if it came to that.

But Jesus, if the BLM pulled the grazing leases . . . They couldn't live without the grazing leases. The whole place would go under if they lost those leases.

Jesus, God! Everything all those generations of Beales worked for, all those years and years, they could have every bit of it taken away just because of some stupid damned wild horses and some bleeding-heart Californians.

Up on the hill they could see the man now. At first there'd just been the skinny woman shouting and flying down toward them. Now the man was chasing her. Grabbed her and dragged her back.

Good. Stay there, damn you. Stay there both of you. If they couldn't get close enough to see, really see and identify them in a court of law . . . just stay right there, okay? Who the hell in this county would take the word of some fairy Californian over a Beale anyhow? The Beales had been here for generations. Just stay right there, dammit, and it would all work out all right. Lie a little under oath, why not? No hesitation at all if it was a choice between that and losing the ranch.

The Californians were an awful long way away up there. They were standing in plain sight, him pulling at her, trying to drag her back up the hill, and her resisting, trying to get loose so she could come down and give them a piece of her mind. As if they needed a piece of that woman's mind down here. Wasn't much doubt what she thought. Lordy. Jim sucked hard at his smoke.

"The guy has his camera with him," JayJay said, shielding his eyes with a hand to block the brightness of the sky above the distant figures.

"He had an awful long lens on that thing," Bill offered. "I remember it from the other day."

"What I want to know is what they're doing here when we sent them over to Salt Spring."

"Don't make any difference how they come t' be here. Point is, they seen us shoot them horses."

"What if they can identify us?"

"If they can identify us in a court o' law, boys, we are shit outa luck."

"If they don't have pictures, it's their word again ours."

"Maybe they didn't get no pictures."

"Maybe."

"We got to figure they didn't get no pictures."

"Won't know till the prosecution lays out its case, will we?"

"First thing we get home, boys, we call Preston Davis."

"Pres ain't a criminal lawyer."

"Well, he's the only lawyer we know. If he can't help, he'll find us somebody that can."

"All right. We'll call Pres. Have him set t' do whatever's needed when the time comes."

"You know damn good and well those Californians are gonna turn us in first thing they hit town."

"Nothing we can do 'bout that. Just remember, boys. We don't know nothing 'bout no horses getting killed. And there hasn't none of us been anywhere near Coffee Hill since last fall some time."

"Right."

"Aw, damn," JayJay complained.

"What is it?"

"That man, damn him. He's fixing to take some pictures now. See 'im? With that long lens on there he'll have proof for sure."

"Shit," Jim said.

Bill looked pale and shaky and like he was going to puke.

"If they got proof, dammit, we could lose everything. All of us lose everything. Everything. Dammit."

"I'll move 'em back away," JayJay said. He lifted his rifle and aimed it up the hill toward the Californians.

"My God, JayJay you can't . . ."

"Hell, I ain't gonna shoot 'em. I'll just kick up some gravel, like. Spray some gravel around and make 'em think I'm trying to shoot them. That'll send them running and there won't be no pictures."

"All right." Jim was still holding his rifle, but he made no effort to raise it. One warning should be plenty, and JayJay was a better shot than he was anyway.

JayJay dropped his Marlboro to the ground so it would be out of his way when he bent to the sights, coughed once and then took aim.

The Californians were staring down the hill in stunned disbelief, or so it looked to Jim, as JayJay pointed his rifle.

Prob'ly the Californians thought JayJay was fixing to shoot them instead of just scaring them. Well, that was fine. Let them believe it and maybe this would work out yet.

JayJay's Ruger fired, a flash of pale flame visible at the muzzle.

SEVENTEEN

HE MISSED A SWIPE at her arm, managed to grab hold of the collar of her vest and hauled back on it. Oliver's heels skidded on the gravel, and they both nearly fell before he got JoLynn stopped.

"You can't go down there, honey, there's no telling what those people might do."

"Didn't you see—"

"Of course I saw, dear, but—"

"You can't let them get away with—"

"I'm not letting anyone get away with anything, JoLynn. Don't try and twist this around so that it's my fault, dammit. I just don't want you going down there and getting into a fight with three armed men. You know? Animals like that might do *any*thing. They're crazy people, JoLynn. They'd have to be mindless, insensitive cretins or they wouldn't slaughter innocent creatures like that. And I don't want you—"

She tried to pull away from him. Once again he hauled her back under protest.

"We'll go straight to the police or the sheriff or whoever it is who's in charge of the law around here. If that doesn't do any good, we can take it up with the federal people. Congressmen, senators, whoever. After all, it's a federal law they've violated. We can make sure they'll be punished. But *you* aren't the one who needs to punish them, honey. They might get violent with us."

"What if they deny it. What if we let them get away from here and they simply deny everything."

"Fine. I'll take some pictures. Then we'll have proof." Actually he was not at all sure he still had any film left on this roll. Even so, he raised the camera and pointed it downhill toward the men. "I'll get proof to take to court, honey, but I will *not* let you go down there and get yourself hurt by those men."

"You are being ridiculous, Oliver. No one is going to . . ."

Oliver's eyes widened, and he pointed.

"What?" she snapped. Then added, "No!"

One of those men down below had his rifle lifted and aimed up the slope toward them. The man was actually aiming a rifle at them. That seemed like a theatrically stupid thing for anyone to do.

"No," JoLynn repeated.

"They're trying to scare us," Oliver said.

"It won't work. I don't care what those people do, we *are* going to report them. We—"

The muzzle of the rifle jumped, and almost instantly Oliver heard a zinging, rasping whine of noise that was amazingly like the bullet sounds in bad movies.

JoLynn grunted—with surprise, fear, whatever—and immediately dropped flat onto the ground.

Oliver stood upright a moment more, half in defiance and half from sheer disbelief that anyone would have fired a weapon so dangerously close to another human being.

Then he followed JoLynn's sensible example and got low to the ground also.

"I think they can still see us here, honey," he said. "Not that they're really wanting to hit us or anything. But even so . . . I think we ought to get back out of sight. We don't want to antagonize them any more than we already have. Come on. Let's go back to the car."

Keeping his eyes on the men down below who now were standing all together in plain sight at the foot of the hill with their rifles lowered, Oliver reached over to take JoLynn by the arm.

She didn't respond to his touch.

Frowning, he shook her.

And still she lay there without moving.

"JoLynn? Honey?"

He edged closer, still trying to remain low to the ground. He raised himself over her—she was lying on her side with her back to him—and took hold of her.

Had she fainted? Damn, he complained to himself. He shook her again. Harder this time.

"Jo*Lynn.*" He was becoming more than a little impatient now. He wanted to get to the Subaru and get away from these people now, before they went completely berserk. "Come *on,* honey."

JoLynn lay where she was.

Puzzled, Oliver drew his hand back away from her unresponsive flesh.

His hand came away from her damp and sticky.

He stared at it in unbelieving horror.

Red. Bright, bright, smeary red.

Blood.

There was blood on his hand. JoLynn's blood.

Dear God, she'd been shot. She . . .

Oliver cried out and rolled JoLynn onto her back.

He felt numb and faintly, fuzzily detached. As if somehow his connection with reality, with sanity, had become tenuous and subject to short circuit.

The oddest thing about it, Oliver decided with an eerily calm deliberation, was that his senses seemed for the moment to have been reduced to one.

He was aware of no sound, no scent, no flavor or feeling.

Only of sight.

And his vision was total, its clarity perfectly acute, every line and texture and color sharp and boldly drawn. He was sure he would hold the memory of these sights—unwanted—with complete and utter recall for the remainder of his life.

Dear God, he hoped he was wrong about that.

He hoped this sight would leave his memory and be lost forever.

JoLynn's eyes were open. Wide open . . . and empty. Staring sightlessly toward the buttermilk morning sky.

Her flesh, so soft and sweet, was still now and pale beneath the veneer of her tan.

Her neck—Oliver stared mindlessly at her neck, willing himself to look away but unable to do so; it was this horror that was and always would be etched sharply into his consciousness—was gashed and gouged, ripped apart by the flying bullet so that the left side of it was laid open red and raw like an obscene extra mouth. Red flesh. Purple and white matter that he couldn't identify, strings and pulp and gooey clots. He could see *inside* JoLynn's neck.

The sight should have gagged him. He should have been heaving and retching. He knew that. The abnormal calm of shock, which surely was where his sense of detachment originated, held him slightly apart from what he was seeing so that the normal impulses failed to rise.

A major artery—Oliver tried to recall the name for that most commonly known of all the body's arteries, but he could not—had been severed.

She must have bled to death within moments.

Blood pooled inside the wound. Drenched the front of her clothes. Ran in stringy, clotting rivulets and puddles on the soil beside her.

Her lips were parted. Just a fraction of an inch. So pale. He had never seen her lips so completely without color before. Her front teeth—incisors those were called, although why he should be able to remember that now was a mystery to him—were partially visible through the narrow gap between her sweet lips. Thin slices of gleaming, polished white open to view.

A fleck of something—dried spittle? flake of dandruff? dirt?—lay on her lower lip at the left corner of her wonderful mouth. Very, very carefully he lifted the offensive bit of stuff off of her, capturing it onto his fingernail and carrying it away from her.

When he touched her lip there was no response from her.

There really should have been some response from her. Shouldn't there?

The question puzzled and confused him. He tried to think it through, but at the moment it was too much for him to grasp.

Later, he decided. He would think about all these things later.

He blinked and realized that his vision was no longer so acute as it had been. In fact it seemed quite blurry at this moment. Misted and foggy as if seen through a sheen of falling water.

How very odd. The sensations he was experiencing now were exceptional. Even unique.

He would have to remember each of them so he could tell JoLynn about them lat—

With a roar of blinding anguish, Oliver Bendix surged to his feet and tried to outrun the torment.

EIGHTEEN

"MAN! Now that's what I call great reflexes."

"Hmm?"

"The broad. You see how quick she hit the dirt?" JayJay chuckled and dropped the lightweight Ruger to belt level, bent and retrieved his cigarette. "Yeah, that skinny woman sure got down quick. Lot quicker reflexes than him."

"Look at the guy run. Damn," Bill said. "He's skeedaddlin', all right."

"Now if she'd just do the same, there wouldn't be no pictures taken."

"You think I should fire another shot?" JayJay asked.

"Yeah, maybe. See if you can move her off that spot. Just get her outa sight long enough that we can slip away."

"That won't do any good," practical-minded Bill pointed out.

"Why not?"

"We got to walk around to where the horses are. They can watch us every step o' the way from up there."

"But from far enough off they can't get a good look, that's the thing. All we need is to create a doubt, right? Any bit o' doubt and there won't be a jury in this county that'd ever convict. Not on the word of some Californian. Right?"

"I suppose so."

"Put another round over her head, JayJay. But high this time. I seen your bullet strike low and raise a dust that first shot."

"Hell yes, you did. I wanted to sting 'em with some gravel."

"Gravel's fine, but I don't want you taking no chance of a ricochet, JayJay. These aren't any soft-nose hunting bullets we're shooting, they're jacketed military surplus and they won't break up on contact like a regular bullet does. These things will carom off rocks like a cue ball making a bank shot."

"Whatever you say, Jim. No gravel this time." He held the Marlboro in his left hand, sighted carelessly into the sky above and to the right of where the thin woman had dropped to the ground, and fired another shot into the air. The little rifle cracked, the sound of the gunfire sharp and businesslike in the grassland silence where there is not even the sound of wind in tree branches to break the solitude.

"Shoot again," Bill said. "She never moved." He had raised the binoculars and was observing the woman when JayJay fired his second round.

"Closer?" JayJay asked.

"Not too close."

The Ruger barked a third time, and dirt and gravel sprayed into the air from a point several feet beyond the woman and just to the side. From the foot of the hill below, Jim and JayJay could spot the point of impact easily without the aid of binoculars.

"That should've moved her," Jim said.

"She never flinched," Bill reported, the binoculars still pressed to his face.

"You don't think she went an' fainted, do you?"

"Scared that bad?"

"Could be. I've heard o' people passing out from being scared bad."

"Never saw such a thing, though."

"Well, I tell you one thing for sure, some sonuvabitch shoots that close t' me, I'm either going to be going hard *for* him or going hard *away* from him. But I damn sure ain't gonna lie there and wait for him to do it again."

"That woman's just laying there," Bill said. "She hasn't moved the first muscle since I put the glass on her."

"Dammit, she must've fainted."

"So why isn't the guy doing something about it? He so scared of guns he won't come back an' help her?"

"Whatever, we can't just leave her laying there."

"What?"

"You heard me. We can't just leave her laying there. I mean, what if she passed out and, say, hit her head when she fell down. She could be hurt or something. We can't go off and leave her like that."

"But if we go up there, she'll recognize us for damn sure."

"We aren't leaving her there. Now that's all there is to it."

"It ain't our responsibility to see to her."

"Tell that to the boyfriend. If you can find him, that is."

"All right, dammit. If we got to."

JayJay glared up the slope with disgust.

Apart from the unpleasantness of being face to face with someone whose pointing finger could get them all in trouble, Jim knew that JayJay —indeed, he and Bill too—would be annoyed at the necessity to travel so far afoot. It wasn't seemly for a man to be climbing hills on his own hind legs. That was what horses and pickup trucks were for, dammit. Still, the horses were more than a mile away and the truck and trailer many miles further than that. If they were going to go up and see to that woman, they were all going to have to do it the hard way.

"Come on," Jim said. "Bite the bullet, boys, an' let's get this over with."

"OHMYGOD!"

Jim felt his stomach lurch and twist itself into knots.

"Jesus," Bill said.

Bill was pale, his skin the color of dirty laundry. So was JayJay's. Hell, Jim's was probably the same too, the only difference being that he couldn't see himself, could just feel the queasiness that was making his gorge rise and turn the back of his throat to acid.

If the three of them were pale, well, that was nothing to how pale the woman was.

But then judging by what was spilled onto the ground and drying there, she couldn't have an ounce of blood left anywhere in her.

The three men stood over her body and stared in shocked disbelief.

"You don't think . . ." JayJay didn't bother to finish the question.

Of course none of them thought it was possible. There wasn't a chance of it. The thin, dark-haired woman was dead as dead ever gets, and no going back to change it.

She lay half on her back, the way the man had left her when he up and run, with her jaw slack so that they could see a white gleam of teeth past thin, pale lips.

Her eyes were open and glassed over. Pointed up at the sky. Empty. There is no second-guessing eyes like that. They only get that empty when there isn't anything behind them anymore. Jim had seen the look before on animals, and now he discovered it was the same with people. Deer, horse, slaughtered cow . . . or skinny California woman. He tried to turn his head away, was drawn back to the look in those dead eyes and found himself shivering.

A noisy clatter snapped his attention around, and he turned in time to see JayJay's rifle bounce off the gravel and slide to a stop a few feet downhill from where JayJay'd dropped it.

JayJay was turned away and bending over. He looked like he was fixing to be sick or something. And maybe he was.

After all, it'd been JayJay who killed her.

"Jesus," Bill repeated.

This wasn't getting it done, Jim thought. It didn't occur to him to follow that thought any further and try to work out just what it was that he figured needed doing. He simply knew that something had to get done. And that this wasn't doing it.

He dropped to his knees and reached a hand out. Then stopped, drew his extended fingers back a bit.

Generally speaking, you want to check for a pulse, you lay the fingertips to the side of the neck, just over the carotid. Except this woman didn't seem to have no carotid left. The bullet—it must've been a ricochet, that first shot when JayJay was trying to spray gravel; he must've by accident hit a substantial rock, and the tough, jacketed slug changed direction instead of breaking apart like a normal bullet should; just a crazy-weird piece of extra shitty luck that it'd hit the woman instead of passing on by.

He shuddered and tried again, this time drawing down the zipper of her vest so he could get inside and try to find a heartbeat.

There wouldn't be a heartbeat, of course. He knew there wouldn't. But he had to try. No point in bothering to hope. But he had to be *sure*.

The skinny woman wasn't wearing a shirt under the vest. Must've dragged it on in a hurry, like. Or, hell, maybe city people just liked to dress like that for some reason. Whatever, the fact was that she hadn't been wearing anything under that vest. Now her titties were right there, bare to the sky and the whole damn world. They were little things and pale. Awful pale. They looked cold, Jim thought. Except he didn't want to touch them to find out. Not even to check for her heartbeat, he didn't. It was bad enough that they'd gone and killed her, wasn't it?

His eyes narrowed and he turned his head and coughed nervously for a moment and then turned back and with grim resolution laid his fingertips on the flat plate of cartilage that was her breastbone, very careful to avoid touching the sides of her breasts. He had the impression, irrational but persistent, that the flesh of her breasts would be as hard and as cold as marble if he were to touch her there.

The thin covering of skin and flesh over bone where he did touch her felt chill to him, although he knew he was only imagining that. There hadn't been time enough for the body heat to leave her.

Mostly though it just felt . . . empty. No response or natural resilience. It just . . . lay there. Cooling meat.

There was no flutter of heartbeat.

Well, dammit, that's what he'd felt he had to know, really know, for himself.

All right, now he knew.

When he looked up, he saw that Bill had walked off a few paces and was standing staring off over the basin toward Oregon.

JayJay was standing close and staring down at the dead woman.

"Jeez, Jim, you're kneeling in the blood. Can't you see? You're getting blood on your pants, Jim. You oughtn't to do that, Jim. You really oughtn't." JayJay's voice was thin and quavering. He sounded like he was sleep-talking. Not really there even though the sounds were coming out of his head.

"It's all right, JayJay," Jim said gently.

"Is she . . . I mean for really and truly sure is she . . . ?"

"Yeah, JayJay, she's really and truly for sure dead."

"Christ."

"Yeah." Jim started to get to his feet, then realized it wouldn't be right to leave her lying there with her titties exposed. Somehow that partial nakedness looked even more obscene than the ugliness of the hole in her throat. He forced himself to hold down the bottom of the vest with one hand while he used the other to draw the zipper closed again. He didn't have any trouble getting the vest to close over her. It seemed several sizes too large for her, so that there was room to spare when he zipped it shut. The woman's body hadn't been very large to begin with and now it looked like it had been deflated. Like it was already starting to sink back into the earth from which it'd come.

Jim finished what he had to do, then lurched to his feet.

JayJay had been right. The knees of his jeans were covered with sticky, drying gore. He was careful to avoid brushing off his britches. That would only have transferred the half-dry blood onto his hands.

"What . . . Christ, Jim, what d' we do now?" JayJay asked.

"I don't know," Jim confessed.

"IT WAS AN ACCIDENT. You fellas *know* it was an accident," JayJay insisted once again. The three men were hunkered near the blue-and-white tent the Californians had set up on the west shoulder of Coffee Hill. From where they were, they could not see the woman's body lying just below the sloping lip. JayJay had been protesting his innocence so often it was almost like he was trying to convince himself. For sure Bill and Jim knew he hadn't meant to shoot that woman.

Jim reached into his shirt pocket for a Chesterfield while Bill obliged ol' JayJay by assuring him once again that they all knew it was an accident.

"I don't see how. . . ." But of course they did. It was those damned jacketed slugs stepping out quick and nasty. That's what had done it. A regular soft-nose hunting bullet would've broken up and been no more hurtful hardly than the gravel it sprayed. It was the fault of the bullet, not JayJay. Jim lighted his cigarette and explained that to JayJay again. Ol' JayJay was about half a mess over this, though. He had a pale look to him still, and his hands were shaky.

Oddly, it was Bill that Jim was really worried about now. Bill wasn't saying or doing much of anything. But then, he hadn't had time to chew on this yet. Bill hadn't been in favor of coming out here to begin with. Now that there was a woman laying on the ground dead, well, there was no telling how he might come to think of it.

Funny, but Jim hadn't thought about all those dead horses down below. Not since . . . Bunch of dead horses hardly seemed important right now anyway.

This was bad joss, and the burden was on him to handle things. Get them all out of it with them and the place intact.

That was what really mattered right now, Jim recognized with a clear and sudden insight.

What was done was done. Dead is dead and can't be changed, whether you're talking horse or human. Or dream or hope or responsibility, for that matter. Dead is dead. Jesus!

Jim drew smoke deep into his lungs and held it there a moment before letting it out. The simple act of smoking helped to calm him. The familiarity of it eased the whirl of confusion and let his mind slow and take hold again. He peered out across the basin toward the distant mountains.

Lordy. Dead. And dead is dead. What t' do now, though. That was the question. Done is done and what comes next?

"I swear I never. . . ." JayJay was rambling on about the same old shit, Bill listening and sympathizing and saying all the same stuff back to him every time JayJay repeated his protestations. Jim tuned the two of them out and tried to concentrate.

Dead is dead, done is done, bad is bad, but where to go from here?

One thing sure. A whole lot of Beales died on this land after living their lives on it. It was Jim Beale's job now to see that the land was still theirs so more Beales could do the same.

That was what it came right down to. And never mind how regrettable it was if some wild horses died along the way. Or a California woman too.

That part was a genuine damned shame, but there it was. If Jim could change it now, he surely would. But he couldn't. So the thing to do now was to put that behind and think about what came *next.*

He cleared his throat and waited for JayJay and Bill to quit yammering at one another.

"You fellas ready to hush up an' listen to me?"

Apparently they were. They both of them shut up and turned their attention to him. Bill spat a stream of yellow juice. JayJay pulled out a Marlboro.

"We ain't bringing the law into this," Jim said firmly. "We go and report this, they'll charge you, JayJay, and let a court shake it out. You'd have Bill and me to stand up for you, o' course. We know what was meant an' what happened. We'd sure say so. But a judge an' jury might or might

not believe us. They might could think we was lying for you. Well, we
aren't gonna take that chance. We just won't take it to law to start with."

"But—"

"Bill, you hush yourself right up and listen to me. This mess comes to
law, boy, they're gonna be pissed. Looking for ways to rattle us around and
prove something on JayJay and on us too. They'd look at that dead woman
and they'd look at those dead horses and next thing you know they'd have
all three of us in jail and no grazing leases. Not ever again no grazing
leases. How the hell d'you think we could get along without grazing?
Huh? How long?" Jim's voice had turned hard now, and his eyes were
boring straight at Billy. Bill couldn't meet that look for long and quickly
turned his head away to spit again. When he was done spitting, he found
something off toward the horizon to look at.

"They'd say we were lying for JayJay just so we could cover ourselves,
dammit. At the very best we'd all go up for federal endangered species
charges. Likely they'd add manslaughter onto JayJay. Maybe onto all of us.
And no leases, Bill. We'd dry up and blow away. Bad enough what would
be happening to us. Think what it'd do to Maureen and Gloria and those
boys of yours if we was all in jail and they had no home t' comfort them
through it. Think about that."

Bill scowled but didn't say anything.

"What we are gonna do, boys, is let this thing end right here an' now.
Just pretend none of it ever took place. Do over that California woman
same as we've always done about the horses we've had to put down. Like a
great big dog turd laying out in the middle of a fresh-raked garden patch,
eh? We'll cover it over with a bit of dirt and forget it ever happened. And
I will tell you boys just exactly how the three of us are gonna accomplish
this. Okay?" To emphasize what he was saying and to ease things along by
going ahead and starting the process of what was required, Jim stood and
walked over to the camera the California man had dropped. It was laying
on the ground just a couple feet away from the dark-haired woman's body.
He bent down, got the camera and found the catch on the back that
opened the thing. He took the film out and exposed it all to the daylight,
ruining whatever pictures were there. Some of the photos could've been of
them, after all. Now those pictures were as irretrievable as that woman's
life was.

There wasn't any challenge. Nobody said anything. Jim had been more
than half expecting a squawk. From Bill, not JayJay.

Jim grunted with satisfaction and coughed once. He stubbed out his
cigarette and reached for another, cupping his hands around the lighter

and bending to it, more giving himself time to think than really caring whether he had another smoke right now or not. He glanced up, fixing first JayJay and then Bill with close, searching looks. Then he nodded. "All right. Here's what we are gonna do. . . ."

NINETEEN

VIOLENT TREMORS rippled through his limbs, making him jerk and shudder in a macabre puppet dance as he lay face down on the ground with his eyes squeezed shut and his breath coming in harsh, ragged gasps.

Too loud. He was breathing much too loud. Those men would come and they would hear and they would shoot him the way they had shot JoLynn and then . . . What then? Then he would die, of course. There would be nothing after then. Not for him and therefore, at least so far as Oliver was concerned, there would be nothing at all.

Oliver trembled and drew his knees tight against his chest, clasped his knees with his arms and rocked to and fro in his anguish.

Dead!

He could still see the sightless stare of her empty, open eyes.

Dead.

Could still feel the sticky-tacky weight of her blood on his hands.

Dead.

He'd touched her flesh and there had been no response. None. She was inert. A . . . thing. A body now. Transformed from a live and vital and loving human being, just that quickly, that easily, by the passing touch of a bullet. Shot down, murdered, by those men.

Dead.

JoLynn did not exist any longer. But Oliver did. And those men did. *And what were they going to do now?*

Dear God. Oliver knew his lips had moved. He had no idea if he had spoken the words aloud or not. Not, he hoped. If he made noise those men might find him. Make him dead as JoLynn. Jesus.

His eyes squeezed shut even tighter, and he began to cry.

But oh so silently lest the men hear and find him.

. . . .

IT SHOULD HAVE BEEN RAGE that brought him out of his state of panicked withdrawal. Rage or perhaps resolution. Rage against those who would so wantonly destroy. Resolution that men like that should be brought to justice. It was neither of those qualities that led Oliver back to full awareness of his surroundings.

Rather, it was sweat. More precisely, it was the repeated minor annoyance of sweat accumulating on the back of his neck and trickling along the underside of his jaw that made him finally sit up and wipe himself off and look blinking around him.

He felt ashamed of himself once he realized. But only for a moment. The fact was, JoLynn was dead and he was not and death was the one place where he did not wish to join her. Oliver shivered despite the heat of the sun on his shoulders, blinked again and tried to make sense of what he could see.

He was sitting now, had been lying, between two small boulders on an otherwise drab and barren hillside. The sharp tip of hill above the place where they made camp last night? He thought so. He thought he recognized below him the place where this morning JoLynn posed against the dawn light for his pictures.

Pictures. Where was the camera? The last he remembered seeing it was when he was holding it in his hands. But then that was before. When JoLynn was standing beside him. Before . . . any of this. He shuddered. His memories were all . . . mixed up. He had no recollection of running here. But all too well he remembered lying beside JoLynn's body. Remembered turning her over. Remembered in unwelcome detail what he'd seen there. Remembered . . . returning to full awareness only here and now on this hillside. There was nothing in between.

He shuddered and looked up toward the sky. The sun, barely off the horizon when the horses appeared, was past zenith now and sinking toward California and home. He must have lain here cowering for hours and hours.

That was all right, he concluded. At least the men hadn't found him. Surely they had looked, but they did not find him.

But where . . . ?

Oliver's breath caught in his throat, and a chill of fear leaped through him.

His head swiveled and craned, searching anxiously for some sign of the men with the rifles.

He could see nothing. Nothing now but earth and sky and vast, vast distances.

He blinked again. He really couldn't see anything that was man-made.

Shouldn't he be able to see the Subaru? He was sure he'd parked it right over there. He looked again, but there was nothing.

Frowning, Oliver climbed shakily to his feet, then began making his way slowly around the hillside.

He moved with animal caution, alert and ready to sink down out of sight at the first glimpse of movement. If the men were still on the hill, he wanted to see them before they could see and shoot him. But he did want to move now. He wanted to return to JoLynn. Gather her up. He wanted to get JoLynn's body and the car. And the camera too; he wanted proof of what had happened here, including pictures of those men if that was possible. Mostly, though, he wanted to get away from this awful place just as fast as he could manage.

There would be authorities somewhere. Police, a sheriff's department, whatever. He wanted to report to them what happened here and let them see that justice was done. The slaughterers of wild horses had become murderers of people, and they must be punished.

But first Oliver had to collect JoLynn's body and get away from here.

He crept one slow step at a time around the pointed cone of stone and soil that had seemed so happy a place until the men came.

There was nothing left on the hill. Nothing but grass and gravel, stone and soil.

No tent. No camping gear. No car. Above all there was no body.

The men—it had to have been the men—had gathered everything up and carried it all away. Even JoLynn. Her body was gone.

Oliver could see—he remembered entirely too well—where she had been lying after the men murdered her.

Now there was nothing on the ground.

Oh, he could see where dirt had been freshly kicked over the clotted blood—JoLynn's lifeblood, emptied out on this spot, squandered here—so that only a few rust-colored stains remained visible. Ants and beetles infested the patch of ground now. Oliver saw that the insects were feasting on the blood that had been JoLynn's life, and he felt sickened.

He turned away and slumped to a seated position on the hard ground, sitting now almost precisely where he had been when the men were shooting down the horses.

The bodies of the horses were still there, he saw now. Too many and too large to hide or haul away.

Yet the men had taken JoLynn's body away with them.

And the tent. The car. Everything.

Oliver was still having difficulty grasping the full impact of the things that had taken place here.

He kept focusing on the one central fact that JoLynn's existence had been extinguished.

Nothing else seemed to have very much meaning at all.

He sat there in the afternoon sunshine and cried.

TWENTY

JIM GRUNTED AND SWORE. The lousy little Jap Subaru was no stout and reliable pickup truck. The station wagon felt like it might break into pieces if he took a bump too hard, and he didn't trust the engine to pull him out of trouble if it started to bog down in the soft spots.

Still, it was creeping and crawling along okay so far.

Jim glanced out the window, looking up toward the sky. No airplanes. That was good. If the sky would just stay nice and empty another half hour, forty-five minutes, he would have everything done that needed to be done here.

There wasn't any low-range transfer case in the Subaru, just the choice of two- or four-wheel drive and a regular transmission. Jim kept the vehicle in first gear now that he was into the arroyo and slipped the clutch when he needed to move really slowly over the roughest places. He wondered how Bill and JayJay were coming. At least an hour back, he figured. Maybe more. He should have driven them to where they'd left the saddle horses instead of expecting them to walk it. Except there wouldn't have been room for them in the wagon, would there?

He thought about the cargo in the back of the station wagon but didn't turn to look. Not that there would've been much to see. The body was underneath the tent and the other stuff back there. Nobody would be able to see it there even if they did spot the car. And that wouldn't be possible for very much longer either.

Jim would feel better once the Subaru was buried, dammit. Then there wouldn't be anything, nothing at all, to even show that there'd been an accident out here. The woman, the car, everything would just up and disappear. There wouldn't be questions to answer and nobody would have to say or do a thing about this, not ever more.

With luck Jim would be able to get that part of it finished with before Bill and JayJay reached him with the horses. Jim didn't want Bill having to think about it overmuch. It wasn't that he didn't trust Bill, hell no. Bill was solid as they came, as good a brother as anybody could ever hope to have. It was just that Jim didn't want to push him about it. Best to just get things done the way they needed to be done and let Bill stay out of it as much as possible.

JayJay of course, well, he wasn't going to say or do anything to bring attention on them. Hell, it was JayJay had actually shot that woman. JayJay would be the last of them to want this thing laid out for everybody to see.

It was going to work out okay. It really was, Jim assured himself.

He lighted a cigarette, reached a reasonably flat and straight section where the sandy arroyo bottom was compacted nice and hard. He was able to shift into second gear for the first time in more than a mile and increase his speed some. The quicker he got to the head of this wash, the better, dammit.

He didn't know why he was still feeling so damned nervous and shaky. After all, it was all going to be okay. They were handling it. It'd been a bad break, but they were handling it. Nobody could do any more than that, could they? Course not.

Jim recognized a place where there were breaks on both sides of the banks just a few dozen yards apart so that horses or cattle could cross there, down into the wash and then back up again onto the flat. He'd ridden through at that spot himself, saving a ride all the way up to the beginnings of the arroyo to get around it or a detour in the downstream direction far enough that the walls weren't sheer and livestock could pass. Annoying damned things, these washes sometimes. If the walls were too sharp to negotiate on horseback, they were worse than fences for keeping a man from going where he wanted.

Still, this here one was turning out pretty useful.

Encouraged to know that he wasn't much more than a mile from the spot he wanted, Jim increased his speed again, and the Subaru jolted steadily forward, its engine pulling quiet and steady and frankly much better than Jim would've expected from such a little thing.

Damn, he was going to be glad to get this over and done with.

. . . .

HE SAT AND SMOKED and studied on the problem for a while.

He'd finally reached the head of the wash, and it was just like he remembered seeing the last time he rode past. That'd been, what? last fall some time. Looking for some stragglers, a couple long yearling steers that they'd missed when they gathered up the Beale cows and moved them back off the BLM graze at the end of the season. Sure that was when. It hadn't changed a lick since.

Nice and deep here because of the way the snowmelt had gathered all along that ridge up there and then run together and somehow for some reason started cutting back into the hill and now had cut all this way. Ten, twelve foot deep at the head of the wash here. And wide enough the Subaru should jam into it just fine.

That wasn't the problem.

Jim sighed and sat on the hood with his boot heels hooked onto the front bumper and lighted another Chesterfield while he tried to work out the best way to handle this.

He was being silly. That was what it came right down to. Silly and, all right, maybe a bit squeamish too.

It was just that it was giving him the willies, the thought that . . . He shuddered and made a face, and the smoke in his throat tasted foul.

He cussed a little in the silence, slid down off the hood of the car and turned to glare at it a moment, then marched up to the sharp wall that was at the extreme head of the arroyo he'd been following all this time.

The loose, sun-baked soil smelled dry. He grabbed a fistful of it and felt the clods crumble between his fingers and sift through.

A man could all too easily touch both side walls at once. It wasn't any stretch at all. In fact, with one arm extended he could touch the other wall with just his elbow. Less than five feet across here, he guessed. But soft enough that with something of a running start he should be able to jam the front of the car pretty much all the way in.

If he backed away and tried leaving the Subaru farther down from the head of the wash . . . well, he wasn't fixing to fill in any more of this arroyo than could be handled with the dinky little folding camp shovel they'd found with all the other stuff.

But, dammit, the side walls were 'most too close here.

What he'd been planning right along was that he should drive the car in nice and deep, then slip out and close the door and leave the windows all rolled up nice and tight when he got out and commenced to bury the car.

Because that, really, was one of the things that was bothering him the most, damn it.

It was bad enough that that woman was dead. He hated that, he really did. But it would be even worse if he went and left it so that mice and rats and snakes and whatever could get inside the car that was fixing to be her coffin. That wouldn't be . . . respectful.

Yet narrow as the wash was up here where he had to park if he expected to be able to cover the car completely over, well, the only way he could drive it in there and still get out again would be to roll a window down and crawl out through that. Maybe even bust out the windshield and go out onto the hood. There might not be enough room even to get out a side window. Yet if he did either of those things, well, the crawling creatures would be able to come and go inside the car even after it was buried. Burying it would keep coyotes out. But not the burrowing things. It would take the steel and glass to keep them out.

"Shit," he said aloud.

He walked back to the car and measured across the front of the hood with his hands, turned and walked carefully with his hands still extended to more or less the same distance apart.

There just wasn't any denying it, the distances were just about the same. There would be barely room to fit the car in and none left over for him to get out afterward.

There was the one other possibility, of course.

But he sure as hell didn't like it.

He would do it, he decided. It was either that or bust the windshield out and let the mice get in.

He was *not* going to trust to luck that he could manage it from inside the car, though. Wouldn't that be a bitch, if he got himself buried inside there and couldn't get out then.

He opened the hatch at the rear of the station wagon and draped the end of a sleeping bag over top of the latch mechanism to make sure the tail door didn't bang down and lock itself closed when the car bashed into the arroyo wall.

He remembered—thank goodness—to get the camp shovel out of the floorboards on the passenger side up front where he'd put the thing so he'd know where to find it when he needed it. Wouldn't it be a bitch to forget that and have to go back after it? He dropped the shovel onto the wash floor. He could come back to it in a few minutes.

Then, quick before he had time to think about it too much, he got in the car and rolled the driver's-side window up. That was the window he'd had down for ventilation while he was driving. He made sure the other windows were all rolled up and the vents closed. He even turned off the fan that was supposed to circulate fresh air inside the car. He didn't know if that kind of vent would allow a mouse to come through, but why take any chances?

Jeez, he felt funny about this.

He put the car in gear, took a deep breath and gunned the engine.

The little Subaru surged forward, drove hard and deep into the narrow gap where the dry wash started. The fenders scraped on both sides, and loose dirt tumbled down onto the hood, half burying the windshield by the time the front bumper impacted on something solid.

The car shuddered and there was a thumping, banging noise from underneath it as the engine and drive train failed to overcome the immovable surroundings.

Jim could hear more dirt and debris falling onto the roof.

The engine died, leaving him in silence save for the soft sounds of loose soil sliding down and the creaks and pops of hot metal beginning to cool.

Jim was acutely conscious all of a sudden of the cargo that rested behind him now.

He grimaced and stubbed his cigarette out in an ashtray that looked like it had never been used before.

He turned and crawled through the gap between the front seats, slithering onto his belly atop the flimsy nylon tenting material that covered the cargo. The stove, food, bags of clothing . . . body.

Jim was crawling over that woman's body. He couldn't remember just exactly where the body was, quite precisely how it lay inside the back of the station wagon.

He wished he could remember.

He didn't want to touch her. Didn't want to think that he was kneeling on her face or . . . whatever.

With a squeaking, shamefully audible gasp he lurched and scrambled for the open hatch at the back of the car.

He tumbled out head first, hit the ground hard and rolled, coming to rest on his back several feet from the rear bumper of the California car.

He was breathing hard and was sweating more than the warmth of the day justified.

But he was out, dammit.

He got shakily to his feet and brushed himself off.

He tried to remember if he had thought to turn the ignition key off after the engine died. He couldn't remember doing it. But he might have.

Not that it made any difference, really. It wasn't like the battery needed to be preserved. It really wouldn't matter at all if the ignition was left on and the battery ran down. Still, he found himself hoping that the switch was off. It would be . . . tidier somehow.

He carefully tucked the sleeping bag inside where it would not intrude on the tailgate latch and dropped the hatch closed. It dropped shut with a slightly tinny clang.

He tugged, making sure the latch had caught, but did not look inside the back window to see if . . . anything . . . was visible there. He turned quickly away, coughing nervously into his fist, and picked up the shovel.

Jim Beale walked down the arroyo looking for a place where one of the banks was broken and he would be able to climb out. He intended to walk up to the head and start working from above. With any luck he should have the Subaru covered and completely hidden from view before Bill and JayJay brought the horses up and joined him.

Then it would be like nothing had ever happened with the woman.

Out here way the hell and gone from anything, why, the car might never be found again. Probably wouldn't be. Or if it was, well, it'd be decades from now at the very earliest and no one would ever know or much care by then how it'd come to happen.

Jim found himself hurrying. He was anxious for this to be over and done with for good and all.

HE SAT AND SMOKED and tried to ignore the aches and the pains while Bill and JayJay finished the job. It was better now that they had joined him. More hands meant quicker progress. Not that Jim's efforts had been so shabby. He'd gotten all the dirt filled in over top of the car so there wasn't anything anybody could see. Now all that had to be done was to lay on rocks in a riprap to keep the loose dirt from washing away and exposing everything. Bill and JayJay were sure as hell welcome to do that part. By the time they brought the horses up, Jim's back was aching, his hands were raw and sore and his legs hurt. He just plain wasn't young enough for this kind of work anymore.

Jim sucked deep on the Chesterfield, holding the smoke in his lungs awhile before he exhaled. He sat with his arms wrapped around his knees and the brim of his hat tilted to keep the afternoon sun out of his eyes. It had turned out warm again. He tried not to think about what the heat of the coming summer would do to the inside of the station wagon, even buried in the dirt like it was. It would be an oven in there.

Funny, he reflected, how none of them'd said a word yet about the chore that brought them here. Not Bill, not JayJay, for damn sure not Jim himself. The car was covered over and out of sight. Better they should pretend it was out of mind too. They all of them worked at finishing the job of hiding it but never a thing said about what it was they were hiding. Or why. Or, above all, about what came next.

'That was the really shitty part, of course.

Jim sighed and drew on the cigarette again. He wished he had a bottle along. But then it was better not to, wasn't it.

He'd already decided to send Bill back home. There were some things that needed doing there. And Bill wouldn't object to being left out of this part of what needed doing. Better by far, Jim figured, to leave him out of it. And to leave some things unsaid. Just in case, like.

As for JayJay, he'd just have to do what he had to do. Hell, he was the one got them in this deep anyhow. He was the one who screwed up a perfectly innocent warning and shot low instead of high like he ought. Now it was only right that JayJay help get them all out again.

But Bill . . . Jim wouldn't have admitted it to JayJay, not for anything in the world, but the simple truth was that he wanted Billy kept in reserve, like. Kept in the dark on this part of it, with never anything actually out-and-out spoken, so that Bill could say without lying that he didn't actually *know* what Jim and JayJay were doing out here. It was necessary that Billy stay out of prison and hold things together. Just in case. If it came down to it, Jim would give up JayJay to the law and himself too. But somebody had to be kept at arm's length, and it had to be a Beale. Which meant Billy. No question about it.

Not that it should ever have to come to that, of course.

Nobody else knew about those Californians. All they had to do now was to smooth the thing over—just like Bill and JayJay were laying the rocks down and smoothing over the head of this arroyo right now—and nobody ever would have to know about the Californians.

Not about either one of them.

But, Jesus, this was a hard thing to come to.

Jim hated it. Hated it worse than having to slaughter the wild horses, hated it worse than having to knock defective calves in the head, hated this whole deal just awful bad.

But he'd do it. Of course he'd do it. There wasn't anybody, not some skinny California woman nor James Adam Beale nor some bad-luck California man that was more important than what all the generations of Beales had built here.

Jim would do exactly what he had to do here, and never mind how much he hated the doing of it.

He smoked the Chesterfield down to a nubbin so short it was starting to burn him, then stubbed out the coal and with his thumb and first two fingers ground the butt into a loose, dry powder that he released onto the breeze. He stood, joints and muscles aching, and went to help finish covering over the car and its cargo.

TWENTY-ONE

IT WAS BEGINNING to get through to him just how serious his situation was.

Oliver stood at the base of the hill, his hiking boots muddy and the knees of his trousers wet here in the midst of the desert, and it gradually came clearer and clearer to him that he was in serious trouble.

It was simple thirst that had pointed the fact out to him. As simple a thing as that. He'd been up on the hill sitting, moping, blindly grieving for JoLynn. And he got thirsty.

Never before in his life had it been anything particularly alarming to be thirsty. You want a drink, you get one. Easy as that. You turn the knob on a faucet or press the button on a fountain, buy a soda pop, sit down at a cafe table and order a cup of tea. Whatever seems both satisfying and convenient. When you are thirsty, you drink. Nothing to it.

Except here Oliver became thirsty. And there was nothing for him to drink. No canned beverages on hand. No jars, containers, bottles or tins. Nothing.

It was not really a problem, of course. He walked down the hill here, stepped carefully wide of the area where the dead horses lay, and knelt to drink from the water hole that had drawn the horses to this place of carnage.

He drank, stood again . . . and stopped to consider his own precarious predicament as it suddenly, overwhelmingly occurred to him that he no longer could take life for granted.

Since early morning Oliver had thought about JoLynn and about the men who murdered her and about the horses that had been slaughtered today. He hadn't given consideration to his own tenuous mortality.

But what if . . . ?

"Jesus!" he blurted aloud into the silence.

Oliver shivered. It wasn't cold yet, the sun still standing high over the mountains to the west, but he felt cold anyway. The chill, he acknowledged, was fear.

Those men knew Oliver was here. They had seen JoLynn clearly enough to kill her. Therefore they had seen Oliver clearly enough to identify him too.

They had to know he would report the murder to the authorities at the very first opportunity.

Yet they had gone to the trouble of removing JoLynn's body, the car, the camp, each and every sign that there had been people here and that one of those people was now dead.

One of those two people. Only one. *So far.* Oliver shuddered.

Simple logic dictated that the continued safety and freedom of the three murderers depended now on Oliver's death.

Why oh *why* hadn't he been thinking about this earlier?

Most of the day was gone now, wasted. He could have been . . .

He blinked again. What could he have been doing today?

He honestly didn't know.

Running? Where?

Or was that what the men were counting on to begin with? It was possible, wasn't it? They might be counting on Oliver to panic and run blindly into the desert to die of thirst or starvation.

No, not starvation, he quickly corrected himself. It takes a very long time for someone to die of starvation, doesn't it? He was fairly sure he remembered that that was so. Of course it was. Political protesters went on hunger strikes for months and months sometimes. Dick Gregory would have been dead a dozen times over if it were possible to die quickly of starvation.

Thirst, that was another story. A man could die rather quickly from dehydration. How long? Oliver had no idea. But right now he could practically see in his mind's eye all the stupid cartoons he'd ever read depicting men crawling on hands and knees through a desert while vultures lurked over their shoulders.

Silly, silly, stupid stuff, he chided himself.

Yet even so, he found himself glancing around to see if there were any vultures gathered.

Not that there were any saguaro cacti in northern Nevada. The cartoons always showed saguaros for some reason, but the distinctive plants grew only in a limited area. In Arizona. Perhaps extending into Utah and parts of California? Oliver couldn't remember. He tried now to recall precisely where the saguaro habitat ended. He . . .

He recognized the mental distraction for the unconscious avoidance technique that it was and forced himself to quit. Who the hell *cared* where a bunch of stupid cactuses, cacti, grew? And of *course* there weren't any stupid vultures sitting around waiting for him to dehydrate and die.

Yet.

He shuddered.

Was that why the men had so calmly gone off and left him alive here?

Did they know that he couldn't get away from this place on his own anyway? Did they reason that they didn't need to hunt him down and murder him immediately because they could return to do that at their leisure or just let the desert do this next bit of killing for them?

Oliver felt the faint stirrings of the same sort of panic that had driven him into mindless flight this morning.

Panic would only play into the hands of the men who needed him to die.

Thoughtlessness would accomplish nothing.

But, dear God, he was scared.

He squeezed his eyes closed and tried to will away the trembling that chilled and weakened him.

OLIVER SAT in the fringes of the cattail stand, deliberately staying low so that the tall cattails would hide him in case the men came back to search for him.

What he needed to do, he'd decided, was take stock of where he stood. List his assets, so to speak. And try to *do* something.

Neither dying of thirst in the desert nor allowing himself to be slaughtered as the horses had been, as JoLynn had been, neither of those held any appeal to him whatsoever.

So what he needed to do was to sit quietly and *think*. Evaluate. Plan.

Oliver believed in planning and reason and tidiness in all things.

He'd always been one of those people who claimed that brain was superior to brawn.

Well, this was certainly an opportunity to put that theory to the test.

A little extreme on the Pass/Fail grading process, he thought wryly. But effective. If he survived, by godfrey, he was a roaring success.

And if he didn't . . .

Damn it, he would not meekly accept a failing grade.

So all right. What did he have here and now that he could use? And how could he use those things?

"Pay attention, stupid," he told himself.

TWENTY-TWO

"YOU TAKE CARE NOW, dammit. And don't you fret. Me an' JayJay will be along directly. Quick as we find the rest of those horses and put 'em down." Which was the fiction Jim had decided upon, the one they could speak of out loud for Bill's benefit just in case Billy someday had to testify to what all was said and done here this day.

Bill reached down to shake Jim's hand and then JayJay's too. Like the two he was leaving behind were fixing to go on a long and difficult journey. And of course so they were. "Are you sure you don't want me to come out and—"

"No," Jim cut him off. "You take care of things at home. Me and JayJay will take care o' things here and be along behind you. If we need anything, we'll come get it. Just make sure you don't do any sympathy hiring while my back's turned. Don't hire on no dwarfs or drunks or drifters, eh? Just good buckaroos this year." Another part of the fiction was that Bill had to hurry home to take charge of things in case any hands showed up early looking for work. Jim grinned up at his younger brother, who was sitting atop his appaloosa but not acting like he was in any rush to rein away.

JayJay chuckled and added, "If any blondes with big tits show up lookin' for work, William, you be sure an' hire 'em. You can take their wages outa my pay, hear?"

That got a laugh and a nod out of Bill, and at last he turned the ap away and took off at a jog toward where they'd left the pickup truck. He would drive it back. When Jim and JayJay were ready to come in, tomorrow with any kind of luck, they would go home on horseback.

There wasn't any laughing, though, once Bill was well on his way.

Jim glanced at JayJay, who had a funny sort of look on his face. Jim suspected he was regretting the comment he'd made about blondes with big tits. That was the sort of casual dumb thing any one of them might say anytime and nobody ever think a thing about it. Except now it was kind of hard not think about a flat-chested dark-haired woman who hadn't been hired but'd been shot instead.

"Well, JayJay?"

JayJay cleared his throat and spat. He stood with his thumbs hooked in his back pockets, the brown horse cropping grass behind him with the butt of one of the Ruger carbines prominent above the saddle. JayJay was staring sightlessly off in the direction of Coffee Hill.

"We got it to do, don't we, Jim?"

"Ayuh. I expect we do."

"You wantin' me to . . . ?"

"No," Jim said quickly. "Not by yourself. I ain't laying that on you, JayJay. Not by yourself, man. I'll be right with you and do . . . my share of things. If you know what I mean."

JayJay nodded and for just a moment there almost looked like he could cry. Instead he scowled and spat again. "Yeah. Shit. Right." He grabbed up the reins of his horse and swung into the saddle with the swift, fluid motions of long habit. "Any time you're ready, Jim."

IT WAS GOING TO BE BAD. Jim could feel it coming, and it was going to be really bad.

It'd been bad enough when they went up and saw that that woman was dead. But at least that had been an accident.

This . . . there wasn't any getting around it. This was going to be cold-blooded. No way they could pretend this was any kind of accident.

No way they could back off of it either. The body and the car and everything were already hauled off and hid. The man would talk if ever he got the chance. One hint of any of this and there would be hell to pay. Worse than prison, they would lose the place. They would lose the grazing leases, and then Gloria and Maureen and Bill's boys would lose the place. And no matter how much care Jim took to keep Bill off at that little bit of arm's-length distance from this part of it. So him and JayJay just had to do this, and never mind if they didn't like it. A man never likes everything he has to do. This example was just a little more extreme than most.

Beside him JayJay shifted position. Jim saw JayJay's hand go to his shirt pocket and then back down again still empty. Good. He'd remembered. But then this was like waiting in a stand for a deer to walk down in front of you, a stand on a really good run where you knew the one you wanted would be along sooner or later. All you had to do was to sit nice and still and not make noise or smoke to spook him, and by and by he'd be yours. Well, it wasn't much different hunting this man, it turned out. All they had to do, Jim was sure, was to wait right here.

"I don't think he's coming," JayJay whispered.

"He's coming," Jim said patiently in a normal speaking voice. Good grief, there couldn't be anybody within a mile of them without both of them being able to see. "Where the hell else could he go, huh?"

"He oughta be here by now if he was gonna come." JayJay was still whispering but not quite so softly this time.

"Give him time. He *has* to come here," Jim explained once again. "This is the only other water he knows about."

"But—"

"I know, dammit, JayJay. This country is thick with water if you know where t' look. You or me, we couldn't pick a thirsty path out here if we sat down and tried to work one out. But to some city fella from California? He only knows two places to get water, and that's Coffee Hill and right here. He's got nothing to carry water in, and he's probably scared so he's running and sweating and using up his fluids quick. I'm telling you, JayJay, he has to come here to drink again. And if it ain't this afternoon, it'll be tonight. Come dark we'll move in closer to the spring and wait for him. One thing I want you to remember, though. When he comes in, JayJay, we both of us take aim, right? I'll give us a three count an' we both shoot together on three. That way we both got the responsibility. Comes to that, we can both think that our bullet missed and it was the other guy's that hit. Right?"

"I know. God, I appreciate this, Jim. I really do. You know? I only wish it coulda been the same with that woman. You know I never meant to shoot her, Jim. You do know that, don't you?"

"I know it, JayJay. You never meant to hurt her."

"I only wanted to spray some gravel. I swear that's all."

"I know, JayJay."

"I never thought—"

"It's all right. Hush now, JayJay. It's all right. You don't have to think about it no more. I understand."

"Yeah. Right." JayJay reached to his shirt pocket again, this time got the cigarette pack out and open before he remembered and put it away again.

"Look, we can see for miles from here. There's nothing and nobody moving out there yet. Why don't we both have us a smoke? Move around a little. Then we can hunker down again and get serious about setting up for this guy. What d'you say?"

"I'd like that, Jim. I really need me a smoke right now."

"All right." Jim forced a smile even though he didn't much feel like smiling at the moment. He set his carbine down and stood to stretch and stamp his feet and move around some. And in truth the taste of the Chesterfield was almighty good. He'd been wanting a smoke about as bad as JayJay.

And hell, they were dealing with a city fella anyway. Likely they could light fires and play loud music if they wanted. It wouldn't be until after dark that it became really necessary to keep from smoking. For right now all they really had to worry about was their own patience. If they could get a handle on that, everything else would work out just fine. Jim was sure of it.

TWENTY-THREE

IT WASN'T AS IF he had so many assets to draw on that inventory management was going to be a problem here. Oliver mentally reviewed the list one more time as he walked.

He had the clothes on his back, which hardly constituted anything worth bragging about. Blue jeans, flannel shirt, jockey shorts, cotton tube socks, nylon hiking boots, jacket—the jacket was little heavier than a windbreaker; why hadn't he been sensible enough to put on something warmer this morning?—yeah, just the thing for the committed survivalist on a trek through unknown desert.

The contents of his pockets didn't seem all that much more helpful either. One handkerchief, unused. One wallet with assorted cards and photos. Forty-seven dollars in cash. His keys, house and car alike, had been left dangling in the ignition switch of the Subaru. There was no telling where they were now. He had nothing really useful, though. No knife or compass or map. No signaling mirror—they always put steel mirrors in those survival kit things, although he didn't know why—or fishhooks—

another popular item in the kits they sold among the camping supplies; fishhooks and line were certainly what he needed here in the damned desert—or . . . or very much of anything else that would be genuinely useful here and now. Oh, yes, he'd forgotten. In his jacket pockets there were two rolls of exposed thirty-five-millimeter film. But no plastic canisters with snap-tight lids that would have allowed him to carry two shots of water for the road, just the yellow and black cans of film.

His face twisted in pain as he thought about the film he carried with him. That film was precious now. That film was of JoLynn, the last pictures he would ever have of her, the ones he'd taken this morning when the world had seemed so fresh and lovely. And hadn't *that* been a joke.

God. JoLynn had been alive then. So very much alive. So beautiful. Now she was . . .

He forced himself to quit thinking about her.

JoLynn was dead. Oliver was not. That was one callous, selfish, ugly way to look at things. It was also necessary.

The truth was, Oliver had already concluded that he would have to somehow survive if JoLynn was to be . . . not avenged. That wasn't at all what he wanted for her. Vengeance wasn't what JoLynn or he was about. It was more that he wanted . . . justice for her. That seemed more accurate if still not quite to the point. Rectification. Yes, that better conveyed the needs he felt now. Rectification.

JoLynn couldn't be brought back. But her death could be made right, at least a little bit, if those men were punished. Even more so if somehow JoLynn's death helped make the shooting of the wild horses stop.

If those men were put in jail for murdering JoLynn, why, they wouldn't be free to murder the wild horses ever again.

If that happened, then JoLynn's death would be a direct and powerful influence on behalf of the wild horses.

She would have liked that, Oliver thought.

Oh, it wouldn't justify her loss. Nothing would ever do that. But it might soften the pain.

So why in hell was he crying now?

His eyes were filming so full of tears that he could scarcely see the ground under his own feet. Could hardly find his way.

HE HADN'T HAD ANY IDEA that it was so far from the hill where JoLynn and the horses died back to the spring where they'd set up before. It hadn't seemed so terribly far when they drove it. Salt Spring, that was the name of the place.

The men who murdered JoLynn had told them what the spring was called. Oh, they'd been so helpful then.

So he and JoLynn *wouldn't* be there to witness the slaughter of the horses? Now, in hindsight, that seemed entirely likely. The men must have deliberately directed them to this poor location in an effort to keep them out of the way.

He stopped practically in mid stride.

There were only two sources of water in this entire, awful stretch of desert that Oliver knew how to find. *And those men knew which ones they were.* Those same men first gave Oliver and JoLynn directions to Salt Spring, then discovered them camped at the other place.

If the men intended to kill Oliver . . .

Dammit, surely they would expect him to run away from the spring where JoLynn and the horses died. That was only logical. And was, indeed, the thing he had chosen to do. If he took a long time to get around to doing it, well, that was simply because of shock and confusion and grief intruding on his normal thought processes. Now, though, he was running.

And where was he running? Why, to Salt Spring, of course. Where else *could* he run? He had no food, no water, no way to carry water.

He had—he wasn't sure; why oh *why* hadn't they bought maps before they left Winnemucca?—seventy, maybe as much as eighty miles to go to reach the nearest wells or habitations. Actually farther than that to reach pavement. But call it seventy miles to the nearest ranch buildings. Could a man walk seventy miles through the desert without water?

Oliver doubted that it was possible. He would try it if he had to. But he really doubted that anyone could do it.

And of course Salt Spring was closer to help than the other, better pond was.

So naturally he would want to drink here before he set off for safety.

Those men would surely expect him to do precisely what he was now doing.

All right, dammit.

That meant they were probably lying in wait for him. Right now. If they meant to kill him too—and surely they must; men who would murder once to protect themselves would have no compunction about murdering twice—then logically they would expect him to present himself for slaughter at Salt Spring. Just as the horses had presented themselves for slaughter at that other spring.

Dear Lord. That meant . . .

He wasn't two miles from Salt Spring now.

Oliver's face twisted in the anguish of indecision.

If he went forward to the water he knew was there in front of him . . . but if he turned back . . . on the other hand if he just were to walk straight on . . .

No, he didn't want to walk on. Not now. Not without some form of preparation and plan. He was already thirsty. And already tired and foot-sore. And that was just from walking ten, fifteen miles, whatever it was from that other spring. Another seventy miles? He was sure he could not manage that.

A Paul Bunyan type might. A jock or a woodsman, a hunter or a recreational survivalist. But Oliver knew good and well that he wouldn't be able to set straight off without water or food and expect to survive a desert crossing.

Oliver was realist enough to recognize his own limitations. He had neither superior knowledge of the desert nor exceptional physical strength and stamina. In this realm he would have been a babe in the woods. If there had been any woods, that is.

He had neither training nor equipment to help him cope with this situation.

And he had three men somewhere close by who presumably wanted him dead.

All in all, he conceded with a wry black humor, he would not at this moment be considered actuarially attractive.

He grunted aloud and sent a glare through the twilight toward Salt Spring.

"All right, damn you. I don't have experience and I don't have gear. But I'm not stupid. And you sons of bitches are going to have to do better than sit there and wait for me to come to you."

He turned and set off at a steady, deliberate gait back the way he had just come. He had no idea what he would do once he got there. But he would think of something, if only because he had to. It was either that or give up. And he was *not* going to give up.

"Damn you," he sent softly over his shoulder as he hiked stolidly away from the spring.

It was less gruesome at night. A little. Enough, he hoped. He stood at the edge of the spring-fed pond, surrounded by the carcasses of dead horses, and tried to steel himself to do what he knew had to be done.

While he had been walking, retracing his footsteps back to this awful place, Oliver had been thinking.

There wasn't any choice. None, at least, that he could think of.

He had to have water and he really ought to have food, and there was only one source of each of those commodities available to him at the moment. This pond. And the wild horses that lay dead beside it.

What he needed more than anything else, of course, was a way to carry water with him while he got the hell away from here and reported the crimes of those men.

Reluctantly he had realized that the wild horses could provide that for him too.

Oliver had no idea just where he remembered reading the idea or seeing it on a television documentary or whatever. Certainly it was the sort of fascinating, even if nausea-producing, tidbit of information that might be seen on PBS or the Discovery Channel or he might have read about it in conjunction with America's early Indians or some South American tribe or perhaps that modern Stone Age band of aborigines someone found in the Philippines a few years back.

Whatever the source of the information, Oliver was sure he remembered from somewhere that primitive man carried water in containers made from the intestines of large animals.

And if there was one item that Oliver did have in abundance right now, it was the ready availability of large animal carcasses.

He shuddered just from thinking about it—he didn't even buy chicken at the supermarket unless the bird was already thoroughly cleaned and disassembled—but he was going to have to revert to a sort of Stone Age primitivism himself and make canteens out of horse intestines.

Either that or allow those men to quite literally get away with murder.

And that was a price he would not agree to pay.

Oliver drank from the pond, then began casting about on the ground nearby for a stone he could use to cut the horses up with, something nice and sharp.

TWENTY-FOUR

HE SANK BACK in a state of near exhaustion and leaned against the stiff, hairy leg of the horse he'd been trying to cut open. The hard shin gouged into his lower back but he was just too tired to care right now.

Oliver felt close to tears from a combination of fatigue and frustration.

His hands and wrists and forearms ached, and his fingers were cramped and quite acutely painful from trying to hold the stone so he could slice and saw with the rough edge.

The stone "tool" was smaller than his palm, reasonably flat and—or so he'd thought to begin with—reasonably sharp.

Yet after more than an hour of intensive effort, he had yet to make the slightest break in the tough horsehide. All he'd managed to accomplish was to wear the hair away at the point where he was trying to cut.

This was maddening. Early man had used stone tools. *Inefficient* stone tools, Oliver was discovering.

Oh, eventually he might be able to wear through with the natural stone edge he'd been able to locate. But slice with it? Never.

It suddenly made sense to him that early man used stone hammers to fashion flint knives.

So where was some flint now that he needed it?

Oliver sighed and flexed his fingers to ease the cramping in them.

It wouldn't matter if there was flint nearby, he conceded. First, he wouldn't have been able to recognize it. And if he had, he wouldn't have known how to turn a chunk of native flint into a cutting tool.

It occurred to him that there had been talk about the cultural influences of modern life on those Philippine aborigines—the Tasaday, he thought they had called themselves—and how uncomfortable they would have been if forced into the modern world. Well, big news, Oliver thought bitterly. Culture shock is a two-way street, fellas. It was no easier for Oliver Bendix to make a Stone Age tool than it would have been for a Tasaday to drive an Oldsmobile.

He shifted position slightly so he could lean against the much softer

belly of the dead horse and spent a few moments running his hands up
and down the legs of his trousers, trying to ease some of the aching.

At least by now he no longer felt any reluctance to touch the dead
horses. Now he would have cheerfully ripped heads and legs asunder so he
could get to some of that meat before it all spoiled past the point of no
return and to get to a length of intestine he could use to make his canteens. Dammit.

Oliver tipped his head back and peered toward the distant stars, so clear
and bright and bold against the night sky here.

Those same stars were seen by city dweller and Tasaday alike. But
modern man could learn about them. What he did not know, he could
seek out. Did the Tasaday even think about stars, clouds . . . tools?

Oliver was capable of thought. He had knowledge that the Tasaday
could not conceive, could not imagine.

But a Tasaday teenager could very likely have a dead horse butchered in
no time at all, while Oliver's superior knowledge and experience were
useless to him in this particular circumstance.

Oliver decided he had just invented a new concept. There was such a
thing as situational ethics? Hah! Now there was Situational Superiority.

Call it the Bendix Concept, he thought. The Bendix Concept of Situational Superiority. Or, the thesis in abbreviation: My flint beats the hell
outa your knife when you ain't got no knife.

Jesus!

He rubbed his eyes, no longer even concerned by how filthy his hands
must be, and tried to come up with some substitute for a knife that a
normal, non-Tasaday human being from modern-day San Francisco could
devise from the materials at hand.

There was nothing in his pockets that would do any good. Not unless
there was some place handy where he could buy a knife. He had money
enough to buy a dandy knife. Whoopee. He sighed.

He'd tried sawing with a plastic gasoline-company credit card. He
might as well have tried biting through the incredibly tough horsehide.

In fact, he had tried to bite a hole in the hide. He'd tried to bite
through at an "easy" spot, an ear. That wasn't any more possible than
cutting with a credit card turned out to be.

What he needed, dammit, was metal. Sharp, rigid metal.

His windbreaker had a zipper. The zipper was made of plastic, some
miracle poly-whatsis. And it didn't work as a saw. He knew because he'd
tried that too.

What he needed was *metal.*

So why in hell hadn't he at least been wearing a belt this morning? Belt buckles are made of metal. His lousy belt was in the car. Along with the kitchen knives and everything else that would have been useful. Wherever all that stuff was.

The only metal he owned right now would consist of the one button and several rivets on his blue jeans—and he sure didn't think he could turn any of those into a knife—and the two 35-millimeter film cartridges in his jacket pocket.

The film cans would probably be too flimsy to do him any good. Even if he decided to sacrifice one of them. God, he hoped it wouldn't come to that.

Please.

But he had to have water if he expected to survive. And he had to survive if those men were ever to be punished and the wild horses saved.

And he had to have metal if he hoped to fashion water containers.

Jesus.

He drew one of the film cartridges out and looked at it. It was difficult to see in the dark. So small, though. Would it do any good even if he did decide to break one apart and try to use the metal?

Not that a knife has to be large, of course. Any tiny knife would do. Just to get a cut started in the tough, thick hide. He was sure he would be able to saw along the grain of the hide if he could once get a cut begun. Even an awl, a lance, little more than a chisel, a . . .

Oliver grunted. Metal. What he needed was metal? Why, he knew where there was some metal to be had. Of course he did. There was one thing—no, a whole bunch of metal items, he bet—that he was sure those men wouldn't have gathered up and taken away with them.

He bounced to his feet, full of energy and enthusiasm again, and ran toward the hill. If only he could remember now where those men had been when they started shooting at the horses . . .

IT WAS EASIER TO WORK now that he could see. Oliver regretted the time he'd lost to sleep. He felt guilty about sleeping when he should have been doing something instead. But there hadn't been any point in pressing his search through the night. He'd needed light to see by so he could find the metal he needed.

Now he had as much as he could ever want.

The brass cartridge cases that those men's guns ejected onto the ground littered the hiding place where they'd lain in wait for the wild horse herd.

There were dozens of the dull yellow metal things scattered on the ground here.

He picked up a handful and then another just to be sure and stuffed them into a pocket.

Each empty cartridge case—the bullets and whatever else they once contained were gone now and the expended casing smelled of a sour, acrid chemical substance—was rounded, several inches long, tapering slightly from the big end to an abrupt bottleneck and then small and straight for another quarter inch or a little more.

Neither the shape nor the odd, cryptic markings on the flat base meant anything to him. But the fact that the empty cases were made of an easily malleable metal certainly did.

He selected two good-sized rocks and laid the small end of one of the cartridge cases onto one of them. Using the second rock as a hammer stone, Oliver was able to flatten the open mouth of the cartridge casing with only a few hard whacks. He pounded the metal vigorously for a few moments, pressing the brass halves so tight together that they might as well have been one piece.

Next he used a piece of rough sandstone to function as a grinder or whetstone. He rubbed the flattened end of the cartridge against the rock, the relatively soft brass material taking an edge quickly.

An edge so easily formed would not be durable, he was sure. But that was no problem. It could easily be restored too. And if this "knife" got used up? Why, he could make another just as easily as he'd made this one.

Oliver felt an inordinate sense of accomplishment over this small bit of progress as he took his crude knife—a Tasaday would probably have been impressed by it even if no one else would—and bent once again over the carcass of the half-grown colt he'd been trying to butcher.

Now, by damn, he could get on with things.

OLIVER SPUN AWAY from his labor and draped himself over the hindquarters of the dead horse.

He hung there retching until his belly ached from the dry heaves and the bile in his mouth was a bitter acid on his tongue.

This was worse than he had imagined it could be. Awful.

The stomach cavity of the dead animal stank, and every slight movement of the carcass vented gases and produced wet, sloppy, gurgling noises.

He didn't know, or want to know, what all the organs were. He would have been much happier if he'd never seen any of them.

At least the intestines were obvious. If ugly. They were long and snake-like and curiously sticky to the touch, not at all the wet and slimy feel that he might have expected. The intestine was a streaked and mottled white-gray that stood out in sharp contrast to the wet purple of the other . . . things . . . that were inside the smelly body.

He cut through a section of intestine and, even though there was nothing left inside him to throw up, gagged again at the stench that rose from this new opening. A damp green and gray substance oozed out onto his hands.

He was going to have to *drink* out of this?

It was too much. He would rather . . .

Oliver's expression turned steely cold. He would *not* rather die than drink from a horse intestine.

"I'd rather die than" . . . whatever. Sure. Easily said when the truth was not so dire. Not so easy as a genuine commitment to perish.

He blinked sweat out of his eyes, wiped his lips with the back of a gritty, blood-grimed wrist.

And leaned forward, reaching deep inside the dead animal to pull more yards of pale gut out onto the ground so he could cut the intestines free.

He ignored the smell that surrounded him and tried to ignore as well the sounds the moving organs made as they tumbled over themselves in a pile of yuck.

No, dammit, he was *not* going to be dissuaded.

He would hack and cut. Squeeze lengths of gut empty and wash them —thank goodness there was plenty of water available for that—and fashion his water bags out of the pieces. There was plenty of stout horsehair to be chopped from the tails of the dead horses. He could use that to close off the ends of the horse-gut canteens. And he could cut meat as well.

The meat—it was a darker red than the beef you saw wrapped in plastic on a supermarket counter—would probably be palatable if he allowed it to sun dry a little while first.

If it wasn't, well, he would just damned well eat it anyway. His stomach had been emptied of the little it had held. He needed all the energy he could muster for the hike overland to civilization and safety. And he would damned well do whatever it was that he had to do in order to survive. It was just as simple as that.

He would *not* be denied, dammit.

He would pack water and meat and walk right on out of here. Away from this desert and away from the people who killed JoLynn, and he would see to it that her murderers were put where they couldn't hurt anyone else, not ever again.

If he could just get control over the annoying damned sobbing that was shooting tremors through his body, that is. And if he could just for a little while keep his eyes from blurring over like they were.

Oliver dragged at the pale gut with one hand and slashed out with the makeshift brass knife with the other and cursed tonelessly, monotonously while he worked.

THE MEAT really wasn't that bad—he tried to think of it as a sort of chunky steak tartare—but the mere thought of the water bags was enough to make his stomach heave.

After all, he had seen and, more to the point, smelled what came out of those sections of gut when he washed them. Now he was expected to drink out of them? What if the water tasted like the intestines smelled? He sighed. He would do what he had to do. He supposed.

He held another piece of gut underwater and swished it around. Experience had shown that the best way to do this seemed to be to cut the bags short, not more than a foot and a half long, with one end already tied closed, then fill them underwater and get the first few wraps of horsehair made and the first few knots tied in place there underneath the pond surface before lifting them out again to finish off the job.

The best that could be said about the resulting sacks was that they did indeed hold water.

But then, that was really all that was important about them, wasn't it?

Well, they did work. But he didn't like them. Or find them to be convenient.

The makeshift water bags felt something like water balloons made from condoms but without the stretch of latex. They were that slippery and awkward to handle, and every time he touched one, Oliver was afraid he was going to puncture or break it.

His first experiments proved that it would not be possible to carry a reasonable supply of water in one or two large bags. Aside from the difficulty of handling a gut container of any size, it would have been impossible to tie a bag end closed again once it was opened. He'd had to conclude that the best procedure here would be to carry a bunch of small sacks and open one—a simple puncture would do—each time he wanted to drink. No, dang it, each time he *needed* to drink. He was going to have to be careful about differentiating between those two.

What he'd decided to do was to carry as many of the small bags as he could manage, wrapping them in his jacket so it would be possible to transport them without having to juggle them. He used his bootlaces to tie off the waist and neck of the jacket, tied the sleeves together and used the zipper opening at the throat to admit his water bags.

The strips of raw meat could be carried in pockets or simply shoved inside his shirt. The meat would spoil soon, he suspected, so he wouldn't bother trying to carry very much of it. Certainly he didn't want to take time to try to dry it before he left the pond. Eventually those men were bound to come looking for him.

Besides, the raw horse meat wasn't so palatable that he wanted to eat any more of it than necessary. Just enough to keep his strength up and let him move along. No more.

The preparations went quickly once he had his tools and had worked out the best methods. Or if not strictly "best" methods, then at the very least functional and therefore acceptable ones. If a Tasaday might have done better, well, so what. All Oliver cared about was getting it done.

And he was discovering that today he was in a fairly optimistic state of mind for the first time since . . . well, for the first time since. He made himself let it go at that. There was no time now for grief.

He filled another water bag, tied it shut and stuffed it inside his jacket with the others.

TWENTY-FIVE

JIM'S JAW shuddered and jerked as he tried to stifle a yawn behind clenched teeth. He was sleepy and he was peeved. Mostly he was frustrated. The city son of a bitch wasn't cooperating. The guy should have been here hours ago. It would soon be dawn but there was no sign of him yet. Surely he couldn't be so stupid that he would try to walk all the way from Coffee Hill with no water. Or so smart that he would know where to look for the small seeps and springs that thoroughly watered this seemingly dry country.

No, dammit. Jim rejected that idea completely. The city fellow had come out here with not so much as a map in the car. Besides what him and the woman said when they talked to them that time, Jim himself had looked inside the car. The only sort of map he'd found was a dog-eared and beat up Rand McNally road atlas. And it'd been years out of date. Anybody dumb enough to head into seriously empty country with no more preparation than that couldn't know much of anything else.

So where was he?

Jim hunched his shoulders against the night chill and wondered if there was any point to sitting here being so miserable when the city man obviously wasn't coming.

Not until after dawn, Jim decided, trying to work it out nice and logical and reasonable. Probably the man had been too scared to move away from Coffee Hill yesterday. Too scared and too confused. So now he'd have all night to think about it and realize he had to move along. Come daybreak he would likely drink himself full at the spring there and then start for Salt Spring. That was where Jim'd miscalculated before, he decided. He'd given the city fellow too much credit for being able to think things through and then start doing them. So it would take him and JayJay a little bit longer to take care of things than they'd thought.

He grunted, satisfied that that was the way things surely must be happening, and reached into his shirt pocket for a Chesterfield.

Oh, he would go right on keeping watch through the night. But now that he no longer believed the city man was fixing to show up until past daybreak there was no point in making himself suffer while he waited and watched. He could go ahead and have a smoke. He'd just be careful not to let the fire show.

He sat up straight and craned his neck for a long, careful look around the horizon, then tucked down low and cupped both hands close around cigarette and lighter. The flame was brief and blindingly intense to eyes long since adjusted to the dark. Lordy, but the smoke did taste good, though. He pulled it deep into his lungs, savoring the taste of it and the sense of ease it gave, and sat up again with the glowing tip still hidden inside a cupped palm. He could feel the heat from the coal on chilled flesh.

"What the hell're you doing?" JayJay stirred and came up onto an elbow.

"I thought you was asleep," Jim countered.

"Can't sleep." JayJay had turned over the watch to Jim at least an hour ago. "I asked you what you're doing there."

"Smoking, what d'you think?"

JayJay didn't bother pointing out the obvious, which was that Jim had forbidden him to smoke while he was on watch. He only sat upright on his blankets and reached for his own pack of Marlboros.

Jim thought about warning him against a show of light, then realized he might better stay off JayJay's back.

JayJay ducked underneath the blankets and came back up again a moment later with a cigarette cupped in his hand and a wreath of smoke pale around his head. "Jeez, that tastes good."

"Yeah, don't it. Look, the, uh, reason I figured it was okay to smoke, long as we're careful, that is. . . ." He explained to JayJay the way he'd worked it out about the city fellow.

"That sounds like it could be," JayJay agreed.

"Once he has light to see by, he oughta come right to us," Jim speculated.

"What if he gets lost?"

"He has to show up one place or the other. These are the only places he knows where he can get water."

"What if he gets lost and trips over some other spring?"

"He isn't gonna do anything like that, JayJay."

"You don't know that."

"He isn't going to. I'm telling you he isn't."

They sat in silence for a bit, both smoking, both hunched deep inside their blankets, neither paying very much attention to the country they were supposed to be watching.

"I didn't mean to shoot that woman," JayJay said after a while.

"I know that." Jim reached for another Chesterfield to light off the first one so he could keep one going without having to flash the lighter again.

"I swear that I didn't."

"Go to sleep, JayJay. I'll wake you up at dawn."

"Right." But JayJay didn't make any attempt to lie down in search of sleep. He sat where he was and chain-smoked while Jim pretended to resume their vigil.

"WE SHOULD OF TOLD BILL to bring us out some groceries," JayJay complained. Breakfast for each of them was a sandwich that had had several days to dry out and turn hard. And there weren't many sandwiches left. If they stayed out much longer, they would be down to rat cheese and Ritz crackers. Less if they hadn't finished what they needed to do by, say, two more days, Jim calculated.

"We'll be all right."

"You don't think Bill will tell anybody . . ." JayJay caught the look of warning in Jim's eyes and let the question tail off into silence. JayJay coughed into his fist and took another bite of his sandwich.

"You look like hell, JayJay. Didn't you get *any* sleep last night?"

"Yeah. O' course I did."

"All right. You just look like you had a bad night, that's all."

"Shit, Jim, o' course I had a bad night. Every time I closed my damn eyes I kept seeing that dead woman. All that blood. An' her eyes . . . I never seen anything like her eyes before. Empty. Staring, kinda. I don't know."

"It wasn't your fault, JayJay. We all know that. It wasn't but an accident."

"Yeah." He chewed slowly, his eyes unfocused and almost as vacant as the dead woman's had been.

The dead woman. They kept calling her that, Jim reflected. She'd had a name, though. He wondered what it was. He could have looked in her purse when he had the chance, but he hadn't wanted to touch anything more inside that station wagon than he'd absolutely had to. Now he almost wished that he had so they would know what to call her other than The Dead Woman. Jeez, that sounded cold. He thought about saying something to JayJay about that, even had his mouth open to do it, then clamped his lips shut again. JayJay really did look like hell this morning. Haggard and kind of jumpy. Better, Jim decided, to let him try and forget about the dead woman—there, he was doing it again—instead of bringing it up over and over and making JayJay think about it more.

"Christ, I wish I had a drink," JayJay complained.

Jim reached for the pot of water he'd carried up from the spring. He hadn't wanted to build a fire to make coffee with, but the pot was handy for carrying water in anyway.

"No, dammit, I mean a *drink.*"

"Oh. We'll have to wait till we get home for that."

"Yeah." JayJay made a face. "I sure wish that son of a bitch'd show up soon so we can be done with this."

"Uh-huh."

"You, uh, figure to carry him all the way to where the car and the woman are?"

"Wander all over hell an' back with a corpse? No thanks. We'll bury him where he falls."

"I never . . . I guess this ain't what I would've thought it'd be like. Not that I ever did think about it, that is. But if I had. You know?"

"Uh-huh. I know."

"I don't know how many times I've got in fights an' thought, hey, I'm gonna kill that so-and-so. But I never really wanted to *kill* nobody. Now here I've already gone and killed one and 'm fixing to do it again. Funny, isn't it?"

"Hilarious," Jim said in a dry voice. "I wish you'd quit talking about it, JayJay. It isn't like we got any choice."

"I know we don't. I mean, I'm the one that's being protected here. I'm the one killed that woman an' could go to jail for it. I know what you're doing for me, an' I appreciate it. I really do. It's just . . . I don't know. Weird."

"I know."

"I never shot nobody before yesterday. Now I'm gonna do it a second time. Deliberate too." He picked up his Ruger and peered at it. "Draw down on that son of a bitch and . . . pow. Drill 'im. What d'you think, Jim? Try for a nice clean head shot? Or just start busting him? Heart/lung shot like you'd try for on a deer? Awful easy to gut-shoot him if—"

"Jesus Christ, JayJay, shut the ▓▓▓▓ up, will you?"

"Sorry." JayJay laid the carbine down again and picked up the plastic wrap that had been on the sandwich he'd carried from home. He wadded the bit of trash into a tight ball and slipped it into a pocket.

Jim shook his head. He wished to hell JayJay would start thinking about something else for a change. Doing the man was going to be bad enough. Jim didn't want to have to talk about it too.

"What color would you say that woman's eyes were, Jim?"

"JayJay!"

"Sorry."

TWENTY-SIX

"I DON'T KNOW, dammit. You think this guy is even more of a pussy than most city creeps? You think he could be holed up beside that pond at Coffee Hill waiting for somebody to come rescue him?" Jim was becoming quite frankly worried. It was near noon and the city man still hadn't shown up at Salt Spring like they'd expected. Like they had pretty much counted on, in fact.

JayJay didn't answer. Jim nattered on into the silence anyway. "I'm beginning to think we screwed up yesterday. We should've chased after him right away, first thing after we saw that woman was dead. You know?" Still JayJay didn't say anything.

Jim took a deep breath. This time he didn't go ahead and say what he was thinking. In spite of everything it was still a damn good thing that they hadn't gone looking for the city man right away. Because this way it was still possible to pretend that Bill didn't know what him and JayJay were doing out here.

What was it they called that on the TV news reports when it happened with the politicians? Jim had to think about it for a minute before he could bring it to mind. Deniability, that was it. You could know something and everybody know that you pretty much had to know it. But no-damn-body could actually up and prove what was inside another man's mind. So if you said you didn't know something, then nobody could prove different so long as you hadn't put stuff down on paper. That was what they called deniability.

Well, this way Bill had deniability. This way Bill didn't actually know what the deal was with the man. Just that JayJay shot the woman by accident and that Jim and JayJay didn't ride home at the same time as Bill did. Beyond that, well, Bill might guess and wonder but he didn't actually *know* anything.

Sure would have been easier if they'd found and shot the man yesterday, though. Jim was starting to get worried about the guy. He should have showed up here before now. There'd been more than enough time for him to walk down from Coffee, even after figuring in extra time for the city man to cry and cringe and gnash his teeth and whatever.

If they'd got on it right away yesterday, though, they could have just scouted around a bit and found him and done what had to be done.

Water under the damned bridge, of course. Yesterday they'd all been fussed up about the woman dying and wanting to hide all the traces of that. None of them would've been thinking too clear right there at first. And anyhow Jim had been wanting to get Bill away from whatever else had to be done. If they'd taken care of this yesterday they wouldn't have had deniability to protect Bill and the rest of the family just in case things somehow went to hell.

So he didn't actually regret not looking for the man until later.

But he surely did wish the guy would hurry up and show himself here now.

"You don't think he'd try and walk out without stopping here for water, do you? I mean, hell, it wouldn't be so bad if he was fool enough to thirst to death for us or something. But I wouldn't want t' count on that. Wouldn't believe it, neither, unless we actual see him laying dead on the ground, for that matter." Jim reached for a Chesterfield. He only had a few left in this pack and two, maybe three more packs in his saddlebags. He would have to start cutting back if the guy didn't show himself pretty soon. Jim hated the thought of running out of cigarettes even worse than he hated the thought of having to cut back on his smoking. It would be far better indeed to run out of food. That would be a minor annoyance. But cigarettes? That would be bad.

"What I think," Jim said, "is that if he doesn't show up somewhere in sight within the next half hour or so, I'll have to leave you here by yourself to watch for him an' ride over to Coffee. Just to check and see if he's there waitin' to be gobbled up. You know?"

Still JayJay didn't say anything. Jim gave the hired man a glance and discovered that JayJay was sitting there staring blindly off toward the north with a vacant, empty look about him.

"Hey!" Jim had to repeat it several times before he finally got JayJay's attention. "I said I'm fixing to ride over to Coffee Hill if that guy don't show up here soon," he said in a voice that was louder and more distinct than normal. There wasn't any point in repeating all that other crap, he decided. JayJay was acting confused enough right now without giving him other stuff to think of.

"I'm not waiting anymore, dammit. I'm gonna ride over there and see if that guy is holed up scared and hoping for the cavalry to come riding in." Jim stood and brushed off the seat of his britches.

"JayJay? D'you hear me, JayJay?"

JayJay turned his head finally and gave Jim a blank sort of look.

It was obvious that JayJay hadn't been paying attention, so Jim had to say it all again.

"You watch here while I'm gone, right?"

JayJay nodded.

"If the guy shows up . . . you do what you think best, hear? I won't mind if you want t' just hold on to him till I get back. You know what I'm telling you?"

JayJay shrugged and stared sightlessly off toward Idaho.

Fat damn chance JayJay would see or do anything while he was gone, Jim thought with more than a touch of irritation. The city fella could walk in and drink his belly full and walk right out again and it wasn't for certain that old JayJay would so much as notice, the way he was acting right now.

Sometimes it seemed like Jim had to do every damned thing himself.

"I won't be gone long."

JayJay didn't answer. He reached into a shirt pocket and pulled out a Marlboro and fired it up, but he never once took his eyes off the horizon up toward Idaho.

Jim grunted and walked down to the seep. This spring wasn't near as good as the one at Coffee Hill, so he didn't drink from it. He would wait and drink there. But he did want to take a look and refresh himself on just what tracks were already there.

It wasn't that he honestly and literally believed that JayJay could miss seeing the city man if the guy marched in and helped himself to a drink. Or see him and not do anything about it. But . . . well . . . Jim wanted to be able to check things for himself when he got back. That was all.

Satisfied that he would recognize any new tracks around the Salt Spring pond, Jim walked on down to where the horses were picketed.

Figuring out what to do with the horses was one of the bad things about laying in wait—all right, laying an ambush, that was what it really was—for somebody at Salt Spring. The country all around was so flat and the vegetation so low that you either had to know which way the quarry would be approaching from and put your animals on the other side of the hill from there to keep them hidden from view or you had to leave your transportation a mile or better away from the spring.

Naturally him and JayJay had chosen to stake the horses on the south side of the hill, figuring the city guy had to come straight down from Coffee to the north. They sure as hell weren't going to walk afoot for two miles every time the horses had to be seen to.

Maybe that had been their mistake though, Jim was concluding now. Maybe the city guy had gotten himself half-lost—lost was something Jim didn't fully understand, not out in open country or in the mountains, where everything was logical and orderly, although he could accept the idea of somebody getting confused in a maze like city streets made; still, it was supposed to be entirely possible for city dwellers to get themselves lost, there were hunters who managed it 'most every year—and come onto Salt Spring from the side. The guy might have spotted the horses and figured there was an ambush and shied away.

That was a possibility they would have to take into account. First check at Coffee Hill, of course. Then . . . well, Jim didn't exactly know what would happen if the guy wasn't at either Coffee Hill or Salt Spring.

It wasn't like a man on foot could be tracked in country like this. You could track a horse or cow. Sometimes. If the soil and moisture conditions were right for it. You could track a pickup truck nearly always. But one guy on foot? Jim didn't think so.

No, dammit, if the city man wasn't at Coffee Hill and didn't show himself at Salt Spring, well, they would just have to start trying to guess at his travel and cast about for him. Try to spot him somewhere out on the grass and ride him down.

If they could once lay eyes on the guy, he was done for. There wasn't any way he could outrun two good horses and two good carbines.

But first, unfortunately, they had to get that one good look at him.

Jim took a little time to lead both horses over to the seep so they could drink. Then he returned JayJay's animal to the picket rope and saddled his own horse.

At least they didn't have to worry about feed for the horses. Jim was down to about a quart of grain for the red horse, and JayJay probably had the same for his brown. When the hot feed ran out, though, the horses could make their own living off the graze that this country was all about. They would be fine no matter how long this took.

Jim snugged his cinches tight, took a handful of mane and slouched onto the seat. Damn but it felt good to be horseback again after laying around waiting for so long. He wished he'd gone and done this hours ago.

He bumped the dun into a jog and pointed it north.

JIM LET OUT A STRING of cuss words that would have made a whore blush.

He stepped down off his saddle, the red horse fidgeting and unhappy with all the smell of death around here, and hobbled the dun so he could leave it at a distance while he took a closer look at the mess beside the pond.

It might not be possible to track someone across open grassland, but it didn't take any kind of expert to read sign that was pressed into soft mud. Or to see plain facts and understand them.

The damned city guy had gone and stocked up with food and water to carry with him.

Horse-gut canteens. Jesus. That was a sickening notion. Horse guts. A man who would drink out of raw horse guts couldn't hardly be human.

That was for sure what the guy had done, though. Jim might not have figured out why the colt had been disemboweled except for the discards that were laying on the bank. Water bags that'd leaked or something.

Washed out, he noticed, and tied with horsehair.

And some meat taken from one of the haunches too.

Damn!

So now the guy didn't need to stop at Salt Spring. Not at all.

No wonder he hadn't come along and stumbled into the ambush.

Jim bent down and picked up one of the discarded sections of gut. It had one end tied off, but there was a cut or tear in the side of the tough membrane where water would have leaked out.

He looked it over close, then tipped his head back and squinted toward the sun.

It was just past noon now, so the sun was high. Bright and clear, the day cool but comfortable. The temperatures would get at least into the fifties by mid-afternoon, maybe tickle the sixties even.

Jim felt of the piece of gut with both hands. It was tacky to the touch. Limp. The sides of the bag kind of glued together where they touched while they dried.

But not very dry. That was the thing.

Not all that very dry, no sir.

Jim grunted, much more satisfied than he'd been when he first saw what'd been going on here.

It had taken the city man a long time to get this done.

That was why there hadn't been any sign of him last night or this morning. He'd been up here butchering the dead colt and fixing himself up to travel.

Well, now he was traveling.

But he didn't have all that much of a head start.

Jim was positive about that.

This piece of gut was still much too moist to have been laying in the sun more than—it was only a guess but a reasonably well educated one—call it not more than two hours for sure and maybe less than that. Maybe less than one hour.

So the city man was within . . . six miles? Six miles away from here at the very most, Jim decided. More likely within four miles of where Jim was standing right this minute.

Four miles away and having to head south to reach the only help he'd know about?

Easy pickings, Jim decided, feeling much better now that he had a handle on knowing what was going on.

With no more of a head start than that and his general direction of travel locked in, why, there was no way the city fella could get away now. The only real question was how long it would take to wrap him up and put him underground.

Then they could all just forget that any of this ever happened.

Jim tossed the limp, sticky scrap of horse gut down, bent to wash his hands at the edge of the pond and then walked around to the far side of the water so he could drink before returning to his mount.

TWENTY-SEVEN

THE POUNDING in his chest was so hard he could feel it, even hear it sort of in his ears as well.

Oliver lay spread-eagled on the hard ground, immediately in front of him the bundled jacket holding his meat and water bags.

It wasn't that he thought he could hide behind the lumpy jacket. But he felt better knowing there was at least that much obstruction between him and the man on the horse.

The horseman was riding from south to north, pretty much on a line from Salt Spring to the bigger hill that Oliver was privately coming to think of as the Dead Horse Place. It was easier for him to think of the horses having died there than it was to think about . . . the other things that had happened there. He had no time to think about those things now. That would all come later. If he lived long enough to have a later existence, that is.

For one awful moment when he'd first seen the horseman coming toward him, Oliver had been elated. He'd very nearly waved and shouted to try to attract the man's attention. His first, foolish thought was that there was another human in sight and therefore he was saved.

Then he'd realized. Any person he saw out here was almost certain to be one of the men who had murdered JoLynn.

Barely in time he remembered to lie flat on the ground and will himself into immobility.

He felt silly doing that. After all, he was lying there in plain sight. Anyone who bothered to look must surely see him.

Yet the horseman was riding right on past.

It really must have been true, then.

Oliver was certainly no expert on the ways of the wilderness. But he had read a great deal. He—they, he and JoLynn together—belonged to the Sierra Club, the National Geographic Society, to half a dozen other organizations and causes just as worthwhile. He had read articles about how to film or photograph wildlife. The consensus was that camouflage was preferred but was not entirely necessary. That an eye is drawn more to movement than to shape or color, so it is possible to hide oneself in plain sight if you simply remain very, very still.

Oliver was putting that advice to the test now, for his clothing was far from blending into the background. The dark blue jacket contrasted sharply with the pale tan colors of the desert floor. His checked flannel shirt and faded jeans were no better a match for the surroundings provided by nature.

Yet the horseman hadn't seen.

Right now the only thing of Oliver's that was moving was his chest. And if he could have thought of a way to stop himself from breathing for a while he would have done that too.

He squeezed his eyes closed to keep himself from blinking or turning his head to follow the movements of the rider. Then couldn't stand not knowing what was happening and opened them again.

The horse and rider were nearly past.

They were, he judged, not more than three football-field lengths away. Perhaps closer than that; he had never been any good at judging distances.

The horse certainly moved slowly. Oliver felt as if he'd been lying here forever.

However long it had been, it was long enough that he could feel bugs crawling on him. He began to sweat. Which probably would only attract more insects. They would want the salty moisture of the sweat. He hoped the ants were not stinging ants. Even if they were, though, he wouldn't dare move and give himself away. Better to be stung by an ant than a bullet.

Lordy, why oh why didn't that horse go any faster? In all the old movies, cowboys went everywhere at a gallop. So why was this bucolic bastard any different?

It occurred to Oliver that of course this man was different. Those cowboys were trying to go somewhere. This one was trying to find and murder someone. Of course he would go slowly so he could keep watch. Oliver shuddered and squeezed his eyes closed again for a moment, then popped them open.

Not that he knew what he might do if he was spotted.

Nothing, probably. He couldn't outrun a horse. Or a bullet. He had no way to defend himself.

Would he defend himself if he could?

He realized that he quite honestly did not know.

All his life Oliver had believed that violence was abhorrent. Killing was wrong. Killing animals was wrong and killing human beings would be even worse. He believed that so strongly that he had differed with JoLynn about her pro-choice abortion stance just on the possibility that the pro-lifers were right and life begins at conception.

But now . . .

Those three men had already committed one murder. Now they were willfully attempting to commit another.

Oliver did not want them to murder him. But even more than his own desire to continue living, he wanted those men punished for murdering JoLynn. And he wanted them stopped from slaughtering the wild horses too.

So if it ever should happen to come down to it—not that it ever could, of course—but if it should ever happen to come down to a question of him allowing them to kill him or else him killing them first . . .

He didn't know. He did not honestly know if his lifelong convictions would hold up. Or if he would abandon his scruples in favor of self-interest.

What he suspected, but truly did not want ever to confirm, was that the choice would lie in favor of violence.

Self-defense. Justifiable in the eyes of the law perhaps. But violence nonetheless and therefore wrong.

Oliver squeezed his eyes closed again, this time almost forgetting the horseman who had by now ridden completely past without seeing him lying there with nothing but short grasses for cover. He was trembling and close to tears. His entire life had been spent in the belief that good was better than evil, that understanding was better than violence, that reason could always prevail over savagery.

Why, why, *why* were these sons of bitches trying to destroy him like this?

Wasn't it bad enough that they murdered JoLynn and wanted to murder him too? Surely they didn't have to tear his beliefs apart on top of everything else.

Unable even to run and hide until the horseman rode out of sight, Oliver lay there and gave in to the miseries of tearful self-pity while the sun began the downward side of its arc toward the distant mountains.

OLIVER'S FEET AND LEGS hurt from the hours upon hours of steady travel. His arms and shoulders and back hurt from having to carry the awkward bundle of water bags and meat scraps. His eyes burned from the constant worried searching that made him continuously scan the countryside all around, front and back, horizon to horizon, lest one of the men see him first. His only defense, he knew, was to see them before they could spot him. And surely they would have the advantage of having binoculars with them. Oliver's own binoculars were God knew where. Possibly even in the hands of the men who were looking for him.

Oliver was hurting, basically, from one end to the other.

And all in all he felt pretty damned good.

The point was, it was nearly dusk and he had managed to escape detection thus far. He was alive. And that truly seemed worth celebrating under these circumstances.

If he could just hold on to that status until nightfall, keep it a serendipitous status quo for just that long, he was fairly sure he could get through the night alive.

And if he could keep moving for another twelve hours, why, almost anything would be possible. Even that he might actually, honestly, genuinely escape intact from this desert hell.

Oliver felt quite good just from thinking about it. His pains and aches diminished. They seemed really quite insignificant anyway. His shoulders straightened and his jaw became firm. His stride lengthened, and he even began to whistle just a little. After all, there was no one close enough to hear. There couldn't be. And now he believed that there wouldn't be.

Oliver felt so jaunty and encouraged that he very nearly died.

He very nearly wasn't paying attention to his surroundings as the sun began its final descent behind the distant peaks.

It was luck rather than caution that let him see a brief flicker of light from a far-off hilltop. A reflection, probably, gone in an instant. But there, bright, unmistakable. A last ray of sunlight striking glass or polished metal. Then gone again.

Oliver whimpered and dropped into a crouch.

There was nothing here to hide behind.

If the person over there had binoculars . . . was looking in this direction . . . it might even have been the lenses of binoculars that reflected the light . . . or merely a bit of native mica? There was no way to know. And the penalty of a wrong guess too severe to encourage a gamble.

He swallowed, his throat gone tight and dry, and let himself down into a prone position with the water sacks by his head. He curled unconsciously into a loose fetal position and tried to will himself into total motionlessness.

Dark.

If he could just stay here unseen until it was fully dark, he could get up and move again.

In the meantime he should rest while he could.

He would assume he hadn't been seen. He had to assume that. And pray for it.

Otherwise . . .

There was no point in thinking about otherwise.

He would just have to stay right here and wait for the protection of the night. Then he could move again. He swallowed once more, although the lump that was lodged in his throat was not the sort that could be swallowed or washed away. And he waited.

THERE WERE A GOOD MANY ADVANTAGES to the night. And perhaps one of the biggest was that he couldn't see what he was drinking. It was bad enough that he had to taste what was in it.

He used a cartridge-case knife to prick an opening in the end of a bag, made a sour face and pressed his mouth to the hole before too much of the precious water was lost.

After riding half a day inside the bags, the water was the temperature of spit. The taste of it was something like the scent of alfalfa tablets. Damp alfalfa tablets gone musty and rotten, maybe.

He deliberately tried to equate it with alfalfa, though, because alfalfa tablets—definitely the pressed tablet, not the sprout—at least were a known and acceptable substance, and the idea therefore lent a measure of palatability to an otherwise disgusting event. Oliver concentrated his thoughts on the remembered tastes and textures of those tablets. The natural vitamin/fiber/protein source had had a run of popularity a while back, less successful than dried kelp or alfalfa sprouts. The scents and flavors came back to him now as he drank from a length of horse intestine.

There was a subtext of flavors that he carefully refused to identify or think about.

He drank every last drop from that bag and considered whether he should open a second. Better not to, he decided. He would wait a little longer.

Instead he groped inside the shell of his makeshift pack and found a bit of meat.

One whiff of it proved it was even better that he couldn't see this than that he couldn't see the water containers.

The horse meat had already begun to taint and spoil, he realized. It was rotting with amazing speed. But then, the process was probably accelerated by the moist environment he was carrying it in. The water bags naturally seeped fluids to some extent. The inside of the jacket would be hot and damp.

Oliver regretted the thought of losing his supply of meat but knew he would be better off doing without solid food for however long this took than risking food poisoning.

He decided he probably could safely eat his fill tonight. Anything he did not consume immediately, though, would have to be abandoned.

He ran his hands through the moist, wormlike lengths of gut to hunt down bits of meat, pulling out all he could locate and forcing himself to eat them. There was no telling when he would have a chance to eat again.

And he was not going to throw up, dammit. He simply would not. No matter what.

Oliver was grimly determined that he would do whatever he had to do here and now to insure his own survival.

No matter *what* that required of him.

IT WASN'T AS SCARY being alone in the desert at night as he'd expected. Perhaps that had to do with knowing that there was no animal alive that was as sure a threat to him now as the men who were also in this desert. Whatever the cause, though, even the sharp yip-yap of the coyotes wasn't frightening him very much. He was able to keep right on with hardly a missed step.

Would a coyote attack a man, anyway? Oliver wasn't really sure. His humor of the moment was such that he would pick up a stone and fight back if one tried. He was sure about that.

So far, anyway, the coyotes all sounded distant and more lonesome than threatening.

Lonely was something Oliver suspected he was going to learn about.

But not now. Not right now, dammit. He had no time to think about that right now.

He moved along at a slow but steady pace. Much quicker than he'd hoped to accomplish, actually. He had always assumed that a flashlight or lantern or some such artificial aid would be necessary to walk across unknown terrain at night.

In the city one gets used to having headlights and street lamps outdoors, electric lights and bright, bright television screens indoors. Oliver hadn't had any idea there could be so much natural light outdoors in the middle of the night.

Why, it was considerably brighter than he had ever expected, ten times as bright, twenty. Starlight alone was enough to let him see fairly well, once his eyes became adjusted to this startlingly complete absence of artificial light. Moonlight, once it became available, seemed almost too bright, almost dangerously bright if any of those men were close by and alert. Oliver actually found himself wishing for clouds to obscure the moon and make the darkness all that much more protective.

He trudged on, shifting his water bundle from one aching arm to the other and then back again. The burden seemed little lighter now than it had been when he started. That was good in that it meant he still had a good supply of water to carry, bad in that he had to carry it. Considering the alternative, he would continue to carry all he had. And would have carried more if he were able.

It occurred to him as he walked that he was making good time and was sweating very little. Much less than he had during the day.

And it was unlikely he could be seen from any appreciable distance at night.

Perhaps he should curl up somewhere at daybreak, ideally in a shaded spot if he could find one, and wait for dark before starting out again.

Lord knew he could use the rest. The idea of stopping, sleeping . . . he tried to work out how long it had been since he last slept. Not that terribly long, he eventually conceded. He had gotten a little sleep last night while he waited for light enough to find the metal cartridge cases. It felt longer than that, though. It felt like a very long time indeed.

And it had been . . . a day and a half since JoLynn had died. Soon two days. An hour, two hours after daylight and it would be two full days.

How was it possible that he could have lived two days without her?

How many more would he have to face alone?

Oliver scowled. He really ought to take hold of himself and think about himself surviving instead of JoLynn dying. Dammit.

But it was so very hard not to think about her. And he was beginning to feel cold now. And that last coyote sounded so awfully close.

He shifted the limp, awkward bundle to his other arm and marched slowly, stolidly on through the night.

TWENTY-EIGHT

JAYJAY was beginning to act as jumpy as a rummy coming off the D.T.'s. Or worse, just going into them. Jim hid his frown behind his hand but probably needn't have bothered. Ol' JayJay wasn't paying attention to very much except his own ghosties and goblins right now, not that Jim could tell.

The foreman's eyes were red-rimmed and baggy, and he kept scratching at his beard stubble so that there was a spot underneath his jaw where blood was starting to show.

"Damn, JayJay. Don't pick at that no more, hear?"

"Pick at what?" JayJay's voice was snippy and peevish.

"Your face, dammit. Don't be picking at it like that, man, you're commencing t' bleed."

"I ain't picking at it," JayJay argued, and all the while his thumb nail was digging and gouging at the underside of his jaw.

"Okay, whatever you say." Jim stood and took another look around the horizon. With the same lousy result they'd had the whole day long. There wasn't anything moving out there except cloud shadows and jackrabbits. And not so many of either one of those.

"Where'd the sonuvabitch get to?" JayJay complained.

"I wisht I knew. I surely do."

"You sure you don't have a bottle stashed away someplace, Jimmy?" JayJay's voice had a whining note in it that had been there more than once this afternoon. Jim didn't like that in a man. He especially didn't like it in JayJay Lawrence right this minute.

"I already told you I didn't. Look for yourself if you don't believe me."

"I believe you," he said without sounding like he meant it.

"Hush now while I look for the guy."

"He's gone, Jimmy. Gone, gone, gone. Flew right outa here. Gone, Jimmy. Gone t' tell the cops. Jeez, man, he's gettin' away right now while we set here an' talk. Goin', goin', gone."

"Shut up, JayJay." This obviously wasn't the time to be bringing it up, but Jim sure as hell wished JayJay would quit calling him Jimmy. That old nickname was reserved for family use. Didn't JayJay know that? Or maybe that was the thing. Maybe he knew that right well an' wanted the reassurance of thinking Jim and Bill would treat him like family, stand by him as far as they would a Beale if that's what it took. Huh. Fat chance. Tell him they would, sure. But there were limits.

Jim sighed. Shit, what they needed was to find and fix that California bastard and then they wouldn't have to worry about any of this stuff. They could just set it all aside and forget it ever happened.

Forget? Hell, nothing *to* forget. Of course not.

If they could just find that slippery SOB and keep him from ruining everything.

"Be dark soon," Jim said. "If he doesn't come t' water here tonight, tomorra morning we'll shift south a ways. Spread out, like, and ride a boundary on him. Crisscross back and forth with the horses, you and me, so that we pretty much have to spot him. I mean, he's afoot and everything. And carrying that shit. He can't be moving very fast. If he don't come to us tonight, JayJay, we'll find him come morning. Guar-ahn-tee."

JayJay didn't respond. Jim looked around and saw that the foreman was digging at his neck with his fingernails again. Jim decided there was no point in saying anything to him about it again. Just let the stupid SOB bleed if that's what he wanted.

"You REALLY oughta lay down and get some sleep," Jim said softly. Sound carries far at night and there weren't any actual guarantees that the California man wasn't close enough to hear. Besides, it just wasn't right to speak out when you were on a hunting stand, even this kind of hunting stand.

"Can't sleep," JayJay snapped in a voice that was perhaps a trifle louder than normal. He was sitting upright even though Jim was on watch and JayJay was free to sleep now. He had his blanket slung over his shoulders like a shawl. He looked like an old granny. With the shakes.

"You didn't sleep last night either, JayJay. What the hell's the matter with you anyhow?"

JayJay turned his head and fixed Jim with a wide-eyed, wild-eyed kind of stare that was eerie in the moonlight.

"What's bothering you that you can't sleep, JayJay?"

"Christ, Jimmy, what th' hell d'you think? Every time I close m' damn eyes all I can see is that dead woman's eyes. She's staring at me, Jimmy. Every time I shut my eyes, there're hers. Big an' flat an' wormy, like. I . . . Christ, it was an accident. You know that. I never meant to shoot her. All I wanted t' do was raise some gravel. Spray it around their boots, like. I never meant to kill her. It was just a accident."

"I know that, JayJay."

"I wish t' hell I'd never come out with you this time, Jimmy."

"I know you do."

JayJay pulled out a Marlboro and lighted it, not even making a pretense of hiding the flame this time. Jim was annoyed, especially since the flare of JayJay's lighter had been bright enough to temporarily wreck Jim's night vision too, but decided against correcting the foreman at the moment.

"You got something t' drink, Jimmy?"

"Just gyp water outa that pond, same as you."

"No, I mean something t' drink, dammit. You got a jug tucked away someplace, don't you? You'll share, won't you? Just one. That's all I need t' settle me down. One drink, Jimmy, that's all I'm asking."

"I told you twenty times today that I didn't bring no damn hideout bottle, JayJay, so quit asking."

"You just don't want me t' have none, do you? Scared I'll get likkered up an' run my mouth, ain't you? Shit, Jimmy, you know I'd never do that. I swear I wouldn't. You an' Billy, you been good to me. You're standing by me even though I shot that woman. Not everybody would do that for a guy. You're all right, you and Billy. I'd never say nothing to get you boys in trouble, I swear I wouldn't. Now lemme have just one swalla, will you do that, Jimmy? Just one an' I'll be able to get t' sleep. You know?"

Jim felt his stomach twist and clench.

Shit, he hadn't even thought about that.

Not until JayJay brought it up his own self.

JayJay was acting bad enough out here in the boonies where he was cold sober.

What the hell would things be like once he hit Talley's and took a load under his belt?

There wasn't any man predictable when he was drunk. JayJay Lawrence in particular. The man might say or do anything once he got shit-faced.

Why in hell hadn't he thought about this before? Jim asked himself. It wasn't like it shouldn't have been perfectly obvious.

They got back to the place, JayJay wouldn't be five minutes changing clothes and grabbing the keys to his truck. He'd carry a bottle with him and be half in the bag before he ever reached Talley's.

And five minutes after JayJay walked into Talley's that very next time, why, the whole county would know that JayJay Lawrence hadn't *meant* to shoot that California woman. And they'd know, too, whatever it was happened to the California man. At least whatever of it that JayJay knew so he could tell them.

Jim felt sick to his stomach at the knowledge.

Damn JayJay anyhow. *He* was the one that started it all. *He* was the one that killed that woman. Jim hadn't fired a shot that time. Just JayJay. And Bill, why Bill hadn't even been carrying a gun.

Yet JayJay open his damned mouth and next thing you knew, the very thing they were trying to prevent would up and happen anyhow. The Beales would be setting behind bars and—worse; Lordy, far, far worse than that inconvenience—the grazing permits would be lifted. The place all those generations of Beales had built and nourished and relied upon . . . it would go under. Dry up and blow away like dust on a hot wind.

And it would all be Jim Beale's fault.

All those generations past. All the ones to come. He'd be letting them down. Every one of them. Because they'd entrusted the running of the place to him as the eldest. To him and not to anybody else. And now he was the one would be letting them all down. All those generations of Beales dead and Beales yet to be born. He was letting them down each and every one.

Sour acid burned deep in his belly, and he could taste the bitterness of it on the back of his tongue.

Dammit, he was gonna have to do something about this. He couldn't just . . . let it happen.

No matter what, dammit, he was gonna have to handle this. No fucking matter what.

He swallowed, warding off an impulse to duck his head and puke.

No matter what, he swore to himself.

TWENTY-NINE

OLIVER STUMBLED to a halt and, gasping, bent over from the waist to set his burden of life-giving water on the ground and stayed there panting for breath. He braced the heels of his hands on his thighs and tried to bring his breathing under control. Slow and deep, that was what he needed.

He felt light-headed, and his knees were rubbery. The rise he'd just come up was nothing, little more than a zit on the earth's face, but it had him wheezing and ready to collapse.

It wasn't that he had been traveling so fast. But he'd been moving steadily. He needed to rest for a bit now even if it wasn't yet dawn.

He picked up his jacket with its load of water bags—fewer now than there had been when he started and lighter—and wobbled the last few yards to the top of the shallow inclination he had been climbing. There he set the jacket down and slumped to the ground beside it. He opened and drank one more bag of the vile, nasty, precious water and tossed the scrap of used gut away. Oliver wiped his mouth with the back of a grimy hand and shuddered with undiminished revulsion.

He felt better now, though. Almost refreshed. He could feel the beginnings of a cramp in his left calf, so he leaned forward and massaged it, then took a moment more to rub the right leg too.

He wished he had some idea how far he had traveled from the hill where JoLynn had died, but he didn't. At the moment he couldn't even calculate the hours he'd been walking, much less the miles. Half a day and most of a night? Something like that, he thought. A lot of hours. Lot of miles too, no doubt. Far enough that he'd crossed a barbed wire fence line already. Surely that had to mean something. Surely that had to mean he was nearing civilization? Or not. When they came out here—the two of them, he and JoLynn together—there had been an awfully long drive from that crossroads store to the last fence, hadn't there? And that had been in the car. How much longer would it take for him to walk out? Another day? Two? More? For sure there would have to be more fence lines crossed before he could expect to get close to the real world. He remembered they'd crossed several getting out here. He couldn't remember how many there had been. More than one or two. So he wasn't there yet. He still had a very long way to go.

Oliver supposed he should have felt depressed by that kind of thinking. In fact, he found it encouraging. Yesterday the thought of finding a fence to cross would have seemed a goal beyond attaining. Tonight he'd already crossed one. There would be more. Fine. As long as his water held out, he would manage.

He sighed. As long as the water held out.

Almost reluctantly he unzipped the jacket and spread the fabric wide so he could count.

The cool, gelatinous sausages that were his lifeline lay like so many fat grubs in a nest. Oliver cleared his throat and touched them one by one as if anointing each, as if giving them benediction.

Seven. He had seven bags of water remaining. Each bag would contain, what, a quart? Less than that probably. A pint or a little more. Seven bags full at roughly, say, a pint and a half per bag. How much was that? It took him a while to work it out. A little over five quarts. A little more than a gallon and a quarter.

How long could he expect a gallon of water to keep him alive? More important, how long would it have to?

Something else occurred to him, and he blinked, frowning. A pint is a pound the world around. Once heard, the singsong quality of it is difficult to forget. A pint is a pound the world around. So a gallon weighs . . . two pints in a quart . . . four quarts in the gallon . . . a gallon weighs eight pounds. Oliver's water supply, then, would weigh, oh, ten pounds?

It felt like an awful lot more than ten pounds. It felt like it weighed more on the order of twenty pounds, thirty. Yet there were only the seven containers, and he didn't think they would average more than a pint and a half per bag.

But surely it was more than a lousy ten pounds of water that was dragging him down so, making his arms ache this badly.

So which calculation was wrong? Was he overestimating the weight because of his fatigue or underestimating the amount of water a section of horse gut holds?

If he was going to be wrong about one or the other, he realized, he would rather find himself carrying more water than he'd supposed. More water was always acceptable. Fatigue severe enough to affect judgment was not. He really and truly hoped that he had more water than he'd guessed.

Still, the simple fact was, he would have to make do with however much or however little it turned out to be.

That was the bottom line.

Oliver touched each of the seven tubby, rubbery bags again, his fingertips lovingly soft and gentle on the cool surfaces, then zipped the jacket shut over them.

Who the hell would ever have thought that a bunch of makeshift water balloons would stand between him and death by dehydration? Life can really be weird sometimes, he decided.

HIS EYES SNAPPED OPEN, and he began to tremble. He had almost gone to sleep there—may even have been dozing for several wasted minutes—and it was still night, still the safe time when he needed to be up and moving. He couldn't afford to waste the little darkness he had left, not on something as inconsequential as sleep, dammit.

Oliver forced himself to his feet, his lips drawing back into a thin, bitter grimace as half-rested leg muscles cramped in protest at the renewed motion.

He really needed to rest more. He knew that. But he couldn't risk dropping off to sleep again. Better to move even more slowly than before than to go to sleep and not move again at all for what was left of the night.

He picked up the jacket, still convinced the water inside it weighed more than ten pounds, and cradled the burden in one arm. His arms hurt about as bad as his legs did. It might be an interesting competition, actually, if he tried to work out which part of him ached the worst.

If nothing else, the comparison would give him something to do while he walked. Something other than thinking, that is.

Why not?

He yawned, staggered sleepily, tried to get his bearings. He had momentarily lost the sense of direction that had brought him this far.

That way, he thought. Or over there?

He frowned, looked behind trying to retrace the route that had brought him here and tried it again.

There. He was sure of it. That way was south. So that was the direction he wanted to go.

So why in hell did he keep wanting to look over that way toward . . . toward what, dammit?

There wasn't anything over there to see.

There wasn't anything *anywhere* to see.

It was the middle of the night in the middle of a desert and of course there wasn't anything to see.

So why did he keep looking?

Oliver was so tired that it took him several minutes of dull, bovine contemplation before he could work it out that his attention was being drawn in that direction—slightly west of due south—by a glow of light.

Light.

Not moon- or starlight, either. Not any sort of natural light.

Man-made light. Artificial light.

Not a direct light like a fire's blaze. But a pale glow reaching into the sky from somewhere beyond the horizon, reflecting there from the bottom of a wisp of low cloud or airborne dust. Just a faint, poorly defined, barely seen glow of light. But there. Most certainly there now that he recognized what he was seeing and paid attention to it.

A city? No, he was pretty sure it couldn't be a city or town. Winnemucca should be . . . he concentrated, worked it out, looked . . . once he was paying attention, he could see another, much stronger glow that would be the halo of light projected by the streetlights and gaudy neon of Winnemucca, right there where it should be, far to the east of due south and partially obscured by a line of low mountains between there and here. That would be Winnemucca. So this couldn't be.

This other glow seemed much smaller and much closer than that.

Reno? The direction would be about right. But Reno was very, very far away. A hundred fifty, two hundred miles. Too far to see the sky glow at all? Maybe, maybe not. Oliver didn't have experience enough to decide that. But he was fairly sure that the sky-reflected light he was seeing now came from some source much closer than that. Really quite close. Twenty miles? It could be that close, he suspected. Closer? He wasn't sure. What then? He knew of no towns that . . .

Ranches? Did ranches have lights?

Stupid, he chided himself. Of course ranches had lights. But would they project light into the sky like that?

He grunted.

*Some*thing was over there as the source of the light he was seeing now.

Whether it was a ranch, a store—surely it couldn't be that crossroads store already; surely he hadn't walked that far without realizing it, had he? or had he? Jesus!—whatever, it hardly seemed important right now what it was. Just that something was there. A man-made structure. A place of refuge where Oliver could find people, shelter, perhaps even a telephone. A way to report those men to the authorities.

He felt suddenly alert and completely awake again as adrenaline rushed through him like an electric charge.

There was something over there. Something close enough to reach in a day's walk, perhaps.

Something . . .

Oliver began to tremble.

For the first time since he set out from that awful place where JoLynn had died, for the very first time he had a measure of genuine hope.

He might actually, honestly survive to rectify the wrong that had been done to JoLynn and to those innocent horses.

Oliver straightened his shoulders and sighted carefully in the direction where he could see the faint glow.

This time he felt almost smug as he set off at a swift walk toward safety.

THIRTY

SO WHAT IN HELL *else* could go wrong? Jim asked himself.

No, dammit, he didn't want to know. Whatever it was—and there would be some-damn-thing, he was sure of that—it would happen soon enough.

He scowled and tossed JayJay the pack of Chesterfields, knowing good and well that sharing them was only gonna make the both of them run short instead of just stupid JayJay. That damned JayJay had gone and smoked up all his own Marlboros; now he was bumming out of Jim's scant supply.

Jim waited until JayJay had a smoke going, then said, "Whyn't you go check on the horses, JayJay."

Damned JayJay stood there for half a minute blinking and fidgeting and trying to work out what it was that needed to be done before he finally got his butt in gear and walked off toward where the horses were picketed.

JayJay was getting worse, Jim saw. Not so much jumpy now as, well, pretty much useless. Stood and stared off into space a lot. A couple times

Jim would have sworn the foreman was crying. JayJay's eyes were sure as hell watery and bright anyhow, and he wiped at them more than seemed natural. Jeez.

The guy moved and even walked around like he was asleep. Which was probably reasonable enough because Jim knew for certain sure that JayJay Lawrence hadn't slept in the past two nights. He was an out-and-out mess by now, so much so that Jim had had to alter his plans.

The best way to've done this would be for Jim and JayJay to split up and both make long, looping sweeps on horseback so they could intercept and take down the California man.

Except with damn JayJay gone so completely unreliable, Jim no longer trusted the foreman enough to send him off by himself. Whatever they did or didn't do, they would mostly have to do it together.

Except now, dammit, there was so much other crap to worry about that Jim wasn't so sure he could even stick to that plan.

Everything was getting screwed up. Now that was the simple truth of it.

They were out of food, out of feed, out of luck and soon out of patience.

And unfortunately they weren't even done yet.

For the past couple hours Jim had had the awfullest, nastiest, most uncomfortable sensation that that SOB Californian had pulled an end run on them somehow. Otherwise why hadn't he yet turned up someplace? And the only way Jim knew the fella might have done a thing like that would be if he was smart enough to follow the tire tracks of that car—it might take an expert to track a horse over empty country, but any idiot could follow a tire track—and uncover it.

Jim was regretting now that he'd left the keys in the thing. At the very least he should've disabled it. Holed the gas tank or smashed the distributor or something. But no, he'd just closed it up and covered it over with the keys hanging right there in the ignition ready to fire up and drive away.

If the California guy had done that, why, he had all the evidence in the damn world right there with him. Body, camera, everything. Even food and water to fill up on before he drove away. Which was another damn thing. Jim should've thought to take some of those supplies and use them, but he hadn't. Hadn't even looked to see if there were any cigarettes among the supplies. At the time that would've seemed like stealing. Stupid. He should've done it anyway, that was all. Now it was too late.

He sighed and peered into the nearly empty Chesterfield package. Not that he really needed to look. He knew good and well how many smokes were left. Just six. And now that asshole JayJay was smoking off Jim's supply too, damn him.

If it wasn't for wanting JayJay to help him with some things yet . . . needed for JayJay to be with him when he did find the Californian was closer to the truth of it . . .

No point in thinking about that, Jim told himself. Not yet.

But there was something he needed to do while he had the chance.

He glanced off toward where Lawrence was checking the picket pins, hunkered down over there and paying no attention at the moment to what Jim was doing. That was good.

Quickly Jim sidled over to their piled gear and picked up JayJay's carbine. Quickly, quickly he stripped out the slender, pointy little army surplus cartridges. Twenty of them in a magazine this size. They slid out nice and easy and just as nice and easy disappeared into Jim's pocket. He could transfer them to his saddlebags later. Or just throw them away where JayJay couldn't see. It wouldn't matter.

He fitted the now empty magazine back into the action of the Ruger and remembered to give the bolt a yank to clear the chamber. One last, bright brass cartridge flipped into the air and dropped to the ground, leaving the carbine no more of a threat than any other heavy object. Jim picked the last cartridge up and put it in his pocket with the others, then returned the carbine to the scabbard where he'd found it.

Lawrence wasn't busy with the horses any longer, but he wasn't on his way back to join Jim either. He was just standing there, staring off toward the south somewhere. Jim didn't need to see any closer to know that the fool's eyes were empty and unfocused. It was getting so that being around him was positively spooky.

"You wouldn't have nothing t' drink on you, would you, Jimmy?" JayJay's voice was petulant, whiny. The sound of it set Jim's teeth on edge as bad as a fingernail scraping on a chalkboard.

"No, I don't, JayJay," he said with a forced, entirely artificial calm. He had been answering this same damned question for about as long as he could remember and still Lawrence kept asking it. Apparently the dummy wasn't capable of remembering that he'd just been told the same thing five minutes ago.

"Okay. Sorry." JayJay tilted his head to one side and squinted against a curl of white smoke that was drifting into his eyes.

Jim saw with considerable disgust that the unlit end of JayJay's cigarette was soggy with spit. No wonder he smoked filter tips. Bastard couldn't handle a real cigarette. If the thing got any wetter, it would fall apart in his mouth. And then he'd probably want another one out of Jim's pack to replace it with. Damn him.

Right now just looking at JayJay was enough to make Jim's stomach knot and gurgle. Jeez!

Jim came to his feet and reached for his saddle.

JayJay blinked stupidly for a moment. "We going someplace, Jimmy?"

Lordy, Jim wished Lawrence would quit calling him that. "I am, JayJay. I want you to stay here and keep watching for that Californian, though. Can you do that, JayJay?"

"I didn't mean to shoot that woman, you know."

"I know, JayJay. Look, I don't want you to shoot the man neither. All right?"

"Sure. I really didn't mean to do that to the woman anyhow. I really didn't."

"I know you didn't, JayJay. And I don't want you to shoot the man. But I do want you t' keep watching for him. If you see him, you can bring him in and set him down and wait for me to come talk to him. You could do that for me, couldn't you, JayJay?"

"I could do that, Jimmy."

"Thanks, JayJay." Jim gave him the same kind of big, happy, insincere smile that you give to a retard kid or to some drunk stranger that you know is too far gone to start a scrap with anybody. In a way JayJay had come to fall into that same sort of category. Not entirely real anymore, at least not in the ways that count for anything.

"You got a smoke before you go, Jimmy? One you could leave with me?"

"I'm out, JayJay," he lied.

"How 'bout a drink then? You got a drink on you, Jimmy?"

"We'll get something to drink real soon, JayJay. I promise."

"Good, 'cause I sure need one right now."

"I know you do, JayJay. But don't you worry, hear? I'll take care of you."

"I know you will, Jimmy," JayJay said solemnly.

"Mind you keep an eye out for that Californian while I'm gone. You'll do that, won't you?"

"I will, Jimmy. I promise you I will."

"Good. And when I get back, we'll see about finding you something to drink, right?" The smile flicked easily on and off again. Why not? Didn't mean anything anyhow. That was just about all they needed now, though, wasn't it; Lawrence drunk and babbling to everybody at Talley's, everybody in town too. Yeah, that was just about all they needed.

"Thanks, Jimmy."

There wasn't all that much of a risk in leaving Lawrence here on his own, Jim had determined after several hours of reluctant deliberation on the subject.

After all, the guy wasn't thinking clearly enough to go off and do anything on his own. So it should be safe enough to leave him here long enough for Jim to ride back to where that station wagon was buried and take a look. Just in case. Just to reassure himself that the Californian was still out here someplace where he could be caught. Just that much encouragement and Jim would be able to press on with all the rest that needed doing. But he did need that much to go on.

And Lawrence, well, he'd been watching for the California guy for so long now that if he did spot the man, he might up and do the right thing out of habit. Programming, that was what Bill's boys would call it. Well, maybe JayJay's programming would take over if the California man did show up. Slim chance maybe, but slim is better than none.

Jim saddled his dun and set off at a steady lope toward where they'd left the car. Far as they'd had to come in their search by now, this was going to take a while—they'd shifted south now, what, three times already today, all the way down onto their own land anyway in an effort to keep ahead of a man moving steadily cross-country—so there were a lot of miles Jim had to ride back to the north again to the wash where that car was buried, but he honestly felt that it had to be done.

Between his concerns over both Lawrence and the Californian, he figured he had to find some relief someplace or else he was going to go as buggy as Lawrence.

He was already an hour gone before he realized that Lawrence couldn't shoot the Californian now if the guy walked up and requested it, because JayJay's damned carbine was empty, even though nobody but Jim knew that.

Hell, though, that would be just like everything else was turning out with this deal. Anything that he hoped to get accomplished Jim was going to have to do himself.

But then, a man shouldn't ever expect anything different, should he? Jim reminded himself without pleasure.

THIRTY ONE

OLIVER GROANED and stirred. The sun had moved around far enough to find him again, and his left ear felt as if it were lying in a pool of sweat, even though it certainly wasn't all that hot. The fabric of his jacket, handy not so much as a pillow as because it was cleaner than resting his head on dirt, was barely warm.

He sat up, feeling loggy and with his nasal passages overfull. He had a low-grade headache and a tongue that tasted like rotten meat. He rubbed his ear, and his hand came away wet. He made a face, turned his head and spat in an effort to clear his mouth. His own saliva, unfortunately, was considerably cleaner and more pleasant to contemplate by now than the water that remained in his bags.

Oliver blinked and knuckled his eyes. He'd been sleeping and that was good, even if he did feel worse right now than when he'd lain down.

He squinted toward the sun. It was dropping toward the distant mountains but was still a fair distance above them. Not yet sundown but well past noon, that was as close a guess as he was capable of making. Quite a while until dark, anyway.

It would be safe for him to move along again once it was dark. Or dusk at the least. As soon as it would be difficult for distant watchers to spot him.

Then he could make the remaining distance between where he now was and the source of the light he'd seen this morning.

Even this many hours afterward he remained excited and eager.

But neither so excited nor so eager that he was going to abandon caution. He'd had time enough to work that out while he marched last night. Too much was at stake here for him to risk helping JoLynn's killers by impulsively rushing ahead in daylight.

JoLynn's killers. It was sad how easily he was able to accept that phrase now. It was no longer so difficult for him to think about her. Or about the fact that she was dead.

She'd deserved a better mourning than she'd received.

But then she'd deserved a longer life too.

If only . . . Oliver clamped down on the thought. Refused to finish it. "If only" was one of the ugliest of all possible word combinations. And one of the most useless. Piss on any sentence that starts with the words "if only."

He rubbed the back of his neck and spent a few idle moments watching the labors of some black ants in the light, sandy soil at the base of the scruffy gray bushes where he was hiding.

The patch of brush covered an area that was larger than a basketball court but smaller than a softball field, whatever that worked out to in acres.

The bushes themselves were chest-high on him and therefore offered both shade and protection from prying eyes. Oliver felt fairly safe here.

He wasn't sure but suspected that the bushes were a sort of sage. JoLynn had told him there were a zillion varieties of the stuff and that it came in all sizes from grass-tall to almost tree-high. Oliver guessed that this was one of those varieties, because the dry, paperlike crinkles that served the plants as leaves smelled faintly familiar. Much like the stuffing in a Thanksgiving turkey. Possibly the herb and these ugly plants were related somehow.

He yawned, spat again. He was still tired without being particularly sleepy. Dull aches made themselves known in his calves and thigh muscles whenever he moved.

What he really ought to do, he supposed, was shift his jacket of water bags into the shade and lie down again. He needed all the rest he could manage. Rest if not actual sleep. Either would be helpful.

Besides, if he didn't move the jacket, those ants would probably be attracted to the horse gut. That was certainly a complication he could get along without.

He took a moment to stand and stretch, careful not to expose any more of himself than his head and shoulders, then stepped a few paces away and took a leak. His urine was an unusually dark yellow and smelled strongly of ammonia. Nothing untoward about that, of course. His water intake had been limited lately and his usage heavy. There wasn't any surplus reaching his kidneys, but a day or two with unlimited fluids and everything would return to normal.

He was thirsty again now, of course—he was beginning to feel that thirst was a constant—but he wouldn't drink again. Not until dark and he was ready to leave. Oliver had decided that before he ever lay down here to rest. He wouldn't drink again until sundown. That would leave him two bags to travel with tonight. The jacket, though, was becoming much lighter to carry than he now found comfortable. At this point he would gladly have exchanged pain in his biceps for a heftier supply of water.

He looked around for a shaded area that was free of ants, found one that he thought would be suitable, then went back to fetch his jacket and water bags.

A cry was ripped out of him when he bent over the loosely folded jacket.

The cloth was wet.

It hadn't been sweat he was sleeping in a few minutes ago. It was water. His water. The bags were leaking.

He clawed at the front of the jacket, snatching it open and reaching for the first of his three remaining water sacks.

The length of gut was limp and floppy in his hands, not at all the stuffed sausage shape it had been when he started out.

Oliver hastily put that one down and lifted out another. It too was losing water.

And there was a smell to the damp inside of the jacket too. Now that he was paying attention. Why, how, had he not smelled it before now?

The horse-gut water bottles were rotting this quickly. Tearing and beginning to separate at the junctures where they were tied. Weeping precious fluid.

Oliver knelt in frightened misery for only a few moments.

But then, he couldn't spare any more time than that for regrets about things that were not or thoughts of things that should have been.

Quickly, very quickly, he picked up a bag. He used his rock-whetted cartridge-casing knife to puncture the cleaner-looking end of the gut and, practiced now, sucked the water from it without losing any more than he already had.

Funny, but Oliver no longer found the water revolting, even though its taste was far worse than it had been to begin with. By now he accepted the water as nourishment and never mind the flavors.

At this point his sole regret was that there wasn't more of the vile stuff to drink.

Still moving quickly, he drank off the last of his water supply, consuming all of it lest he lose any more.

When he was done doing that, he licked up whatever moisture he could from the fabric of his jacket and chewed on the cloth in search of the last recoverable drops.

Then he stood and took another look at the slowly—too slowly—sinking sun. He felt uncertain and afraid. If he left this sagebrush shelter now, he could be seen by anyone who might be watching. But if he started out too late, with no more supply of water to draw on, he might not make it to safety at all.

After all, he had no idea how far it was to civilization and rescue, how far to the source of the night-sky glow. And no experience on which he could fall back to make a guess.

Oliver felt more alone now, more frightened, than at any time since he'd left the pond where JoLynn had died.

He had to do the right thing here or die.

And he didn't have any idea which of his two apparent choices would turn out to be the right thing.

"Not to put any pressure on," he whispered aloud to the vast Nevada desert. "Of course not."

THIRTY-TWO

"SHIT!" The epithet ripped out of him in a spurt of sudden anger and he sawed at the dun horse's reins, yanking the animal's head around cruelly as he spurred it into a run.

That was a lousy thing to do. Jim knew it even when he did it. At that particular moment, however, he just didn't much give a damn. He needed some way to vent his frustrations, and the red horse was the only creature within reach or hearing.

"Shit," he repeated as he swept closer to the place where he'd positioned JayJay Lawrence earlier in the day.

Jim stood in his stirrups, chin tucked low so the brim of his hat would be pushed down by the force of the wind, eyes narrowed against the thrust of the breeze made by the horse's quick passage. Even with his vision partially impaired, though, he could see that there was nothing in front of him to see.

Not a single, stinking damned thing.

There should have been Lawrence and his saddle and other gear, and his horse ought to be beyond the rise but likely wasn't, not if that damned

Lawrence wasn't up here where Jim had left him. Where Jim had told him in no uncertain terms he'd damned well better still be when Jim came back from checking on the buried car in that wash.

Lordy, Lordy. What next?

Jim was commencing to feel like the whole world was ganging up and working against him. Like nothing had gone right, nothing was going right, nothing was fixing to go right.

Except that couldn't be, and it was up to him to make sure that things turned around again and started going the way they were supposed to.

Lordy, Lordy.

Jim took the dun to the top of the rise at a fast pace and then pulled it back as he leveled out on top and he could see the exact same spot where he'd sat Lawrence down those hours ago and given the man his simple instructions. Set still; stay put; watch for the California guy. That was all there'd been to it. So why in hell hadn't the man been able to follow those orders? Damn.

Jim hauled the dun to a stop and sat there a moment to peer at the ground. There wasn't any sign to hint where Lawrence had gone or how long ago it was that he left. There weren't even any cigarette butts, because Jim hadn't left any of his smokes for the idiot foreman. Good thing too, because Jim only had two left his own self. If he'd shared with Lawrence, he would've been out by now too.

He bumped the dun forward again and took it down to where Lawrence's brown had been the last time Jim had seen it.

There was sign on the ground there, all right. Two manure piles. No, three of them within the scope of the picket rope that'd been pegged into the ground. Jim dismounted and checked each pile closely. The freshest of them was glazed on the surface but still moist and loose inside. Cold, though. An hour old or longer, he guessed. He wiped his fingers on the seat of his jeans and lighted one of his remaining two Chesterfields while he tried to figure out what in hell had happened to Lawrence.

Had the guy discovered that his carbine was empty and worked out why Jim would've done a thing like that?

Not likely, Jim decided. Even if Lawrence did figure out that the gun was empty, he'd only believe that he wasn't trusted with ammo now. Hell, he had to know that his thinking was all screwy right now. Surely he'd recognize that much. So he wasn't likely to know why the gun had been emptied without him knowing.

Could he've spotted the California guy and gone off after him?

No, that didn't make much sense neither, Jim realized. If the California guy had been walking close enough to be seen from the hilltop, him and Lawrence would both be in view from there still. Even if the guy tried to run for it, he couldn't have gotten far enough that Lawrence's brown horse would've been out of sight from that hilltop. And Jim had just been up there and looked around. There wasn't anything in view or he would've seen it already. So it wasn't really likely that Lawrence's leaving here had anything to do with him finding the Californian.

He must just have . . . left. Just up and left.

To get a drink, Jim guessed. To get himself blind drunk. That was what he'd been wanting ever since he'd gone and shot that woman. He wanted some liquor and he wanted some ease from his nightmares.

Shit, they couldn't afford for old JayJay to go and ease his conscience at the expense of the Beale Ranch and the Beale family, dammit.

The son of a bitch really wanted an excuse. Have a few belts and let his tongue flap loose and then he could get it off his chest to the whole damned world about how he hadn't meant to shoot that woman.

Man, Jim could see how that conversation would go. Didn't take no kind of genius to figure that.

Didn't mean to shoot a woman, JayJay? What woman did you go an' shoot, JayJay? Oh really, JayJay? Tell us s'more 'bout this, hey?

Jesus, they couldn't let that happen.

No, not that *they* couldn't let this happen. As the eldest Beale and head of the family, it was the responsibility of James Adam Beale to see that it didn't happen. Him and no other.

But jeez, he hated to do this. He really and truly did.

He confirmed his suspicions with a close look at the ground near where the brown horse had been staked out.

The hoofprints leading away from the spot lined straight and true for home.

JayJay Lawrence was heading for the barn. And then right quick for his pickup truck and Talley's Corner and God knew where else to spill his gut after first loading it with liquor.

And Bill wouldn't know to stop him even if he did see JayJay there.

"Shit," Jim said again, louder and with more force this time.

He gathered his reins and swung onto the saddle of the red dun that he favored.

This was gonna be a good test of whether he had reason to favor the horse. The dun had already been all the way up to the dry wash—and what a waste that trip had been; there wasn't a track put down since Jim and Bill and JayJay were all there together, not one track except for coyotes, no sign whatsoever of the Californian—and now back again. The horse already had thirty, forty miles on it today, and now Jim was gonna ask it to catch up with Lawrence's brown against whatever head start Lawrence had.

That was a lousy deal, but it had to be done.

Jim at least knew a thing or two about getting the most out of a horse. Once he was settled comfortable atop the dun, he reached down and loosened his cinch strap, letting the mohair cinch hang free under the horse's belly so its wind wouldn't be restricted any by the girdlelike pressure. The rider, of course, would have to stay upright on sheer balance, because the saddle would slide free to either side if ever he tried to depend on it.

And the biggest thing about forcing a horse is the old saying about making haste slowly. Or at least deliberately. So he set off at a nice lope first, trying to remember the pattern his father had told him about from the long-ago times. Lope most of the time, gallop much of the time, get off and lead the horse at a walk at least five minutes out of every hour. And don't quit. Not for nothing.

Not even if Lawrence got home before him and he had to take up the chase on wheels, too, if that's what it came to, dammit. Just don't never quit. That was the ticket. Don't never quit.

FIFTY-FIFTY. Not bad odds. Until you gambled and came up a loser.

Well, Oliver had gambled. And he'd come up a loser.

He pressed his cheek against the dry grit of the sand and fought off the dizziness that washed through him.

He'd fallen down for, what, the umpteenth time and wasn't sure if he had strength enough to get to his feet again now or not. Wasn't sure either if it mattered whether he got up again or not.

His belly hurt—Lord, how it hurt—and his head was pounding and there was a cold sweat that was soaking his shirt and wasting away some of the precious fluids he'd managed to retain.

For the past half hour he hadn't hardly been able to make any progress walking because of having to stop so often to throw up.

And he couldn't afford, he just really couldn't, the loss of all that strength and fluid.

He hadn't eaten anything in so long that he knew the reaction wasn't from the horse meat. So it had to have been from the last water he'd taken. The last out of those rotting bags. It was more than just the gut sections that were going bad. There had been something in the water, and he'd drunk it, and now he was paying the piper.

Another fiery cramp knotted and twisted in his belly, and he felt himself tremble.

If only he hadn't started off so quick. If only he'd stayed back in that patch of sage where he'd had shade and shelter. He was sure he would have felt much, much better, would have been able to better cope with this, if he hadn't been on the move when the nausea and the hurting struck. But he'd decided to trade speed against the risk of daytime movement, and now he was paying for his mistake.

Now he was a few miles closer to where those lights had to be, but what of it? Right now Oliver was convinced he wouldn't live long enough to make it the rest of the way to safety.

His stomach churned and rumbled in protest of whatever intruders were attacking it there, and Oliver could taste bitter, acid bile rising into the back of his throat once again.

There wasn't anything left in his stomach to heave, but that didn't stop his body from going through the reflexes of rejection.

Oliver lay on his side with his eyes closed. He could taste vomit and sand.

He felt empty. Of hope as well as everything else.

Dying was going to be a bummer. But that seemed little more important right now than a minor annoyance. Much worse than that was knowing that he was failing JoLynn.

One last thing he might have done for her, and he wasn't going to manage it.

She was dead and now no one would ever know. Not really.

With Oliver gone too, there wouldn't be anyone left who might tell.

JoLynn Weaver, dear and joyous, a contributor to all that was good and decent in life, would simply cease to exist. No one would ever know why. No one would ever even know for sure that she was gone. She would fail to show up for work. People would wonder. There would be regrets. But people disappeared of their own volition every day of the year. With no real proof to the contrary, why, the people JoLynn and Oliver had known would probably assume that the two of them had turned their backs on society and run away. With both of them gone that probability would seem all the stronger to their friends and coworkers. And especially considering the lifestyle JoLynn and Oliver had shared. Not alternate, certainly. But not conforming either. No one would find it all that strange if Bendix and Weaver drifted away to do their own thing.

No one would think it all so terribly strange. And next year they would be forgotten. The Christmas cards would go unanswered. The phone would be disconnected and the apartment reclaimed, the furnishings sold at auction. Oliver supposed a few of their more personal possessions might be held in storage. For a while. And then those would be discarded too. Sent to a charity, probably. He hoped so. Better that than to a dump. Better that some homeless person receive the benefit from the things he and JoLynn had cherished and shared.

And once all that was done, why, there would be no legacy remaining. No trace of their passage through life.

The footprints Oliver left on this desert would have as much permanence as the impact JoLynn and he left on the world they loved so much, wished so desperately to protect and preserve.

Had it all been worthwhile, then? Their hard work on behalf of baby seals and AIDS victims? whales and waterfowl? dolphins trapped in tuna nets and newts endangered by dam builders?

Oliver found himself laughing. Which was better, if only marginally, than crying.

Because the simple, stinking truth was that there wasn't any one of those things, not any entire class or category of those things, that was as valuable to him right now as JoLynn's life had been.

And his own life?

Well, that hardly seemed to matter anyway.

He opened his eyes and tried to make himself comfortable in spite of the twisting, debilitating pains that jolted through him in irregular spasms. Between pains it really wasn't all that bad. Bearable. Bidable. Not really so . . . a scream of raw agony tore out of him, and the tendons of his neck corded and strained. Sweat beaded his forehead and soaked the collar of his shirt, and he cried out again.

"Holy Mary, Mother of . . ." His mumbling swelled for a moment and then faded. "Now and at the hour . . ."

Now and at the hour. That hour wouldn't be long in coming. He was sure of that.

It was almost dark. Sometime tonight his hour would come. Soon. He almost hoped for it to be soon. At least then it wouldn't hurt anymore.

But, Jesus, he hated to be such a failure to JoLynn.

Hated too to be calling on Mary now after so many years without the church, without so much as a thought of all the things he'd been taught so long ago. Taught by rote, rejected by choice, ignored by habit.

Until now. Now it was Holy Mary, Mother of God.

Oliver felt ashamed of himself for having these thoughts now. Turning to prayer now was kind of like cheating, wasn't it?

So all right, he wouldn't do it. There were some things he could handle with pride and decency. Even if he didn't know how to handle himself in the desert like some Rambo/Boy Scout cross.

So all right. He would hold on to his dignity and go out with the strength of his convictions, anyway. Not try to hedge his bets or weasel out of anything.

". . . now and at the hour of my death," he whispered.

THIRTY-THREE

CLOSE. So close. The question was whether he could catch up with Lawrence before he got to the home place.

Jim felt the dun tremble between his knees, felt the horse falter as its gait became even more ragged.

So close, dammit.

But Lawrence was close too. Within a dozen miles of the home place. And still a good quarter mile ahead of Jim's exhausted dun. Lawrence's brown jogged on without any idea that it was being chased. And the red horse had no more to give.

It had come dark, but Jim could see Lawrence and the brown tantalizingly close ahead in the moonlight. Could smell, damn near taste, the dust the brown's hoofs raised for Jim and the dun to plod through.

Jim had to catch Lawrence before he reached the yard. Before they got where everybody could see. *Had* to.

There was only one more thing Jim could think of to do. And that was a gamble.

Life is a gamble. Next year there may be drought. Disease. You just never know. Hell with it. He wasn't getting it done this way.

He pulled the dun to a stop. The weary horse seemed grateful for the rest. Its head sagged, and its flanks heaved for breath. It was so tired that it didn't bother picking at the grass where it stood. Just stayed there, head down, nostrils flaring, its coat dark and soapy with sweat.

"Just a little more, that's all I'm asking of you," Jim mumbled as he snatched his already loose latigo completely free and slipped the buckle on the belly strap. He pulled the carbine from his scabbard and lifted saddle and gear free of the tired horse's back. "Feel better, boy? Damn straight."

He dumped the forty or fifty pounds of saddle and accouterments onto the ground but held on to the carbine. With a swift, fluid motion he sprang onto the dun's back. Even as tired as it was, the red horse tossed its head and tried to sidestep away.

"Easy, boy, easy now." Jim was neither surprised nor annoyed by the horse's reaction. Hell, this dun maybe hadn't never been ridden bareback. For sure it had been years and years since Jim Beale got onto anything without a saddle. It was the only chance he had to catch up with Lawrence. "All right now," he said softly. "Just this one more time, fella. Then you can rest."

He bumped the horse with his spurs, urging it first into a walk. And then a gallop.

Lawrence and the brown had gotten out of sight while Jim was stopped. He had some catching up to do. And then some.

HE COULD FEEL the dun paddling, its feet flailing haphazardly in all directions as the horse lurched and staggered forward from instinct rather than purpose.

Sixty, seventy yards. As close to JayJay and the brown horse as that. But now the tough dun was giving out. Jim Beale had never in his life ridden a horse to death. Until tonight. God, he hated that.

He felt the animal's legs go out from under it. Shifted his weight to the high side and stepped off the dying horse even as it slumped to the ground.

"JayJay! JayJay Lawrence." His shout seemed loud in the stillness of the night. Loud enough to be heard, that was all he could hope. Loud enough and that Lawrence would heed and turn back. If he hadn't figured out what Jim intended, there was a chance that he might.

"JayJay! Come help me."

He sprinted forward, toward the receding horseman, and raised the carbine. The gun barked, and a yard-long spear of flame leaped out of the muzzle.

Out ahead JayJay heard finally and pulled the brown to a stop.

"JayJay, it's me. Jimmy."

Jim saw Lawrence wave and start back toward him.

Thank goodness.

He stood, feeling much, much better now. It was going to be all right after all. First he'd get JayJay straightened out. Then him and Bill could go look for that Californian. It was a shame to have to involve Bill, but it was working out that way. They would make it work, though. They'd have to.

"Jimmy. I . . . I didn't expect . . . you ain't mad at me, are you, Jimmy?" JayJay stopped beside him and got down off the brown.

"I'm not mad, JayJay."

"I . . . look, hear me out, will you? Listen to what I got to tell you before you say anything. Will you do me that, Jimmy?" JayJay sent an odd, inquiring look in the direction of the dying red horse but didn't say anything about it. There was too much else that needed talking about at the moment. Anything as inconsequential as a dead horse could be discussed later. "Please?"

"All right."

"I been . . . I know I been a mess since . . . you know. Since I shot that lady. I ain't been much use to you, Jim, an' I apologize for that. But see, I can't forget about it. You can't know. I mean, it wasn't you that shot her. An' those eyes. I can't quit seeing them. Every time I try an' sleep, even just rest. Don't even have to have my own eyes closed an' I see hers, Jim. I sit an' look out across the grass for that husband o' hers and what I see is that woman's eyes staring back at me from outa the grave. Except she don't even have a proper grave, Jim, and that's tearing at my gut too. I mean, it's bad. You know?"

"I know, JayJay. I know it is."

"So what I worked out, Jim, setting there and keeping watch like you told me to, what I worked out is that I got to go turn myself in."

"JayJay, you—"

"Dammit, Jim, you promised me. You promised you'd listen t' what I got to say here."

"Sorry."

"Now I know what you're thinking, Jim. You're thinking this is gonna mess you up. You and Bill an' the ladies an' Bill's boys. But it won't. I'll see to that, you understand. I won't say nothing about anybody else being out there. Just that I was out shooting them horses on my own. For fun, like. An' that I got scared when I seen those people up on that hill an' that I only shot to warn them off so's they wouldn't take pictures. I'll tell them just the way it was about that. I won't make up nothing in that part. Won't have to because I never meant to shoot that woman. God knows I never meant to do that."

JayJay's face had twisted, and his lip was quivering. His voice cracked and quavered, and he was crying like a baby but never tried to cover it up.

"I'll tell them how I panicked when I seen what I done and that I hid the body and the car all by myself to try and keep anyone from ever knowing. Nobody ever has to know that I wasn't there alone, Jim. I swear I won't never mention anything about you and Bill. Not to anybody. And God knows it'll be all right going to jail a while if it'll just let me quit seeing that woman's dead eyes staring at me. You know? They got doctors in jail that can help me with that, I bet. Be worth it just for that, Jim, I swear it will." He was smiling now. The idiot was actually smiling now, still crying but smiling at the same time too.

Jim felt nothing but disgust for the broken, mewling excuse for a thing that used to be his foreman.

The asshole wasn't even thinking straight. Feds, state, county, everybody would want to put his two cents in. And grab off whatever glory would be in it for him and his department. There would be one hell of an investigation. The car would be found first thing. And there wouldn't be a single fingerprint in there that came off JayJay Lawrence. Just the dead woman and the California man and Jim Beale. How would JayJay explain that away? Did he really expect to convince anybody that the man was making it up about seeing three fellows at the water hole? Because surely the man would be found still alive if something wasn't done about him pretty damned soon.

Shit, Lawrence just wasn't thinking this through.

Which wasn't a problem Jim Beale could afford to have.

He had to think these things all the way through.

No matter what that led to, dammit.

He sighed.

He'd have to change the story he'd worked out for Billy. No way he could protect Billy from knowing things now.

Probably not, anyhow.

Maybe. Just barely maybe, though. If he could keep Billy and everybody tight to home for the next day or two while Jim took care of everything else by himself. Jim's thoughts worked fast and furious as he tried to work up a story that was plausible enough and that would do what he needed done.

He sighed. "I'm sorry, JayJay. I truly am."

"Don't say it like that, Jim. I've thought it out real good. I promise you I can handle it. Nobody will ever have t' know anything but what I tell 'em. I can do it, Jim. I got to do it. I can't go on like . . ."

"I know you can't," Jim agreed sadly.

"Don't fun me like that, Jimmy. Put that thing down, will you? That gun is pointing right at me, man. Put it down now."

Jim pushed the safety off. The catch made a thin, metallic click in the sudden quiet.

"Jimmy! Jesus God, Jimmy!"

JayJay spun away, snatched his own carbine out of the scabbard and pointed it with both hands. He yanked at the trigger, cursed and fumbled for the safety and yanked again.

Jim sighed. Jeez, he really hated having to do this.

His carbine barked, the sound of it loud and sharp. He was standing so close to JayJay when he fired that the cloth of JayJay's shirt caught fire on his chest and began to smolder. A flow of blood put the flame out, but the smoke of it stank and lingered in the air.

JayJay dropped like he'd been poleaxed. Jim could hear a gurgling in his throat, and the heels of his boots drummed on the ground in a wildly macabre dance performed to the music of JayJay's jingling spur rowels.

Jim felt mercifully detached from the whole thing. Disconnected from it somehow.

He found it more . . . interesting . . . than horrifying.

But then, after all, he'd seen dead people before but was never this close to anyone who was in the process of actually dying. Not even a peaceable death, which this one certainly wasn't.

Jim waited until the body was laying nice and still, then walked over and looked closer. JayJay was dead, all right.

Bill would have to know, of course.

Jim figured he could make up a story. JayJay caught up with the California man and tried to talk to the guy. The Californian shot ol' JayJay with his own gun. Then tried to get away. And Jim coming along too late to do any good.

Why hell, Jim realized with considerable pleasure, with that kind of excuse he could even get Billy to help him find and gun that Californian. Bill would be willing to do that to get even for JayJay.

And to protect the ranch—Bill would go along with it once Jim explained the way things had to be, mostly the risks they'd run if they tried to do things any other way—why, Bill would help him cover it all over.

They could pack all JayJay's things and hide them and his body and his old pickup just the same way they hid the woman's body and the little station wagon.

Tell everybody that JayJay'd taken a notion to move on. To Canada, maybe. JayJay'd been around a long time, but everybody knew how bucka-roos moved. Any breeze was apt to set them to drifting. This was even the right time of year for it, with hands looking for work from Alberta clean down to Sonora.

Nobody would think twice about it if Jim and Bill said JayJay had left them and moved along. Nothing, that is, except to wonder who'd be lucky enough to catch on as the next foreman on the Beale.

As for the Californians, well, that would work out, too, just so long as the man was found.

With luck Jim might even be able to do that himself with Bill never knowing anything about it.

He could give that one more try before he tried to get Bill to believe that the Californian killed JayJay.

Jeez, but Jim was commencing to feel tired. So much he had to do yet. So much responsibility.

He could handle it, though. Dang straight he could.

He felt better just from realizing that.

What he could do, he decided, was go by the house—he was sure close enough, less than a half-dozen miles from right here—and get more sup-plies.

He'd have to remember to get enough for two. And JayJay's Marlboros as well as his own Chesterfields. Couldn't let Bill know that JayJay was dead. Not until the Californian was taken care of. But he could tell Bill that JayJay was still out keeping an eye on things and Jim had come back on his own to resupply.

Hell, that was logical. Jim, after all, was the one with an old lady waiting for him at home. It was only natural and right if there was gonna be one stay out and one come in that it would be Jim coming in so he could grab some groceries and cigarettes and have a couple minutes of privacy with Glory before he headed out again.

Have to switch horses too, of course. If Bill came out and noticed—hell yes, of course he would—explain the dun got a stone bruise. So he'd borrowed JayJay's horse. And, um, the saddle was already on it. They neither one hadn't felt like switching gear. Have to remember tomorrow to go back and get his own rig where he'd left it laying on the ground.

Then find that bastard Californian. Take care of him and bring him back here to where JayJay was. Then get Bill and tell him the story. Get him to help covering it all over.

Jim smiled, satisfied that he had it all worked out. He had a faintly nagging sense that this wasn't quite the same story that he'd intended to work out. But no matter. This one was better, he was sure. This one would work. Dang straight it would.

He felt good again. He was taking care of things. Just the one little detail to get past now, and everything would fall in place.

Nobody would ever have to be the wiser. None of this would have to disrupt what they had going for them here.

Jim was starting to feel really quite good now that things were falling into place so nicely.

He gathered up the reins of JayJay's brown, dropped his carbine into JayJay's scabbard and swung onto the saddle.

He still had that one last Chesterfield that he'd been hoarding. His mood was so fine right now that he celebrated by pulling it out and lighting it. Why, he'd be back home to a fresh pack in no time at all.

Jim Beale wheeled the nose of JayJay's brown in the direction of the strong sky-glow that came off the mercury vapor lamps they'd installed in the ranch yard to discourage coyotes from coming after chickens and rabbits and whatever other 4-H projects might be under way at any given time. For that and, the rest of the truth, to keep the children from getting the willies when they went out to chore after dark.

One nice thing about those lights, though. A fella couldn't miss finding the Beale place no matter how drunk or confused he ever got. You could see them for miles.

Jim clucked softly to the brown and bumped it into a walk. There was no need for a faster pace. Not right now there wasn't. He could afford to relax for a few moments and enjoy the flavor of his smoke.

Later would be time enough to worry about duty and detail. He smiled and sat back against the cantle of JayJay Lawrence's unfamiliar saddle.

THIRTY-FOUR

OLIVER SLIPPED and fell heavily onto his side. The breath was driven out of him with a loud grunt.

So close and now . . . He started to laugh. No wonder. Why, it was no wonder at all.

He'd slipped in mud. Mud. Imagine that. Real mud. He touched it, enjoying the cool, malleable feel of it.

Ah, and where would mud come from in a desert.

Oliver laughed again. The pipe protruding from the mud puddle was answer enough. He reached up, turned the valve and let the cold, wonderful water spray right over him. He opened his mouth to it, sat beneath the spigot and let icy water pour into his throat and down his body.

Wonderful. Marvelous. He drank until he choked and then drank some more.

His stomach lurched and rejected this sudden cold intrusion. Oliver didn't mind a bit. He simply drank again. After, however, moving out of the flow to kneel beside it. The water from this well was wonderful but it was also damned cold.

He stood, laughed, bent to drink a little more before finally, almost hesitantly, turning the water off.

He was sopping and sodden from head to toe. Whatever hadn't been drenched in water was coated with mud.

Oliver didn't mind. If the people who lived here did, well, he wasn't so much interested in their approval as in their assistance. One little telephone call. One short telephone call and everything would be right again.

He sobered, frowning. No, not right. Not really. That telephone call would not bring JoLynn back, and that was the only way things could be made truly right. But then, justice only provides balance and not renewal, doesn't it? Funny, he thought, how that can be so difficult to grasp until there is a personal involvement to point out the shortcomings of the concept we call justice.

Oliver sighed and walked around the set of livestock pens where he'd discovered—the hard way—the freeze-proof outdoor water faucet.

It seemed hard to accept, but he really had reached the source of the lights in the sky. He had begun to think of the quest for those lights as never-ending, a search for a phantom grail. Now here he was, and it was real. It was only a ranch, he supposed, or a small ranching community, but right now it certainly looked like a town. Almost a city. There were houses, house trailers, outbuildings, barns, pens, sheds . . . lights, cars . . . wires! Electric wires. Telephone wires too. He was almost sure that one of those sets of wires he could see on the poles that led off toward the road was for a telephone. Why, the people in one of the houses had a satellite dish. Surely people who had television would have telephones too.

He made his way past the stock pens and paused at the edge of the yard. Only two of the houses showed light. He decided to ask first at the one with the satellite dish. It was the nearer place anyway.

He limped forward, invigorated by the elation of success as much as he was revived by the water.

For the first time in what seemed a very long while he became aware of his own appearance.

What if the presence of an apparition at their door frightened the people? What if they refused him entry?

He could stand outside and beg them to make the call.

That would be all right.

If nothing else, dammit, he would stand outside and shout. Make a nuisance of himself to the point that they called the police. Any way the police came to be here would be just fine, thank you.

He wouldn't blame the people if they refused to let him in, though. He must look a sight. Especially now that he was muddy and dripping wet. What kind of imbecile walks out of the desert covered with mud? Oliver almost wanted to laugh at himself. Leave it to him to do such an ass-backward trick. Wouldn't JoLynn laugh at him for that one. Why . . . He sobered, no longer at all inclined to laughter. JoLynn. He wouldn't ever be able to share anything with her again. He suspected it would be sharing all the good things that he would most miss about not having her beside him. No one to repeat quips and foibles to. No one to sit beside and point with awe or joy or wonder when life and nature showed off.

Oliver felt close to tears.

He didn't even know what they had done with her body. Had they even bothered to bury her? Or just left her lying somewhere to be disposed of as carrion?

He shuddered. God, what a lousy thing to think about now that he was saved.

But then, how could he not think about JoLynn now that he himself was saved?

He waddled across the packed earth toward the lights of the house, legs held wide to keep the wet cloth of his trousers from rubbing together. Having wet britches felt almost as bad as when he was a little boy and wet himself. Worse, perhaps, in that this water was cold. He really should have known better than to sit beneath a faucet. It was just that it'd seemed such a wonderful idea at the moment. Now it seemed to have been considerably less than wonderful. Understandable perhaps. But short of wonderful.

His feet and legs were hurting again now too. For a little while there he hadn't been aware of that at all.

His feet hurt, his legs hurt, his hands hurt from falling so often and abrading them raw, his stomach ached abominably and his head was pounding.

But to look on the bright side, his tongue no longer felt swollen and he wasn't the least bit thirsty now.

He reached the front door of the house and stopped there for a moment to wipe his feet on the coco mat laid out for the purpose.

There really wasn't much he could do about his appearance, but he made the effort. Ran a hand over the mat that his hair had become, then smoothed it through his beard. It occurred to him that all the awful things that had happened out here had happened so quickly that he still didn't need to trim his mustache. And he hadn't trimmed it since they left San Francisco. That seemed really quite incredible. He felt as if he had aged half a lifetime and yet his mustache hairs hadn't had time to grow a quarter inch.

He lifted his hand and tapped lightly on the door.

JIM MUTTERED under his breath as he pulled the brown to a stop and stepped off of it. Just his luck to ride practically into his brother at a time when he would've preferred that Billy not see him on JayJay's horse.

"Heard you coming in," Bill said softly from the shadows of the tack shed. "You're alone."

"JayJay stayed out. We, uh, got some more stuff to tend to. I come in for groceries, cigarettes, like that."

"Uh-huh."

"You wouldn't have a smoke on you, would you?"

"You know better'n that. Give you a dip if you want one, though."

Jim smiled, feeling calmer now that he was with his brother and no hard questions were coming out. That was good. Jim didn't want to have to lie any more than was strictly necessary. Not with Billy.

"I think I got some in the cab o' the truck," he said. The truck was considerably closer than the house. He tossed the reins of the brown to Bill and went to get a fresh pack of Chesterfields.

The taste of the smoke was wonderful. Even better was the feel of the fresh pack lumpy and firm in his shirt pocket. He was always nervous and irritable when his supply ran low. He couldn't remember actually running out of cigarettes since . . . practically since he'd taken up smoking, and that had been when he was a kid still waiting to get his first acne pimples. Long time ago now.

"You both needing fresh horses?" Bill asked when Jim came back to the shed where Bill had been oiling some harness, getting it ready for the spring working that would start in the next few weeks.

"Ayuh," Jim said. "My horse got a stone bruise. Figured I'd take the borry of this one. Woulda sent JayJay in but . . . ," he looked toward the old house where Gloria had a bedroom light showing upstairs, likely where she was reading in bed, ". . . you know how it is."

Bill chuckled and nodded. "I expect I'd of done the same."

"One o' the advantages of being boss."

"I figured there had to be one in there somewhere. Glad to know you proved my point, Jimmy. Personally, I was beginning to think there was only responsibilities went with that title."

"Now we both know better," Jim agreed.

"You, uh . . ." Bill hesitated. Jim could see that there were things he wanted to ask. Things he knew he shouldn't ask but wanted to anyway.

"Don't worry 'bout it, little brother. Don't you worry about nothing, hear?"

"I hear you, Jimmy."

Jim grinned. "Damn right you do." He tapped another cigarette out of his pack and used the coal of the old one to light the fresh one. He felt like he'd been running short on his nicotine needs and would have to smoke double-time for a spell just to catch up again.

"It's good t' see you, Jim."

"Good t' be here, bud."

"Thinking of which . . ."

"Mmm?"

"Bud. I think I got some Budweisers in the toolbox of that truck there. You want one?"

"Does a bull slobber?"

Both of them laughed, and Bill went to fetch a pair of beers.

Jeez, Jim felt better now. It was all okay again, everything back to being just the way it was supposed to.

"LORDY A'MIGHTY, mister, what happened to you?" The woman's round, big-eyed face reflected sympathy and concern with no trace of fearful suspicion.

She shoved the door open and stepped outside to wrap a strong arm around Oliver, completely unmindful of the filth that would be getting on her.

"What is it, Mama?"

"I don't know. The gentleman has had an accident. Something like that."

"I didn't hear any accident."

"Well, he didn't get like this on purpose. Help me with him now."

Two boys, early teens or thereabouts, appeared at Oliver's other side. The three of them supported him in.

They shouldn't have done that. Really they shouldn't. His feet were all muddy, and he would be tracking it onto the rug. They should have left him outside. Getting the rug muddy seemed to be all he could concentrate on at the moment.

He tried to protest.

Somehow he couldn't get the words to come out right. Not then and not when he tried to tell them what had happened.

He was there, thinking and doing just fine—or so he'd believed right up until that moment—and then the next thing he knew he was filling up with sorrow and tears, feeling the moist heat gather behind his eyes and spill outward, feeling the trembling in his mouth and cheeks, the utter uselessness of knees that had gone weak.

Oliver let go. He slumped forward and would have fallen except for the support of these good people.

The woman and young boys half carried, half dragged him through their living room and into a huge kitchen that looked like it was probably the most lived-in room in the house.

Oliver felt a little better once he realized that the kitchen floor was not carpeted. At least the mud off his feet would be easily cleaned up here.

That was nice.

Everything was so very nice.

So why couldn't he stop crying?

This was ridiculous. And he was wasting time when he should be calling the police. Or asking them to. Except he couldn't ask them anything. He couldn't make himself stop crying long enough to fit his tongue around a single coherent utterance.

The people sat him down in a wooden kitchen chair. The woman gave her boys a nervous look and motioned them away.

"Mama!"

"Go on now. This gentleman doesn't need you staring at him on top of whatever other troubles he has."

"But Mom. . . ."

"James Albert, Tod William, you do what you're told now. I want you both to run find your father and tell him there's a man here in trouble. Then both of you go on over to Aunt Gloria. Tell her I want you to stay there a while. I'll let you know when you can come home again."

"Mama."

"Do it. Now."

"Yes, Mama." "Yes'm."

Oliver felt even more rude, all the more an imposition on this family. Now he was forcing the children out of their own home.

But oh dear . . . so nice . . . these people were being so nice to him . . . and he didn't . . . he couldn't get a word out . . . couldn't make himself stop . . . just as soon as he could get hold of himself . . . take a deep breath . . . quit this silly blubbering . . . as soon as he could just make sense of some of this . . . call the police . . . or ask the lady to . . . there was a phone on the wall . . . right there . . . practically close enough to touch . . . if he just reached his hand out . . . practically touch it . . . call the police . . . report . . . everything . . . JoLynn.

He began to cry harder.

The lady gave him a look that she probably thought he couldn't see. Half pity. The other half disgust. He didn't blame her. He was disgusted with himself.

All he needed, dammit, was to get control of himself. Just for a minute. Then he could pick that telephone up and call in the police.

Tell them everything. And go home. Right now he wasn't even sure he wanted to stay in Nevada long enough to know that those men were found and arrested.

Right now he only wanted to make that phone call and end this so he could go home and begin the grieving he hadn't yet had time to give to his beloved. Was that too terribly much to ask?

"You wait here, mister. I'll go find something dry to put on you. A robe, maybe. Sit right there. I won't be long."

Oliver nodded, still unable to form words to agree with the lady or to thank her.

Just another minute or two. That was all he needed. Just one more minute. Possibly two.

The lady clucked her tongue and patted him gently on his shoulder, then turned and scurried out of the kitchen, leaving Oliver alone at the table there with the telephone not five feet away.

THIRTY-FIVE

NOW JUST WHAT in hell was this? Jim could see Jimmy and Tod come trotting up beside the truck all excited and begin telling their dad something. Then kind of arguing with him, both of them looking like they wanted to run back to the house but Bill telling them off and sending them to the old house instead. Surely Bill could see that the lights were all off downstairs and that Gloria had gone to bed. Yet he was sending the boys over there instead of back home.

Bill made them go, then glanced in the direction of the shed where Jim was waiting.

Didn't come over and explain it though, whatever it was.

Instead he acted like he hoped Jim hadn't seen.

It occurred to Jim that he was standing in the deep shadows inside the shed. From out in the yard it wouldn't be possible for Bill to know where Jim was or if he was watching.

Bill set the beer cans down on top of the toolbox and wiped his hands nervously. He took one hesitant step in the direction of the tack shed, then turned and went instead toward the house. His own house, not Jim's. The one where he hadn't wanted the boys to go just now.

And wasn't that mighty curious? Jim asked himself.

A notion came to him. A premonition? Maybe. Whatever it was, just that quick Jim knew what it was.

The California man was here. Right here at the home place. The brass-balled son of a bitch had come right here.

Jim's first impulse was to rush after Bill.

He could come up with some kind of story. Or course he could.

Except the California bastard would have a story too.

But not if Jim's was the only story that got told.

They . . . of course. Jim could explain how the thing with the woman had been an accident. And of course it was. That was no lie. But then this man came after them. That was it. The guy stalked them. They tried to talk to him. Explain to him. But he'd been a crazy-wild person. The

Californian grabbed JayJay's gun. He was the one killed the foreman. Then he came here. To the ranch. Still stalking them. Still trying to get revenge for something that'd only been an accident to begin with. Jim was scared of him. Knew this guy had already murdered JayJay and wasn't right in his head. Shooting the California man would be nothing but self-defense under those circumstances.

It would work. People would buy it. It would be the word of a Beale, after all. Beales had been a part of this country since the first white men came to stay. The voice of a Beale counted for something here. And there wouldn't be no other voice arguing against what was said. Jim would be the only one to speak, the only one who knew what had happened and could tell about it. Of course it would work.

But quick. Before the guy had time to say very much. He couldn't have time enough to be telling lies to Maureen and her boys. Not any more lies than he'd already told, anyway.

Jim felt something clench and twist and churn down deep in his gut. He wanted to shout. *I never meant it to be like this. I swear to God I never.*

But there wasn't anybody to tell it to.

He took the carbine down off JayJay's saddle and began trotting across the yard after his little brother. He was the head of the family, dammit. He'd do what he had to do. Now as always.

OLIVER HELPED HIMSELF to a paper napkin from a ceramic dispenser on the kitchen table. He wiped his eyes and mouth and loudly blew his nose. He was feeling better now. At least that asinine crying jag had ended and he could act like a responsible human being again. He didn't know what had set him off like that, but he was awfully glad it was over with now.

He stood, legs aching, and reached for the telephone.

Probably that was rude, not waiting for the lady of the house to come back and give him permission to place the call.

But he just didn't want to wait any longer.

The telephone was one of the old rotary-dial things. Oliver hadn't seen one like that in an awfully long time.

He dialed. 9 . . . 1 . . . 1 . . . Waited. Nothing happened. He frowned, depressed the disconnect button and tried again. There were the expected clicks and whirs, but those resulted in no sound of ringing.

"That's that emergency number, isn't it?"

Oliver jumped. He had been so intent on making his call that he hadn't heard the man come in.

Of course, though. The lady had sent her boys to get their dad. This man would be the father.

He would be . . .

Oliver recognized the thin, wiry, mustachioed cowboy who was stand ing in the doorway.

This was one of the men.

Dear God!

This was the home of one of the men he was trying to get away from. *This man was one of JoLynn's killers.*

"I . . . I . . ."

"That number don't work out here. We're on a party line. Maybe that's got something to do with it. You want t' call the sheriff, mister, you dial 555-6419. It ain't long-distance. If you can't remember it, I think it's on a sticker pasted to the side of the phone there. See it?"

Oliver felt numb. His mouth gaped, but no sound wanted to come out.

He had the distinct impression that if he turned his attention away from this man, to dial the telephone, say, he would be shot down. Bludgeoned from behind. He knew for sure that this person could not allow him to actually call the police and report the crimes that had been committed.

The man in the doorway, though, looked like he expected Oliver to do just that.

He looked, Oliver thought . . . tired. And perhaps relieved? For whatever reason, he did not look at all threatening or hostile.

"Bill? Honey?"

The woman had come back into the kitchen, but Oliver's disorientation was so complete that again he hadn't heard her arrival. He really was going to have to start getting a grip on himself here, dammit.

"It's all right, hon. I'll handle it. You go over an' set with Gloria and the boys, hear? An' honey . . . you stay there. No matter what. You stay right there till I come get you. All right? Will you do that for me, please?" The man's smile was sad but tender too.

"Bill, I'm getting worried now. What is going on here, honey? Who is this man?"

"This fella isn't no danger, Maureen. I promise. And I already told you I'll handle it. Now trust me, hon. Go on an' go like I asked."

The lady named Maureen frowned and gnawed at the insides of her cheeks while she hesitated, standing in the living room doorway there while her husband stood framed in the outside door.

"It's all right," he prompted in a low, soothing tone. "Go on. Please."

Maureen paused a moment longer. Then nodded. She turned and walked away, a plumply pretty middle-aged woman who was confused but trusting. A woman, Oliver reminded himself, who was married to a murderer.

Oliver took a deep breath and looked at the telephone receiver that was clenched in his fist.

"It's all right, mister. Go ahead an' make your call. I won't try an' stop you." The man, Bill, sounded sadder than ever.

He lurched, almost lost his balance and took a long step forward to right himself. In the doorway where Bill had been standing there was another man now. Another one of the murderers.

This particular murderer had a rifle in his hands.

One of the guns they'd used to kill JoLynn and those wild horses? Oliver felt his chest well up with fury.

"You sons of bitches," he spat.

The newcomer, slightly the taller of them, a little older-looking and with less hair than Bill, didn't bother to answer. He simply raised his rifle and pointed it at Oliver's chest.

"No!" Bill stepped in between them. His hand groped for the muzzle of the other one's rifle and shoved it aside. "We aren't gonna do this, Jim. What's done so far was an accident. This here would be murder. I won't have you committing a murder."

"What the hell d'you think me and JayJay been trying . . ."

"I know what you been trying, Jimmy, and I know that practically since I last seen you I been praying that you wouldn't make good. An' I see that you haven't. If it makes you feel any better, come morning I was gonna go out in the truck and look for this fella too. Except I was gonna find him and carry him to town before you an' JayJay could get to him. I won't have murder on my head, Jimmy. Nor on yours. I think too high of both of us to allow it."

The one named Jim seemed to go pale.

"Put the gun away, Jimmy. It's over. Mister, you can go ahead an' call the sheriff now. Me and my brother won't bother you."

Oliver wasn't sure if he could believe them or not. Wasn't going to let this chance slip by, though. He shifted closer to the telephone and bent to look at the sticker on the plastic casing, listing numbers for the sheriff, volunteer fire department, volunteer ambulance service. 5 . . . 5 . . . 5 . . .

"No."

There was a stamping of feet and loud, ugly grunting. Oliver turned in time to see the two brothers grappling with the short-barreled rifle held between them.

"No, Jimmy, don't. You can't, dammit."

"You don't understand," the older one moaned. "You just don't understand, boy." He wrenched at the rifle and threw himself backward.

Bill clung to the weapon with both hands, dragging it down so the barrel was pointed toward the floor. "I ain't gonna let you do this, Jimmy. I swear I ain't."

Jim elbowed his brother in the mouth, kicked at him viciously, jammed the instep of his boot hard along Bill's shin in a move that must have been horribly painful. Bill cried out but kept his hold on the rifle.

Oliver knew he should try to complete the call to the sheriff's office. He knew that. Yet he stood rooted in place while two strangers, two murderers, fought over whether he should die or not.

Jim drew back, kicked again, harder this time, and at the same moment heaved backward, spinning Bill around and slamming him against the kitchen counter. Bill grunted and one hand slipped off the rifle. Jim tugged and succeeded in pulling the weapon free.

He pushed Bill back against the counter with one hand and with the other groped for the trigger of the little rifle.

Oliver could see the muzzle thrash from side to side, its lethal tip slicing back and forth in wild, sweeping arcs.

Jim pulled free of his brother and stepped forward. He had both hands on the rifle now, and his eyes were cold and determined.

"Damn you," Oliver hissed. He steeled himself against the impact of the bullet and threw himself forward in an attempt to strike out at this man who would kill him.

At the same time Bill recovered his balance and launched himself onto Jim's back.

The gun discharged, the sound of it unnaturally loud inside the close confinement of the kitchen.

Oliver flinched and fell to his knees but felt nothing. The bullet hadn't struck him.

"Jim! Don't."

"Got to, Billy. Got to. You don't know, boy. Got to."

"No."

The two of them wrestled over the gun again. Grunting, straining, their faces red and expressions grim.

"Billy!"

There was another explosion, a second gunshot ringing out in the kitchen. But this time the sound was muffled and dull, so unlike the sharp and vicious crack of the first shot that even Oliver's untrained ear could differentiate between them.

Bill cried out and stiffened.

"Billy? *Billy!*" Jim put his arms around the younger man and kept him from toppling onto the floor. "Jesus God, Billy, what've I done?"

Oliver saw a smear of red high on Bill's belly. Bill's face had lost all color, and Jim was every bit as pale. Jim lowered Bill gently to the floor. Jim was weeping now. "Billy?"

"We kinda ██████ up this time, Jim boy," Bill whispered.

"Don't you die, Billy. Don't you dare go an' die." Jim looked up as if coming out of a daze. His eyes found Oliver and focused on him.

Oliver was still on his knees from where he'd fallen moments earlier. He wasn't going to stay there, dammit. This bastard Jim might kill him, but the man wouldn't find Oliver on his knees when it happened. Oliver came shakily to his feet while Jim picked up the hateful little rifle that had dropped to the floor beside Bill.

It occurred to Oliver that he could have grabbed for the gun while it was lying untended there for those several moments.

Which pretty much answered the question of how far back to cornered-animal reactions he was likely to go, didn't it? He found himself vaguely regretting the answer he'd gotten. But proud of it too. JoLynn would have been proud as well. He knew she would have been, and the knowledge comforted him.

Jim examined the rifle, did something to a catch on the underside of it and pulled a boxlike steel thing off the bottom. He tossed that part aside with a clatter when it hit the floor, then pulled on some other part of the gun and a bright brass bullet thing flew out onto the floor as well. Jim looked at the rifle with distaste, then threw it aside.

"Damn you," he said to Oliver.

Oliver stared at him, loathing Jim for a murderer but unable to avoid feeling a twinge of sympathy for a man who had just shot, perhaps even killed, a loved one.

"Call, damn you!" Jim snarled.

"Call?"

"The sheriff. And . . . an ambulance. I won't ask you to call for the ambulance first. Lord knows you don't owe us nothing. But call . . . the ambulance . . . for my brother quick as you've finished telling the sheriff t' get out here. Please?"

"I'll call the ambulance first," Oliver said in a dull, wooden, disbelieving voice.

Jesus, he thought. And Mary. Holy Mary, Mother of God.

He looked again at the emergency numbers pasted to the base of the telephone and began to dial.

About the Author

FRANK RODERUS is the author of nineteen Double D Westerns, including *Leaving Kansas*, which won the Western Writers of America's Spur Award in 1983. He has been a Spur Award finalist five times, and his work has been reprinted in Great Britain, Germany, Italy, Norway, and Finland. He lives in Sarasota, Florida.